The Weight Of What Was

THE DEBUT NOVEL BY
PIP LANDERS-LETTS

ROUXMAUS PRESS

Copyright © 2024 Pip Landers-Letts
First Edition May 2024
Published by Rouxmaus Press

ISBN: 978-1-738543007

Cover Design and typesetting: **Bookcoversonline**
Editing and proof-reading: **Sophia Blackwell**

www.pipwritesfiction.com
Instagram: @pipwritesfiction

For Shannon,

Glenda, Roberta,

and all of the awesome women in my life

CHAPTER ONE

June 2002

Anna whipped off her sweaty bra and rifled through her laundry basket for a clean-ish top to wear to a party she really didn't want to go to. Tiredness seeped through her body from the last few coffee-fuelled nights of revision but she'd promised Rupert she'd show up.

A promise is a promise, especially if it's to Rupert. And for better or worse, the final exam of her second year was done, so she supposed there was some cause for celebration.

The summer scents of cut grass and charcoal barbecues hung heavy in the evening air as Anna arrived at the scruffiest in a row of terraced houses. She raised her hand to knock on the peeling black door of number forty when it swung open and two rugby lads staggered out.

"We're out of Jägermeister already! You need anything from the shop?" the taller of the two bellowed at Anna.

"Er no, I'm all set, thanks." She smiled and held up the cheap bottle of Sauvignon-something she'd brought with her.

"Alrighty then, I'll see *you* in a bit," leered the tall guy. His shorter mate grunted a laugh.

"Great. Can't wait," she muttered and proceeded into the long, cramped hallway. Her nostrils were assaulted by a heady mix of

Jägerbombs, marijuana, and musky incense sticks; an obvious effort to mask the usual eau-de-rugby-lad aroma of the house.

Noise spewed from the kitchen up ahead, where cheers from a lively drinking contest competed with the thumping bass of *Hot in Herre*. *Nelly is not wrong*, she thought as she squeezed herself past the small crowd gathered around the narrow staircase.

A figure pounced on her from the fairy-lit living room to her left. "Anna, daaahrling. You made it," said Diana, Rupert's haughty forty-something next-door neighbour, pink lipstick smudged on her teeth, red wine swishing in her glass.

Diana embraced her, the over-familiar hug giving away that she'd already had far more than just the glassful in her hand. Over Diana's shoulder, Anna smiled at David, Diana's affable, chino-sporting husband.

"Great to see you both," Anna said, awkwardly extracting herself from Diana's mantis-like arms. "I didn't expect you to be here. Have you been dragged along to re-live your student days?"

"Well, if you can't beat them, join them." Diana snorted and slapped David's arm.

"Rupert really is very polite. He asked us along to enjoy the party, so we thought we'd pop in. He said to let him know if things get too rowdy," said David.

"Oh, I do like them rowdy! Rupert is such a lovely young man. Charming, lovely. Very, *very* lovely." Diana swayed like a reed in a light breeze and tried to focus her glassy-eyed gaze.

David's eyebrows rose as he looked from his wife to his wine and took a large gulp. Anna shuddered internally at Diana's embarrassing and obvious crush on Rupert and made a mental note to tease him about it later.

"Okay, well, it's been good to catch up with you both. Have you seen Rupert, by the way?"

"Ah yes, last seen charming the ladies *dans le jardin*," said David.

Anna rolled her eyes. "Of course he is."

"You and Rupert must join us for dinner again soon. We want to hear more about what's next for the delicious pair of you," Diana slurred.

"Sure, yeah. Sounds great." Anna smiled, politely took her leave and ventured past Rupert's jam-packed ground-floor bedroom, the apparent source of the marijuana cloud wafting its way through the hallway. She wove through the drinking games and noisy chaos of the crowded kitchen and finally found her way into the slightly cooler garden.

For student digs, the garden was surprisingly neat; Rupert and the lads had gone to some effort to make it look nice. Picnic blankets were spread across the lawn, tealight candles flickered in old jam jars, and strings of fairy lights sparkled in the trees, setting the ambience for a midsummer's eve.

Smiling and nodding at the faces she knew, Anna scanned the garden for Rupert but there was no sign of him. A gathering of mostly girls sat around Rupert's housemate, Craig, as he strummed out Oasis songs on his acoustic guitar. Joe, Rupert's other housemate, had assumed the role of chief sausage cremator on the barbecue. Anna smiled over at him with a thumbs-up; he returned the gesture with gusto. Black smoke curled up from charcoaled chunks of meat, and

Joe flapped his arms around to little effect.

Then she saw her.

Anna's stomach somersaulted as their eyes locked. The air fizzed and everything around the edges faded out. Only a second or two could have passed, but as everything shifted back into focus, Anna realised she'd been staring at a stranger, and probably with her mouth open.

Oh God. Okay, breathe. Breathe. Stay calm. Be still my beating heart, be cool my stupid mouth, Anna coached herself, as she was magnetised towards the most stunning human she'd seen in her entire nineteen years of being alive.

"Hi," said Anna.

"Hi," the stunning human replied, with a curious smile flirting on her lips.

They continued to look at each other; *mutual permission to stare.* Anna drank in every detail of her face. Her green, almond-shaped eyes, her wavy auburn hair. The piercings in her left ear, which her hair was tucked behind. The tiny, silver loop in her right nostril. Her perfect teeth, behind those perfect lips, now arranging themselves into a perfect smile.

She's just perfect, Anna thought, as her brain ran out of adjectives. She broke eye contact as Craig – the lost Gallagher brother – crooned the chorus of *Wonderwall* to his adoring fan club on the lawn.

"Sorry, I mean hi… I mean… I already said that. I'm Anna. We haven't met before, have we?" Her cheeks flamed.

"No, I'd have remembered you. I'm Grace." Her lilting Irish accent made Anna's heart race a little faster.

4

"Grace." Anna repeated the name that paired so perfectly with that face. "Would you like a drink? Your glass is empty and I have wine… no corkscrew, but I have wine." Anna nervously laughed and held up her bottle of Sauvignon-something. She blushed again, remembering it cost her less than three quid and would probably taste like donkey's piss.

"Yes, please. I've been waiting here for someone to come back with another drink for me, but that was more than fifteen minutes ago. I'll have died of thirst." Grace rummaged in her bag. "Please don't think I'm an alcoholic but I happen to have a bottle opener in here somewhere… ta-dah!" She grinned and presented Anna with a corkscrew.

"Well, aren't we the perfect match?" *Shit! As if I actually just said that.*

With a squeaky pop, Anna removed the cork and filled up Grace's glass.

Grace took a sip and offered the glass to Anna. "We can share," she said.

Anna's heart fluttered as she drank. She immediately wanted to spit out the most awful wine she'd ever tasted. It didn't matter because she was looking at Grace and Grace was looking right back at her, and they were sharing a glass. *Nothing could spoil this moment.*

CHAPTER TWO

November 2021

Anna surfaced from sleep to the buzz of her mobile phone vibrating on the bedside table. Without cracking her eyes open to look at the screen, she answered with a groggy, "Hello?"

"Morning, Banana! Sorry, did I wake you? You weren't working late, were you?"

"Hey, Lexi. It's okay. What's up?" Anna sat up and combed her fingers through her hair.

"I have a mock exam today, so I'm on my way to school, but I wanted to speak to you before Dad does."

Anna exhaled a laugh. "What have you done to upset him now?"

"No, it's nothing like that. Gran called last night and she was going on about a trip. It sounds epic but for some reason, Dad was being a bit of a dick about it. He and Mum had a blazing row… *again,* and Toby got upset. Anyway, has Gran spoken to you yet?"

"Er, no, not yet." Anna winced and massaged her palm into her forehead. "Sorry, rewind. Is everyone okay?"

"Yeah, they're fine. It was like the Arctic in the kitchen this morning though, minus the penguins."

"There aren't any penguins in the Arctic."

"Sure, whatever. There weren't any in our kitchen either, but it was frosty! Mum was being a total ice queen and Dad acted like he hadn't even noticed. Brutal. As usual, Toby was making an absolute mess with his cereal, apparently too busy with Minecraft to steer a spoon into his mouth. But other than a little spilt milk down his school shirt, he's fine."

"Okay, good. So, what's this trip?" Anna juggled the phone as she pulled a woolly jumper over her pyjamas and padded her way to the bathroom.

"I should let Gran speak to you first… but seeing as I've called you now, and I tell you everything, I guess it doesn't matter."

"I'm all ears."

"She wants to take us to Norway and Sweden on this train journey, I think it's called the Polar Express?" Lexi blurted.

"Who? You and Toby?" asked Anna, whilst trying to pee quietly.

"No, all of us. She said it'll be a celebration for our big birthdays next year. We'll be there for my eighteenth." Lexi paused. "Also, she said it's because we should all go to pay our respects. She said it's been too long, and Toby and I haven't been there yet. Mum agreed that it was a good idea. The grizzly bear did not, obvs."

Anna yawned and flushed the toilet.

"Banana! OMG, are you on the loo?"

"Sorry, but I had to pee." She laughed. "Sounds like Gran has made up her mind. Why did your mum and dad argue about it though?"

The stairs creaked as Anna made her way down to the kitchen.

"Dad doesn't 'have the time for this shit'. His words. Mum says he never has time for anything aside from work and so on, blah, blah, blah." Lexi groaned. "Ugh, you know what they're like. Mum slammed some cupboard doors, so Toby cried, and Dad stormed off to sulk in his study. Standard."

"Hmm." Anna's mind turned to Grace. She flicked on the kettle and wedged the phone between her ear and shoulder as she rinsed a mug under the tap. "Okay, well let's see what Gran has to say. I could do with a break. It's been a tough few weeks; we're down a vet, thanks to bloody Covid, so I've been covering emergency calls. Last night it was a cow with a broken leg."

"Poor cow." Lexi giggled.

"Who, me? Or the actual cow?"

"Both!"

"Oi, watch it, cheeky. Have a good day at school and smash that mock exam."

"Love ya, Banana."

"Love you too, Lex."

∗ ∗ ∗

Anna sipped her mug of coffee and tapped out a text.

> Morning. You OK? Lex just called. She said
> you and Ru had another fight. Call me if you
> want to talk. You know I'm here. Always x

Seconds later her phone vibrated on the wooden worktop where she'd put it down. Her screen announced a reply.

> Hey you. Yeah, I'm fine, don't worry. Let me
> know when you've spoken to Gran xxxx

CHAPTER THREE

June 2002

S he heard him before she saw him. Rupert came bowling out of the back door, beer in hand. He was dressed in a rugby shirt, denim shorts, and flip-flops. His cropped blonde hair was even more ruffled than usual, and his Nordic blue eyes looked striking against his sun-kissed skin.

"Joe, my man!" he bellowed. "How are the bangers? Are you keeping the hungry hordes well-fed?"

"I got this," mumbled Joe through a mouthful of hotdog.

"Okay, just let me know if you need a hand, mate." Rupert squeezed Joe's shoulder.

He made his way over to the crowd sitting around a table covered in barbecue spoils, sticky drink spills, and a plethora of empty bottles. He must have cracked a joke, as there was an eruption of laughter and people gathered closer to him, pulled in by his gravitational field. The mate of all and the crush of most; he loved attention, and he got it.

Lots of backslapping and beer-slopping later, he finally made eye contact with Anna. His face lit up and he bounded over and bear-hugged her in the way he always did.

"I'm so happy you made it! You needed to get out of that dark little room and see the daylight. I was worried you were becoming a vampire." He pulled his lips back to expose his teeth in his best Dracula impression.

"Yeah, I'm really pleased I came," she said to Rupert, the whole while smiling at Grace. "Rupert, this is—"

"I'm so pleased you two have met. I knew you'd get along. Anna, this is that gorgeous little creature I mentioned to you last week. I found her skulking around the library." Staring at Grace with big eyes and an even bigger grin, Rupert appeared to have lost his train of thought.

"What did you—? I mean, why were you—" Anna stuttered and shook her head in the hope it would shake her words into coherence. "You never go to the library," she managed.

"I know, right? Well, pity the fool because I've been missing out. Turns out there's more to libraries than books. Hot girls are also abundant. No wonder you love it in there so much, you crafty little fox."

Rupert reached to ruffle Anna's hair but she jerked away, her brain reeling as she tried to process what he'd just said.

"I'm sorry, how is it that you two know each other?" Grace's face clouded with confusion and her cheeks burned red.

"Oh shit, sorry, Grace. Anna is my sister. Remember I told you I had a twin? Anna-Twin Skywalker, as I like to call her." He laughed hard at his own joke.

Grace slowly nodded. "Right. Twin *sister*. I don't know why, when you said *twin*, I thought you meant…" Her eyes flicked between them as if tallying their striking resemblance – blonde hair, blue eyes, same face.

Anna cringed but Rupert smiled on, blissfully unaware of what he'd just gate-crashed. Of his faults, a lack of self-awareness was top of the list.

CHAPTER FOUR

November 2021

Anna poured her third cup of coffee of the morning; resigned to her failed attempt to catch up on sleep, she resorted to caffeinating the problem. Still in her pyjamas and cosied up under a blanket, she took a sip from her steaming 'World's Best Auntie' mug and called Edith.

"Oh hello, darling. Aren't you working today?"

Anna smiled; to hear her voice was always a tonic. "Hey, Gran. I was on call last night, so I've given myself the morning off. Tomas has everything in hand."

"Ah, he's a good egg… and I'm pleased to hear you're looking after yourself. Anyway, I wanted to talk to you about an idea I've had for a family trip."

"I know, Lexi called this morning."

"Ah, Lexi! There are no surprises then," she chuckled. "I've been thinking about us taking this trip for a while. Now it's time to stop thinking about it and just do it, especially as the worst of it with the pandemic seems to be over."

"You say that, but my vets keep dropping like flies!"

"All the more reason for you to take a break. It will do you the world of good." Her words were accompanied by the rhythmic clinking of a teaspoon in a china cup.

"Honestly, you don't need to convince me, Gran."

"Well, you're being more positive about it than your brother. I don't know what's gotten into him lately," Edith sighed.

Anna shifted in her chair but passed no comment.

"I've spoken with a tour company and they have availability on an Arctic Circle tour in January. We can just about make it work with the school holidays. I think it'll be the perfect time to go. Northern lights, lots of snow; you might even be able to get some skiing in whilst we're in Narvik."

"Lexi and Toby will love that. It's been ages." Anna grinned at the prospect, casting her mind back to their last family ski trip, when they'd hired that lovely chalet in Samoëns.

"I've asked if the tour company can arrange an extra stop in Torghatten." Edith paused.

Anna comprehended the weight of her silence and wished she could envelop her in a hug. Grace flashed into her mind, and she wished she could hug her too.

Edith continued, "I want us to take the children there. They haven't been to Torghatten yet, and gosh, it must be twenty years since we last…" Her voice tailed off and then, a little too loudly, she asked, "Do you think you can take the time off work?"

"I haven't had a proper holiday for two years. Leave it with me and I'll square it with Tomas. Hopefully, we can sort out an extra locum."

"Wonderful. Would you mind speaking with Rupert? You always know how to set him right. I will sort out everything else."

Anna sighed. "I'll try my best, Gran, but I haven't spoken to him for a while."

"If he talks to anyone, darling, it'll be you."

CHAPTER FIVE

August 2002

Dear Grace,

As always, I have so much to say to you, but as we can't talk this week, I decided to write. I hope you're having a great time in Greece, and your family isn't driving you too mad. Thanks for the postcard by the way. I look at it before I go to sleep and imagine us there, together, on that beautiful beach.

I can't believe it's been over a month since the end of term, a whole month since we last saw each other. I miss your face so much it hurts; I can't wait to hold it in my hands and kiss your perfect lips again.

The weather has been lovely here. Gran and I have been on a couple of hikes; she's sixty-three but gives me a run for my money. I hope I'm that fit when I'm her age. I've been desperate to tell her about you, tell her I've met someone amazing. Although she suspects something has changed with me; she keeps asking why I'm in such a good mood!

I can't wait to tell the world that we're together.

I know, no pressure, I'm sorry. I understand you're not ready for that yet, and I promise I will give you all the time you need. It's just a struggle to keep all these feelings in.

You'll be pleased to hear that Rupert is finally talking to me again. I know he met you first (he really needs to grow up) but with a hundred girls fawning over him, it hardly broke his heart. I think he was more pissed off at me than anything else, he thinks I corrupted you... if only he knew!

Also, you won't believe this. He told me that at the house party, he snogged his next-door neighbour. She must be at least forty-five... and she's married! She's always had a bit of a thing for him; it was so obvious. She was absolutely smashed and according to Rupert, she pounced on him when he went to the loo!

Rupert effectively cheated on you before you were even really going out with him, so please stop feeling bad. You have nothing to feel bad about. I'm the terrible twin who steals his girlfriends. Girlfriend! I haven't stolen any others before you, just to be clear! His ego took a bruising because the most beautiful girl alive thinks his twin sister is hotter than he is.

Grace Ryan, it's official – you've broken me. I can't stop thinking about you. You're like a song on repeat, looping round and round in my head. Even the thought of you looking at me in the way that you do makes my stomach do somersaults. Those last couple of weeks at uni were incredible. I would trade years of my life to live that time over again.

I can't believe we didn't leave my room for three whole days. It's not even a nice room, but with you in it, there's nowhere else I'd rather be. Who'd have thought we could survive on just tea, toast, and Pot Noodles? I've never smiled and laughed as much; you are the funniest, silliest, and most gorgeous person I have ever met.

How does it feel like I've known you my whole life when it's only been weeks? How do I still have so much to say to you even though we talked all night, for three nights? I've never had so much to say to anyone before. You just get me. Even Rupert doesn't get me like you do, and I shared a womb with him!

I still haven't washed your hoodie yet; I wear it all the time so I probably should. It smells of you… in a good way! Until I can smell you in person it probably won't get washed. Haha – that sounds creepy and a bit grim now that I've written it down! OK, enough of the mushy stuff. I haven't written a love letter since I was twelve years old. Is this a love letter? It feels like it might be. There go the stomach somersaults again.

Anyway, I have some news...

The good news – I smashed my end-of-year exam. The results were posted this week, and it turns out I did far better than I thought. I got 84%, top of the class, proof that I am an actual genius haha. I studied so hard for it though. Why do I doubt myself so much?

The amazing news – my application for the study exchange was successful. I've been invited to go to Australia on a placement! There are only a handful of places, I can't believe they picked me (see, doubting myself again).

The timing literally couldn't be worse though. I've done nothing but dream about being back at uni with you. Hanging out, eating our bodyweight in noodles, going out on proper dates, when you're ready of course... but instead, I will electively be on the other side of the world. I feel so torn, I just want to be with you. On the other hand, Australia has koalas. You're exceptionally cute but you aren't a koala, are you?

You're going to tell me I must go because this is something I've always dreamed of. It will be an incredible experience. Also, next year is your final year and I will be nothing but a huge distraction for you if I'm around. The good part is that it's only for six months. Although that will feel like an eternity.

Well, I better get this posted, hopefully it will have arrived by the time you're back. I can't wait to see you again, until then I'll be thinking about you, I never stop.

Love, love, and even more love,

your Anna (Banana) x

Anna held the paper to her lips before folding it and slipping it into the envelope. She plucked Grace's postcard from under her pillow and traced her thumb over the spot where she imagined Grace standing. Warmth spread through her as she pictured Grace's auburn hair flowing free over bare shoulders, freckles dusting her smooth skin, and those ocean-green eyes with their mystical ability to disarm Anna in a single glance. *How did I get so lucky?*

CHAPTER SIX
November 2021

Crunching to a halt on the gravel driveway outside the practice, Anna cut the engine and rested back into the seat. She closed her eyes and drew in a deep breath through her nose. The sun had barely risen above the horizon and she'd already had a long day. Retrieving her phone from the pocket of her wax jacket, she tapped on her notifications and sighed. Still no response from Rupert.

On the off chance he might pick up, she pressed call. A crackly line connected after three rings.

"Hey Rupert... Ru?" The line crackled. "Rupert, are you there?"

"An... wait... I can't... hold. On. Anna? Can you hear me?"

"Yes, I'm here. I've been trying to get hold of you for days."

"Sorry, I was just coming out of the station. Hello, can you hear me now?" His brogues clacked along the pavement; heavy traffic hummed in the background.

"Yes, I think I've still got you. Thanks for finally picking up! It's been bloody ages. Are you okay?"

"Yeah. Sorry, Sis, I've just been swamped. Work is manic. I've barely been home. I saw that you'd called and honestly, I meant to call you back, but you know how it is. Time is money and all that. I'm sorry." He breathed into the phone.

A pelican crossing squawked down the line, followed by the sound of him walking again. Anna could almost feel the heaving bustle of commuters pressed around him.

"How are you?" he asked. "How are the sheep? Cows? Or whatever it is that you're elbow-deep in these days?"

"Yeah. Good. I'm good. All good here. We haven't spoken for ages." She paused, hoping he might offer some further explanation, but only silence met the void. "Gran called."

"Oh yeah? Was she on about that trip she wants us to go on? Ugh. I'm so busy at the moment, I haven't even had time to think. But, thanks to Gran, the kids haven't stopped harping on about it."

"Ru, you should come. Gran is right, it's over twenty years since we last visited. The kids have never been. I think it will do you all good. And you… you need to take a break now and then. What did you use to say? All work and no play makes Rupert a dull boy."

"Ha! Well, I guess I'm pretty dull these days." He sighed. "Look, okay, I'll think about it. I suppose I could do with a few days off. January is pretty busy so I can't promise anything."

"Come on, Ru."

He sucked in some air and clicked his tongue. Anna could picture him ruffling his hair with the fingers of his free hand, the way he always did when thinking. "Er, okay. I'll get my assistant to work through my diary and see what can be pushed out. There isn't a snowball's chance in hell I can come for the whole trip, but perhaps I can travel as far as Torghatten and then fly back from there. Do you think that'll get everyone off my case?"

"Oh, woe is me; my frightful family is forcing me to take a much-needed holiday. Seriously though, you just need to make sure you're there for Lexi's eighteenth, Ru. You shouldn't miss that."

"Most of the time Lexi just seems to loathe me anyway, so I'm not sure she'll care whether I'm there or not. But you're right, I should be there."

"She doesn't loathe you specifically, by the way. She's a teenager, loathing is their default setting."

He huffed. "She doesn't loathe *you*."

"Well, I'm cool Auntie Banana; the hip and happening alternative to her lame-arse parents."

"Don't let Lexi hear you refer to yourself as 'hip and happening' or she'll disown you." He laughed.

Anna smiled to hear him lighten up.

"I miss you, Ru," she said, speaking right into the distance that had grown between them.

The air on the line tightened with a stiff silence.

"Yeah, I know. I'm sorry." His voice caught and he coughed to mask it. "I have to dash, things to see, people to do." He chuckled at his own joke. "Look, I'll get my people to speak to your people." The line went quiet again. Anna sensed there was more he had wanted to say.

He drew in a breath. "Bye, Sis," he said and ended the call.

Anna swallowed the lump in her throat. She stared down at the phone in her hand and tapped it. A photo from their Samoëns ski trip illuminated her locked screen. A cloudless blue sky, snow-dusted fir trees, and them in the foreground. All goggle tans and big smiles; it seemed like a lifetime ago. A dull ache squeezed her chest. *This trip will do us all good.*

CHAPTER SEVEN

January 2003

A nna shuffled through the mail and memos she found stuffed into her pigeonhole. Her breath quickened at the sight of a blue airmail envelope addressed in the curling loops of Grace's handwriting. The urge to tear it open and greedily consume every word almost overwhelmed her, but instead she stashed it in her pocket and started her shift. First up, a sulphur-crested cockatoo with an upset stomach, followed by an obese domestic shorthair, in for its routine jabs. Even the impossibly cute, orphaned joey with a broken paw couldn't take her mind off the letter in her pocket.

With Grace's unread words waiting for her attention, the clock ticked slower than ever. By the time its hands made their way around to her morning break, she practically skipped outside. The heady smell of eucalyptus and the loud hum of cicadas filled the air as she sat on a bench in the shade of a gum tree. She sipped from the mug of coffee she'd just made, and carefully peeled open the envelope.

Dear Anna,

I'm writing this letter whilst you're at thirty thousand feet, out of touch, beyond reach. My heart feels so heavy. By the time you receive this, you'll have arrived, and you'll be settling in… and I will be missing you beyond measure.

I'm wearing your hoodie and it smells of you. I will not be washing it, nor will I be taking it off for six months. I will be a stinky mare and I don't even care. I'm so excited for you and the amazing adventure that awaits you. You are going to see and learn so much, but I can't believe you're on that plane, going what feels like a million miles away from me.

Also, I'm a little worried for the koalas, you know you won't be able to bring them back, right?

God, I am going to miss the bones of you, I already do. Watching you go through those departure gates is one of the hardest things I've ever had to do. It sounds so melodramatic but it's true.

Thank goodness Rupert was there today, handy with the tissues, bless him. Otherwise, I'd have been alone with all the ugly tears and the snot bubbles, looking like a right eejit. I told him not to worry, but he said he'd check in on me later, and he'll bring pizza because 'pizza makes everything better' (I'd tend to agree if he didn't insist on putting pineapple all over it). The truth is that he's missing you too and he just wants the company of someone else who has the biggest Anna-shaped hole in their heart right now.

I know you'll only be gone for six months, 184 days to be exact (Yes, I worked it out). I need to pull myself together, concentrate on my dissertation, and get through this. In the grand scheme of things, the time we've had together has been brief, but I've never felt like this before.

Meeting you changed everything for me: girl meets charming boy (which was a little inconvenient as she'd been thinking for a while that it might be girls for her, not boys) but then, as if by magic, appears boy's gorgeous twin sister. It all clicked into place. It all made sense. Anna, you make things make sense.

Thank you for being so patient with me. Sometimes I get a little scared by the intensity of what we have between us, I think it's because I'm still figuring things out.

It's going to be really hard with my family, they're going to struggle with this. They're just so Catholic and they take it all very literally. I don't want them to hate me, I'm afraid of what's to come. I wish I was strong like you. I wish I didn't care what people think and I could trust the universe that it'll all be OK. You are the most courageous person I've ever met, Anna Banana; you know who you are and what you want. With you beside me, I'll be OK.

I haven't said it to your face yet, but I'm going

to post this to you today so that when you get this it will be said, and I won't be able to get scared and not say it…

I'm in love with you, Anna Edwards!

As if it wasn't already obvious, but now I've written the words I've been wanting to say. By the time you get back, I will be ready to tell the world.

Until then, wonderful you, be happy, be safe, and stay away from all those hot Aussie girls!

Love, love, and love with a scoop of love on top,

your Gracey x

Grinning like an idiot, Anna read and re-read the letter until she could practically recite every word. She pressed the single sheet of blue airmail paper to her nose in case there was the faintest hint of Grace's perfume. She desperately wanted to wrap her arms around her; she yearned to feel the perfect fit of their bodies pressed together. The distance between them felt like it had doubled, as did her longing for the girl who had just declared her love. *Only 163 days to go.*

CHAPTER EIGHT

January 2022

Despite the early hour, the airport bustled with holidaymakers jetting off to exciting destinations. Anna wove her way through the throngs, her exhaustion somehow compounded by the buzz of excited energy. After a week of covering nights on emergency call, she couldn't wait to get some sleep on the flight.

Over by the Scandinavian Airlines desk, Gran was chatting to a middle-aged man wearing a neatly pressed shirt. His lanyard and clipboard suggested he was their tour leader.

"Ah, Anna, you're here. The others haven't arrived yet. Roy, this is my granddaughter." She planted a kiss on Anna's cheek.

Anna smiled and shook Roy's clipboard-free hand. "I'll just check this in."

She eased her heavy backpack off her already aching shoulders and inwardly cursed Roy for the extensive kit list he'd urged them to bring. *Ice grippers, thermals, hand warmers, a torch for goodness' sake? All set for an Arctic expedition, but perhaps a bit over-kitted for the trip we're actually taking.*

She returned from the check-in desk to the arrival of Rupert and Grace. Lexi and Toby trailed behind, mid-squabble about an almost-dead battery and the rightful proprietor of the power bank.

"Right, that's it. Give the feckin' thing to me now," Grace snapped.

Lexi pouted and Toby thumped her.

"Ouch! Toby just hit me." Lexi rubbed her arm.

Grace glared at Rupert. Preoccupied with his phone, he failed to notice.

"Enter stage right: the rest of the Edwards party," Edith exclaimed, apparently for Roy's benefit. They hugged their hellos. Roy ticked them off his list and handed over their welcome packs. Once checked in, they headed through to the terminal.

"Coffee! I need coffee now," Lexi said once they'd passed through security.

They made their way to the nearest coffee shop and set up a base camp. Rupert was the first to excuse himself, grunting that he needed to, "find somewhere quiet to make a few calls." Edith went soon after, lured by duty-free shopping, Lexi and Toby in tow, keen to follow in case she was feeling generous.

Surrounded by the group's small mountain of carry-on, Anna pulled her jumper sleeves over her hands and cupped her mug of coffee. Grace picked at an almond croissant.

"How are things?" Anna asked, breaking their easy silence.

"Oh, you know, fan-*feckin'*-tastic!" The quiver in Grace's voice revealed that things were anything but. "The man-child is here at least – well, here but not here. He'll probably be on his phone or laptop the whole time." She exhaled a deep breath. "But we've made it this far and I'm not going to let him ruin this trip for everyone," she said, with a conviction not nearly as strong as the airport coffee.

Anna drew her lips into a tight smile. It was hard not to feel torn when they moaned to her about each other over the years. The 'twin-betweener,' Rupert used to joke. *Not funny.* She covered Grace's hand with her own and squeezed it.

Grace stared down at their hands. "God, I've missed you."

"I'm here now. Talk to me."

"At first, I thought the lockdowns might do us some good. All of us being at home together, more time as a family. Yet somehow Rupert manages to be physically there but not actually present. Tell me, how is that even possible?"

Anna raised her eyebrows and sipped her coffee. "I think it has been a tough time for everyone."

Grace sighed. "I'm not sure whether or not things are worse than they were before. Perhaps I just started to notice it more? Life seemed grand when we were plodding along, doing our own thing, in our own space. I guess I could ignore the cracks until I was forced to look at his miserable face every day."

"Why didn't you call me?"

Grace shrugged and picked some more at her croissant. "When the restrictions ended, just like that – he's off. Sometimes even just the sight of him gets me raging, so I don't know why I complain about him not being around." She scoffed. "You're lucky you live alone."

The muscles in Anna's jaw tensed in response to Grace's callous remark. *This is not about me, let it go.* "Well, it's a blessing and a curse," she muttered.

"I'm hoping this trip will make him realise what he's been missing out on with Lex and Toby. He used to be so much fun. I mean, if nothing else we'd have the craic. Not any more, he's been like a different person lately." Grace chewed the inside of her lip. "I'm hoping spending some proper time with you will work its magic like it used to. He's a better person when he's around you."

"Aren't you all?" Anna grinned.

"Yeah, you're not wrong." The corners of Grace's green eyes crinkled as she smiled.

CHAPTER NINE

July 2003

After two long-haul flights in twenty-eight hours with a nine-hour layover in Bangkok, six in-flight meals, five in-flight movies, at least four vodka and cokes, and only about two hours of sleep, Anna didn't have a clue if it was currently today, tomorrow, or yesterday. But she'd finally arrived home.

Retrieving her backpack from the baggage carousel, her stomach flipped at the thought of Grace, literally metres away from her on the other side of the airport barrier wall.

Six months had passed since they'd seen each other. Six months of emotionally charged letters and crackly long-distance calls, and now they were about to be reunited. She couldn't remember ever feeling this excited, or this nervous. She was even shaking a little, but she reasoned that could be the jet lag kicking in. Insecurities crept in with her tiredness. *Will things still feel the same as they did before I went away?*

As eager as she was to just run into the Arrivals hall, she decided to freshen up first. She brushed her teeth whilst staring back at her reflection, her blue eyes striking against her sun-kissed skin. She splashed cold water onto her face, sprayed on some deodorant, and did what she could to tame her hair. *If nothing else, I have a great tan.*

She flashed herself a smile, pulled on her heavy backpack, and took a few deep breaths.

Anna's heart leapt; Grace was waiting with a bunch of sunflowers and a hand-made sign reading, 'Welcome Home Banana'. Grace chewed her bottom lip as her eyes scanned the faces of the arriving passengers, searching for Anna amongst them. Finally, meeting her gaze, Grace beamed, ran over, and threw her arms around Anna, nearly toppling her. Laughing and crying at the same time, Anna shrugged off her backpack so they could properly embrace, and she could feel the jigsaw fit of her missing piece.

Grace broke away first, her tears still coming.

"Anna, I need to—" She stopped and looked around. "I know you probably just want to be getting home, but can we get a cup of coffee and sit down for a minute? There's something I—" She stopped again, her face creased with worry.

"Yeah, sure we can. Are you okay?"

Grace looked down at her sandals and nodded.

Anna frowned. "Come on. Coffee sounds great. I'm going to need all the caffeine I can get today." She put an arm around Grace and lugged up her backpack with the other.

* * *

In the corner of a busy airport café, Grace stared into her cappuccino. Anna stared at Grace, letting her eyes remind her brain that she hadn't just imagined that perfect face.

"It's so good to see you," Anna said, her nerves multiplying with every second that Grace didn't look at her. "It feels surreal to actually be here. I've been dreaming about this—"

"I'm sorry, Anna. I'm so, so sorry but I've messed everything up," Grace choked as heavy tears started to roll down her cheeks and plop into her coffee.

"What do you mean?" Anna reached across and touched her arm. Grace pulled it away and buried her face in her hands. "Grace, what's wrong? Please just tell me what's wrong."

Grace finally looked at her.

"I didn't mean for it to happen. Neither of us did. It just happened and as much as I want to, I can't undo it." Grace let out a sob. Anna reached for her hand again. "I don't want to lose you, so I have to be honest. I couldn't tell you before now as you were so far away, and I needed to tell you to your face." Grace wiped her nose with a napkin.

"Okay, tell me what, Grace? Please, you're scaring me. What has happened?" Anna's eyes searched Grace's face for answers.

"Rupert and I… we slept together." She spat the words out fast, as if they were as dirty as the deed.

"You… you what?" Even though she'd heard her loud and clear, the words Grace had just said made no sense, like she'd spoken in another language. "Sorry, what did you say?" she repeated, snatching her hand away.

Grace's cheeks were flaming red, and her tears started to fall again – plop, plop, plop into the foam of her untouched coffee.

"Please don't make me say it again." Grace looked like she wanted the faux-leather tub chair to swallow her up. "I would do anything to take it back, for it not to have happened…"

Anna squeezed her eyes shut as anger flared inside her. But she had questions, so she swallowed her rage to ask them. "I don't… I mean I can't… okay, when? When did it happen?"

"It was about three months ago, before the Easter break." Grace buried her face in her hands again.

"Oh my God!" Anna's hand rose to her mouth. She looked at Grace through wide eyes, momentarily paralysed with shock. *Fuck, fuck, fuck. I'm asleep and this is just a nightmare.* She pinched her arm hard, and it hurt. Her rage burst forth in a torrent. "I can't believe this. What the actual fuck, Grace? You've spoken to me dozens of times since then. You've written me letters. You told me that you love me. How could you have said that to me?"

Anna's voice was very raised, along with the eyebrows of most of the people sitting near them. "You don't love someone and then sleep with their brother. We're not a buy-one, get-one-fucking-free, Grace!"

"Anna, I know, I know, I'm sorry. Please don't shout." Grace sank into her chair and cupped her hands around her face.

Anna stared into the distance. "I've spoken to him so many times and he said nothing at all. Nothing. I'm going to kill him. I think I'm actually going to kill him." She took a deep breath and looked back to Grace. "I thought we had something, I really thought we had something…"

"We do, at least… we did…"

"Was this your plan all along? Have us *both*? Did you tell him that you love him?"

Grace quietly sobbed and shook her head.

"This is too much; I can't do this." Anna stood. She tried to pick up her backpack, but her hands were shaking and the straps tangled around the chair leg. *For fuck's sake.*

She shoved her bag down and flopped back into the chair.

"Fine. I have to know. I need to know everything. You owe me that at least."

"Anna, it wasn't like what you think. It was a mistake. I'll tell you what you want to know, I'll answer your questions. It happened before the Easter break, like I said. I went to see Rupert as I was missing you, I was feeling really low. We were about to go home for the holidays so I knew I wouldn't be able to talk about you as freely because of my family and—"

"Great! You were missing me, so you shagged my brother," Anna said through gritted teeth.

"Anna, please. You said you wanted to know so I'm trying to tell you."

She folded her arms and Grace continued. "I knew Rupert would understand, he was missing you too. Being around him was comforting. He reminds me of you in so many ways." Grace smiled sadly at her. Anna looked away.

Grace took a breath. "I went over to his place. We watched a silly film, had some pizza and a couple of beers. It got late. He suggested that I stay over. He was going to sleep on the sofa, but then… we kissed, it's like a blur but one thing led to another. Honestly, I didn't mean for it to happen, and like I said, I would give anything to undo it."

Afraid that those six in-flight meals could make a reappearance at any moment, Anna shifted uncomfortably in her seat.

"Afterwards, I realised what we'd done. I left and I cried all the way home. Rupert came after me, but I told him to leave me alone, so he did. I haven't even spoken to him since, although he has tried to call me. I swear to you I haven't said any of the things to him that I've said to you. It's you that I have those feelings for…" Her voice cracked. "It's *you* that I'm in love with, Anna," she said between sobs.

CHAPTER TEN

January 2022

Trondheim

After two short flights – Heathrow to Oslo and Oslo to Trondheim – they collected their luggage and boarded the coach transfer to their hotel.

"It's pitch black out there already and it's only three o'clock," Lexi said as she shuffled into the seat next to Anna.

"You better get used to it, Lex. There isn't a lot of daylight here in winter."

"We could be anywhere." Lexi closed her eyes and pulled on her headphones.

Anna pressed her face closer to the window. Squinting, she could just about make out the outline of a mountain range in the distance. *We could be anywhere, but there's nowhere else quite like here.* She rested her head back and didn't wake until the coach pulled up to the hotel.

* * *

In the lobby, the tour group crowded around Roy as he handed out room keys. "Dinner will be served at 6 p.m. in the hotel restaurant.

That gives you some time to freshen up and make yourselves at home."

"Tobes, you're in with Gran," Grace said and passed him his bag. He pulled a face and Edith put her arm around him.

"I've brought Alexandre Dumas along with me," Edith loudly whispered.

Toby's eyes lit up, and no further protest ensued as they made their way to their rooms.

* * *

Anna made the mistake of allowing Lexi to have the first shower, meaning she ended up being the last to arrive for dinner. Edith waved her over to the seat she'd saved between her and Toby at the long table, shared with three of the other groups travelling with them.

A cheerful Rupert, whisky in hand, was already making friends.

"Everyone, this is my sister, Anna. Anna, this is everyone!"

She smiled and glanced over the group as Rupert delved into further introductions.

"Okay, so we have Jeff and Stephen from Bolton, no, wait... Bradford." Jeff and Stephen smiled at Anna. *Matching polo shirts*, she noted and grinned.

"This is Deb and Dave from Cardiff." The Welsh couple waved. "Last but no means least, Sue and, wait... no, don't tell me, I've got this." Rupert squeezed his eyes shut. "It's Sue and Paddy from deepest, darkest... Portsmouth." Laughter rippled around the table and Rupert looked smug. Grace groaned, Lexi rolled her eyes, and Toby remained engrossed in the game he was playing on his Nintendo Switch.

"Hi, everyone." Anna smiled and waved.

"What took you so long? I thought you were meeting me in the bar," said Rupert.

"Despite being naturally gorgeous, like her aunt, your teenage daughter has a rigorous beauty routine that just can't be rushed." Anna winked at Lexi, who playfully poked her tongue out in response.

"Yeah well, I had to make 'friends' with that lot." He gave a side nod to the people he'd introduced and grimaced. Engrossed in conversations of their own, thankfully no one noticed.

"They all seem perfectly nice, Rupert. Don't be rude," said Edith.

"Dave spent twenty minutes telling me all about his train set. Riveting stuff!" Rupert gulped down his drink and signalled to the waitress that he'd like another.

* * *

A hearty pork stew served with herby mashed potato was followed by a red berry tartlet and vanilla ice cream. As coffee was being served, clipboard in hand, Roy stood and cleared his throat.

"Good evening, everyone. On behalf of myself and Great Arctic Adventures, welcome to Norway. We made it!"

Rupert let out a big whoop and clapped, prompting a sedate round of applause.

"If I can have your attention for a few minutes. I'm going to share a bit of information about Trondheim and give you some details about the next part of our itinerary."

Rupert cheered and clapped again. This time the others did not.

"Okay, great. Trondheim is one of Norway's oldest cities, more than a thousand years old, dating back to the eleventh century." Roy consulted his clipboard. "It was once the capital of Norway and some of you may be excited to hear that Trondheim was founded by Vikings!" He looked over towards Toby. Toby stared back with a blank expression.

"I don't think he's as excited about Vikings as you are, Roy," Rupert muttered loudly. Grace glared at him.

Roy nudged his thick-framed glasses back up his nose and powered on. "The city was founded by a Viking *king* to be specific, King Olav. You will see King Olav's eighteen-metre-high statue on our walking tour tomorrow, as well as the most visited attraction in Trondheim." He paused. "The impressive Nidaros Cathedral. It is the largest medieval building in all of Scandinavia."

This cued some nods and murmurs from the group.

"No more spoilers though." Roy chuckled. "You will learn much more from our local guide tomorrow. We'll be meeting in reception at 9 a.m. sharp, please. I will introduce you to our guide and we'll set out on our tour."

"And, er, how long does this tour last, Roy?" asked Rupert.

"Good question. Thank you, Mr Edwards. The tour will take about three hours, then the rest of the afternoon and evening will be yours to enjoy as you wish. Any other questions?"

Roy looked over his flock; no questions were forthcoming.

"Great. Well, in that case, I hope you all get a good night's rest, and I will see you in the morning."

"Thank you, Roy!" bellowed Rupert. He clapped and the others joined in this time. The group's chatter picked up again. Lexi and Toby resumed their respective activities. Edith became engaged in a conversation with the couple next to her, which Anna half-listened to before being distracted by tension rising between Rupert and Grace.

"Why do you have to be so loud?" Grace hissed at him. "You're embarrassing when you're like this."

"Oh, lighten up, Grace!" He drained the dregs in his glass. The ice clinked as he heavily put it down on the table. "You wanted me to come on this trip and have a good time, so here I am – life and soul!"

"Well, if you're going to be an obnoxious prick the whole time, I'd rather you weren't here."

Rupert scoffed and got up from his seat. "Are you joining me at the bar, Anna?"

Anna looked at Grace's burning cheeks, then back at Rupert, who was staring down at her. "Er, no thanks, Ru. I'm going to get an early night."

"Sod you then," he huffed and stalked off.

"Are you okay?" she asked Grace when Rupert was out of earshot.

Grace sighed. "Yeah. I'm sorry you had to hear all of that. I shouldn't have said anything, not here anyway. He's just all or nothing and to be honest I don't like either version of him right now."

"I'll talk to him."

"It's not fair to drag you into all of this. You're on holiday too."

"It's the least I can do. Besides, I won't have a good time unless you do."

CHAPTER ELEVEN

August 2003

"Why don't you join me for a hike?" asked Edith. Her eyes darted between Rupert and Anna. "There's a trail I'm keen to do, but I've been waiting for the right weather. Tomorrow looks promising. Enough of this moping around; the fresh air and exercise will do you both the world of good."

Rupert didn't normally join them on hikes but on this occasion, he'd eagerly accepted the invitation. Anna hadn't spoken a single word to him since she'd returned from Australia. In fact, she'd barely spoken a word to anyone, choosing instead to seek solace in the quiet of her bedroom.

Bruised and betrayed by the two people who were closest to her, she wanted time alone to wrap her head around it all before facing the world again.

Over and over, she relived the conversation with Grace at the airport. Her mind fixated on the sorrow-filled look on Grace's face as she turned to walk away from her. Echoes of Grace's dreadful confession bounced around in her head. She wished she could rewind to the moments before those words had been spoken, when she was still in love. When Grace was still perfect, and her heart hadn't been broken.

Since her return, Rupert had tried to speak to her on countless occasions. It usually started with a soft knock on her bedroom door, which she refused to open, followed by an attempt to engage her in conversation.

"I made you some tea, Skywalker. I even bought Jammie Dodgers – they're still your favourite, right?"

Piss off! her mind screamed, but the words were unspoken. He sighed as he lowered himself to the floor. The old wooden door creaked in protest as he leaned against it.

Him on one side, her on the other. Just two inches of oak and a huge fucking betrayal between them.

Hours were spent like that. She knew he was still there; she could hear him breathing. She listened out for the big sigh he made when he gave up – only to return a few hours later.

* * *

After a couple of weeks of being ignored, Rupert changed tack, acting like nothing was amiss. Chipper and buoyant, he chatted away when she was in the room, answering for her when she didn't respond. So when the opportunity of the hike came up, he almost fell over himself to accept on behalf of them both. *Pathetic!*

"I'll make us a picnic. I'll even carry it up that bloody hill! Cheese and pickle for you, Anna? Yes? Great. Gran, where's the big flask?" he'd asked, way too cheerily.

Prick! Anna had rolled her eyes and carried on reading her book.

Of course, they'd fallen out before, but in their twenty years of life together he'd always managed to penetrate her silent treatment with his puppy-dog antics. Usually, she found it virtually impossible to stay mad at him, but never before had he hurt her as badly as this, and he knew it.

* * *

The weather forecast promised a hot day, but steam rose from the dewy ground in the cool air, not yet heated by the sun.

Nearing the summit, Anna stopped to catch her breath and admire the views of the rolling green landscape as it bathed in the glow of the early morning light. Edith had powered on ahead; she always liked to reach the top first, as if it were an act of defiance against her ageing body.

Anna pulled off her headphones; she'd kept them firmly on her ears since they'd left the house, opting for The White Stripes over Rupert's attempts to talk to her. Now he puffed up behind her; he'd obviously made an effort to catch up.

"Hey," he said between breaths, bending at the waist. "All those hikes you and Gran did without me have paid off. I can barely keep up."

They stood in silence looking out over the vista until she almost forgot he was next to her.

"Listen, I know you don't want to talk to me, I get it. If I were you, I wouldn't want to talk to me either… but I need to speak to you, Anna. There are things I need to say."

She forced herself to look at him. *If looks could kill*. She opened her mouth and spoke the first words she'd said to him in weeks. "I heard what I needed to hear from Grace. I need some time, so please stop trying so hard and leave me alone!"

"Anna, please. I can't force you to speak to me. I know I can't force you to listen to me either, but there are some things you need to know."

She shrugged and stared off into the distance, but she didn't move away. Rupert took this as a cue to continue. "Firstly, I am sorry, truly sorry. I know how you felt about her, so what I did was unforgivable. I made a mistake. *We* made a mistake, and if I could change it I would."

Anna shifted on her feet and sniffed. Tears burned in her eyes. She kept her gaze fixed firmly ahead as she couldn't bear to look at him again.

"I've spoken to Grace. A few times actually—"

"Oh, you've been chatting, have you? That must be very nice for you both."

"Anna, you wouldn't return her calls. She's written to you, emailed you… she probably even sent a fucking carrier pigeon for all I know." Exasperation strangled his voice. "No, we haven't been chatting, not like that anyway. She needed to speak to you, to me. *To us.*"

"I don't know why. There's nothing else to say." Anna turned and started to walk on.

"She's pregnant," he called after her. "Grace is pregnant."

* * *

As she listened to the phone ringing in her ear, her heartbeat pulsed in her throat.

"Anna." Grace eventually picked up, slightly breathless. "I've been trying to call you."

Oh fuck, the sound of her voice. A sharp pain spiked in her chest. Anna squeezed her eyes shut and forced out some words. "I know you've been trying to get in touch with me… and I know about your other news. Rupert told me."

A heavy silence weighed down the air between them until Grace's shaky breath followed the sound of her opening her mouth to speak. But no words came forth. She sniffled.

Fuck, she's crying. Anna shook her head and fought the urge to comfort her.

"I wish I could see you and we weren't having this conversation on the phone," Grace said, her voice unsteady.

"This is so fucked up, Grace." Anna sighed. If Grace were in front of her right now, her barely-healed wounds would rip right open.

"I know, I know, Anna. Believe me, I know. I made a huge mistake, and now this. It's punishment, it has to be."

"I don't think you should think of it like that. You're not being punished. Besides, I'm going to have to live with it too," she said sharply, then winced at her words. *This is not about me.* She drew in a breath. "How did your parents take the news?"

"Jesus, I'm sure you can imagine. On a list of the worst things an unmarried Catholic girl can tell her very Catholic parents, it's pretty near the top."

"Yeah, I bet."

"It helped a lot that Rupert called my da and asked if he could marry me."

"He did what?" Anna laughed in disbelief. She envisaged Rupert being all sheepish and sincere in the gesture. *What a twat. A big, lovely twat.* Her smile faded when she remembered she was still fuming at him for sleeping with her girlfriend and, to top it all off, getting her pregnant.

"It settled everything down. I think my ma might even be a little bit excited about it now. She has a wedding to plan, which seems to have taken her mind off her eldest daughter going and getting herself knocked up. With the timings of it all, she doesn't think anyone will work out that the cart came before the horse. I'm not so sure of that, I'm getting fatter by the minute—"

"Wait, what? So, you and Rupert are *actually* getting married?"

"Oh. He didn't tell you that?" Grace asked.

No, he fucking didn't. Anna felt the colour drain from her face.

Taking Anna's silence as a 'no', Grace continued. "I know it's a very traditional thing to do. Times may have changed elsewhere but not so much here... I'm only going along with it because of my family, they care about that sort of thing. If things were different then…" She sniffled again.

Anna had no words; her brain jammed with shock as she tried to process this latest blow.

Grace sighed. "God, I wish things were different. I'm sorry, Anna. I'm sorry you're stuck with me in your life… although to be honest with you, I'm not entirely sorry about that. I think that's the only good thing about all this."

CHAPTER TWELVE

January 2022

The Polar Express

Following two nights in Trondheim, they were packed up and on their way to board the Polar Express. On the short drive to the train station, Roy took to the coach microphone to fill them in on the journey ahead.

"We'll be travelling on the Nordland Line. It's the longest railway line in Norway, stretching 452 miles from Trondheim to Bodø. It's an epic journey that takes around ten hours," he said, with far too much enthusiasm for the early hour.

Undeterred by the group's muted response, Roy continued. "However, we won't be travelling to Bodø today. At the special request of the Edwards party, an extra two-night stop has been added to this particular tour. So, after around four and a half hours on the train, we'll be disembarking at Majavatn station, where we'll venture onwards to Torghatten via coach and ferry."

* * *

Stepping gingerly, Anna made her way along the dark, icy platform with two cups of hot coffee. She handed Rupert a cup and added her backpack to the luggage he'd piled up next to their carriage. Elbow to elbow, they looked on as Toby checked out the hardy red train.

"They don't make them like this back home, do they?" Anna said.

Rupert scoffed. "Perhaps if they did, the country wouldn't grind to a halt every time there's even so much as a sniff of a snowflake."

"That's the disdain of a regular commuter right there." Anna winced as she sipped too-hot coffee through the plastic lid. "How's the head?"

"Still banging, but not from the booze. Grace's non-stop nagging over the last two days has been driving me nuts."

Anna pressed her lips together. She didn't want to appear to be taking sides, as he'd instantly put up his defences.

"She's worried about you, Ru."

"Funny way of showing it."

"Well, you are acting a bit odd. I mean, you're not yourself. I know things have been full-on at work and you're trying to unwind but... I'm worried about you too." She touched his arm. He sniffed and looked away.

"Banana!" Toby darted towards them and skidded to a halt. His bright blue eyes – a copy and paste of Rupert's, and her own – beamed with excitement. "Have you seen the snowplough on this train? I think we're going to be hitting some mad powder on the track, what d'ya reckon?"

"I'd say so, Tobes. Not that we'll be able to see much for another few hours." Anna ruffled his messy blonde hair.

"Roy said this train goes through a village called Hell. Do you think it'll still be dark when we go through Hell?" Toby asked.

"Probably," Anna said.

"Go to Hell, Dad." Toby laughed.

"Haha, very funny!" Rupert made to chase him, and Toby skidded off along the platform again.

The sound of Grace's voice snatched Anna's attention away. Edith, Grace, and Lexi shuffled along the platform towards them, laden with snacks and drinks for the journey.

"Let's catch up on the train," Rupert said quickly. "I need to talk to you away from everyone else. I think there's a restaurant car on here, we'll grab a coffee in a bit, okay?"

She smiled at him. "Yeah, of course."

They loaded their bags into the luggage racks and found their seats as the train trundled off into the darkness. The lights inside the carriage made it impossible to see anything other than reflections in the windows. Despite this, Roy announced they would be passing through Hell in about thirty minutes. Once again Toby seized the opportunity to remind everyone they were going to Hell.

"We're going *through* Hell, not *to* Hell," said Lexi with a roll of her eyes.

"You got that right," Grace loudly muttered and shot a dirty look in Rupert's direction.

* * *

It wasn't until mid-morning that the light started to creep in around the edges of the horizon. Rupert stretched up out of his seat and eyeballed Anna – her cue to join him for their chat. They made their way through the carriages to the restaurant car, set out like a retro diner with shiny red seats and lots of chrome. Empty of other passengers, they had their pick of the booths and slid into seats opposite each other. A round-faced lady with a kind smile served them coffee in proper mugs.

Rupert stared out of the window. A frozen landscape of white trees and snowy fields whizzed by in the dull morning light.

"So?" asked Anna.

"So," he replied and continued to look out of the window.

Anna examined the pained expression on his face. *Come on, open up, Ru.*

He took a deep breath and slowly exhaled. "I've met someone."

"Oh!" She looked at him through wide eyes. "You mean...?"

Rupert pinched his lips together and nodded.

"I met her a while ago... at work." He turned his attention to his coffee cup. "She doesn't work for me. Well, I guess she sort of does. She's a contractor. Her name's Nicole." The corners of his mouth twitched in a struggle to suppress the smile her name had summoned. "Nicole," he repeated with an odd accent.

Anna raised an eyebrow.

"She's French," he said.

"Oh, is that what that was?"

Rupert let out a laugh like the sound of a balloon popping. He leaned back in his seat, again smiling at his coffee cup. His goofy grin fell away when he looked up and saw that Anna wasn't smiling. "We've been working on the Edison Project together." He cleared his throat.

"You've been working on that for years. How long has this been going on?"

"The project started at the end of 2018, but Nicole wasn't on the team right away. She was brought in sometime in 2019… before the whole global pandemic bullshit happened. I got to know her, she got to know me, and we're… close." His stupid grin returned.

Anna squinted her eyes, analysing his face. "How close?"

He shrugged. "It's complicated."

"Yes, it is *complicated,* Rupert. You're married. You have two children!" She glared at him. "Three years? You've been having an *affair* for three fucking years?"

"No, I said I've *known her* for three years. It only got intimate about two years ago. Grace certainly hasn't been interested in me for far longer than that. Arguably, she was never interested in me."

"Don't try to justify it. How have you kept this from me for so long?"

"I've been avoiding you because I knew you'd be upset with me." He closed his eyes and pinched the top of his nose. "Look, the longer it's gone on the worse I've felt about it."

"No shit! That's how deception usually works; the more you lie, the worse you'll feel. That hasn't stopped you though, has it?"

"Anna, I don't need your judgement right now. I'm telling you because..." He inhaled a deep breath which puffed up his chest. "I think I'm in love. I've never felt like this before. This isn't just some affair, or a fling, or whatever because things are shit with Grace and I'm bored. I love Nicole. I want to be with her. She wants to be with me too." He cradled his head in his hands.

Anna sat back in the seat. "Wow!"

Outside a blizzard whipped up around the train. Glimpses of the white landscape blurred by in the breaks. "What about Grace? What about your family?" she asked, turning her gaze back to him.

"I know, I know. I feel so guilty just being around them. I take it out on Grace a lot, I know I do. I'm just so frustrated." He ruffled his fingers through his hair. "I feel sick to my stomach most of the time. The only time I feel good about myself is when I'm with Nicole. When we're together it feels like nothing else matters."

"Your family does matter though. Grace matters." Anna shook her head. "You have to tell her how you feel. You have to figure out what you're going to do so you can both move on with your lives. This isn't fair on Grace."

"I knew you'd take her side." He folded his arms across his chest.

"Grow up, Rupert. That's not fair. I've always been there for *both of you*, despite everything." She clenched her jaw in a battle to keep her cool. "For what it's worth, I think Grace is as unhappy as you are. So maybe it's time to stop trying to do what everyone expects of you both and start living your lives as you want to."

"I've ruined everything." He melodramatically buried his unshaven face in his hands.

"Don't be a twat," Anna snapped. He peered through his fingers with doleful eyes and she instantly regretted her choice of words.

"I am a twat. I'm sorry." He rubbed his cheeks with his palms. "I'm scared, Anna. It's going to change everything, isn't it?"

"You know it is… but you can't go on like this."

The hiss of hydraulics interrupted their conversation and the carriage door slid open.

Grace nodded towards their cups and grinned at Anna. "Top-up?"

CHAPTER THIRTEEN

October 2003

Under a steely sky, drizzle blustered around the quaint stone church. The wind howled and hurled brown and yellowing leaves against the leadlight windows of the sacristy.

"Shit! It's hardly the weather for it." Rupert adjusted his hair in the mirror for the fifteenth time in that many minutes. "Is it stuffy in here, or is it me?" He flapped his jacket and looked over at Anna. She shrugged.

They were dressed in matching dark grey wedding suits complete with long tails, waistcoats, pressed white shirts and emerald-green cravats. Despite being twins, this was the first time they'd both worn the same outfit and they looked more alike than ever before.

Rupert tore himself away from the mirror, looked at his watch and paced around the small room. Anna tried to straighten the decorative white carnation pinned to her buttonhole by Grace's mum.

"Ouch!" she yelped, pricking herself with the pin. Rupert came to her aid and fixed the flower into place.

"There. Now it's straighter than you'll ever be." He chuckled.

Anna smirked despite herself.

"Thanks for being here, you know, for doing this today. I can't imagine how hard this is for you," he said, staring at her intently.

Anna looked away.

"I should've asked Craig, or Joe I suppose, but I didn't want them. I wanted you. The unorthodox choice caused a stir with Grace's lot. But you'll be proud of me; I insisted that the role of 'Best Man' is a job title, not a gender. Also, my Best Man, so my choice. Nothing else has been, so I was at least having that." He picked a piece of fluff off her lapel. "You're my best friend, Anna. Always have been, always will be…" he choked on the last couple of words and enveloped her in a bear hug.

"Steady on, you'll crush the flowers!" She patted his shoulder before stepping back and checking their buttonholes for damage. "I have a choice. I can stay angry at you both or I can try to let it go. Yeah, my feelings are hurt, but I'm here because I've had enough loss in my life already, as have you."

Rupert nodded.

"We need each other, Ru. So, instead of bitterness, I choose you. I choose her. I choose to be part of this baby's life when it's here. I'm not missing out on being an auntie because I'm too busy sulking about you stealing my girlfriend." She softly poked him in the chest.

"You're amazing, you know that?" He grinned at her before resuming his nervous pacing.

"I'm scared, Anna. It's the right thing to do, isn't it? Her family expects us to do the right thing. For *me* to do the right thing by her and the baby but…" He swallowed. "I don't love her. Not like you do… or at least, not like you did. That's awful, isn't it?" The colour drained from his face.

Anna focussed hard on the flagstone floor, trying not to feel the salty sting of Rupert's words in her barely-healed wounds.

Oblivious to the pain he was stirring in her, he continued. "I mean, I love her, in that she's great. She's a lovely girl… but I'm not *in love* with her. Maybe when the baby comes? Maybe then I'll feel something more?" He ruffled his fingers in his hair. "We were so young when we lost our dad, I don't even think I know how to be a dad. Shit! I don't have a clue what I'm doing."

Rupert leaned his head against the wall and tugged at his collar.

"Breathe, just breathe. That's it." Anna rubbed his back. "You are going to be a great dad, Ru. You know how to do it, it's already in you. You've been a great brother to me, well, most of the time. You know how to look after someone, how to protect them and make them feel safe. You know how to boss them about. As for Grace, as for love…"

It crossed her mind to tell him that she loved Grace more than enough for the both of them, but that wasn't what she should say to him – not now. *Not ever.* "You're right," she said instead. "Grace is lovely. It won't be hard for you to love her. When the baby is here it will bind you together. You'll build a life, you'll make a home, and love will grow for both of you." She took a deep breath, hoping it might soothe the ache in her chest.

He turned and looked at her. His piercing blue eyes stared right into her own. "I'm so grateful you're here. I couldn't have done this without you. I don't deserve you. *We* don't deserve you."

"No, you really don't!" She laughed, and he beamed at her. "I wouldn't have missed it for the world. Stop worrying about me, I'll be okay, and one day you'll be doing this for me. Except I won't have got the girl knocked up first."

Rupert took a deep breath and punched the air.

"You've got this, Edwards," he muttered.

Anna proffered her arm and they walked out to take their place at the front of the church.

Arrangements of white carnations adorned the ends of the pews which were full of their guests: Grace's family, Gran of course, and a handful of friends. Rupert fixed his gaze on the small flower arrangement on the altar, set amongst a sea of flickering tealight candles. They stood with their arms still looped together. Rupert was rigid with tension, so Anna gave his arm a reassuring squeeze with her own.

The wait finally subsided when the creaky church doors swung open and admitted a gush of damp autumn air. *Ave Maria* piped from the lofty organ, as Grace was escorted by her father and followed down the aisle by her two younger sisters, serving as bridesmaids.

Standing as stiff as a statue, Rupert's eyes remained fixated on the altar. Anna, however, could not take her eyes off Grace. She looked ethereal in an understated white dress of satin and lace. A delicate headdress rested on her head and cascaded tiny white flowers into her wavy auburn hair. Amidst the flowing fabric of her dress, her six-month baby bump was only visible to the knowing eye.

Grace smiled at the faces of the wedding guests beaming back at her, before locking eyes with Anna. *Mutual permission to stare.* The air fizzed and everything around the edges faded out.

CHAPTER FOURTEEN

January 2022

Brønnøysund

The frigid evening air bit at their faces as they walked the few steps from the coach into the lobby. Similar to the one in Trondheim, the hotel had a contemporary Scandinavian style: monochromatic, minimalistic, and practical yet comfortable.

Lexi chucked her suitcase by the wardrobe and flopped back onto one of the beds. Anna called dibs on the first shower and Lexi grunted in acknowledgement. Judging by her frantic thumbs and the clamour of swishes and pings, the hotel's free Wi-Fi access was as welcome as rain after a drought.

Anna leaned back against the slate-tiled wall and let the hot water flow over her. She always found this soothing after a difficult day. It shouldn't have been a difficult day; the journey itself had been incredible. She'd forgotten Norway's rugged beauty in the time since they were last here. However, Rupert's revelation had sent her mind reeling.

On the train, she'd found two vacant seats in a different carriage, away from the rest of the group. She'd spent the remainder of the journey alone, looking out of the window but not seeing anything.

Similarly, for the long coach drive that followed, she sat by herself at the back, insisting it was so she could sprawl out and sleep. But that was a lie. She hadn't needed to sleep; she'd needed to think.

She couldn't be around Grace until Rupert had told her everything. *How can I look her in the eye, knowing what I know?* She didn't want to be complicit in Rupert's deceit, although somehow she felt like she was. Unease burned in the pit of her stomach.

She lathered up a cake of musky-scented soap between her hands and washed herself. As the soapsuds swirled around the plug hole, her mind spiralled with emotions: from anger, mainly on behalf of Grace, through to worry about the impact this would have on their close little family.

What if Grace decides to move back to Ireland? What if she takes the kids away? What if she takes herself away? She couldn't bear the thought of losing them. Nausea crept in if she let her mind rest on that thought for too long.

Above all, Anna was disappointed. She thought Rupert was better than this, *better than her*. All those years ago, he'd done the honourable thing, even though it hadn't been what he'd truly wanted. Learning that he was a liar and a cheat completely undermined her sacrifice. Now she begrudged every ounce of guilt she'd felt over the years. Guilt for the times that intense magnetic force between her and Grace had become too much for them and they'd crossed a line. They had a pact to fight their feelings and bury deep the instincts that felt as natural as breathing because it wasn't fair on Rupert. *He was a good man. He was the good twin. He'd done the right thing. Except, he hadn't.*

Rage bubbled up and she squeezed the cake of soap so hard it slid out of her hand and thudded onto the shower's floor.

"You okay, Banana?" Lexi yelled from the bedroom.

"Yeah, all good. I just dropped the soap."

Her mind turned to Rupert's expression on the train as he'd said the other woman's name – *Nicole*. She'd never seen his face illuminate at the mere mention of a girl's name before, he was clearly smitten. Her anger gave way to pity and oddly she felt a bit sorry for him. *Maybe he is actually in love with her? It has been two years after all.*

"Two fucking years!" she said aloud and then clapped a soapy hand over her mouth.

"Sorry, what was that?" Lexi yelled out.

"Oh, nothing. Sorry, just talking to myself."

Lexi laughed. "You know you can get some help for that, don't you?"

"Apparently it's okay so long as you don't answer yourself back," she said with forced cheer.

Rupert had better tell Grace soon. It all needs to be out in the open, otherwise it'll be a big cloud hanging over us. It had clearly been a cloud over him, which is why he'd been acting like he had.

"Are you going to be much longer? You've been in there about six hours, what are you even doing? There isn't that much of you to wash." Lexi opened the door a crack, and steam billowed out.

"You're a fine one to talk, Lex. Give me five more minutes, will you? And close that bloody door, you're letting a draught in."

As she dried herself in a fluffy white towel, Anna resolved to give Rupert an ultimatum to tell Grace about his affair whilst on this trip. As he was planning to fly home from Bodø instead of staying until the end of the tour, she'd only have to live with his lie for another forty-eight hours, at the most.

It dawned on her that the reason he was so keen to truncate his trip had nothing to do with work commitments, it was so that he could get back to Nicole. "What an absolute bastard," she muttered to herself in the mirror, not for the first time disliking that she also saw Rupert looking back in her reflection.

* * *

Hoping that a strong drink would ease her knotted stomach, Anna made her way down to the hotel bar. Relieved to see that none of the other guests had made it down from their rooms yet, with an over-priced vodka and coke in hand, Anna settled into a comfy seat by an open fire.

Moments later Grace appeared, alone. Anna's stomach lurched.

"Hey, you." Grace flopped down in the seat next to hers. "I hoped I'd catch you on your own. His lordship is still upstairs, he said he had a few work calls to make before dinner, so I left him to it."

Anna kept her eyes fixed on the fire. *Work calls? He'll be calling Nicole.*

"I think your chat with him worked wonders by the way. He's been in a great mood ever since. He seems lighter somehow. What did you say to him? What did he tell you?"

Great. If it isn't bad enough knowing about his affair, now I have to lie about it too.

"He just offloaded about the stressful project he's been working on." She shrugged and felt her cheeks burning.

"Are you okay?" Grace asked. "You were quiet today… and you went off on your own. I was going to come and find you on the train, but you seemed a bit—"

"Fine. I'm fine," Anna said, her tone sharper than she intended. She finally looked at her; Grace's eyes were full of concern. "Sorry, I'm fine, really. Funny tummy, that's all." *Technically not a lie.* She pulled her lips into a flat smile.

Grace narrowed her eyes. "Okay, as long as that's all it is."

Anna sank into her seat as if wilting under Grace's gaze.

"Talk of the devil," Grace said. Anna looked around at Rupert striding towards them.

"Hey, hey!" he said cheerfully. "Grace, Toby is looking for his jeans. He thinks they're in your bag for some reason. I looked but I couldn't see them, sorry." He shrugged and held his palms up. "He said he has to wear those particular jeans tonight, and only they will do. I swear he's like Lady Gaga with his wardrobe demands. Would you mind taking a look?"

Grace groaned and got to her feet. "No rest for the wicked."

Rupert sat in the seat she'd vacated. The orange glow of the fire flickered on his face. Grace was right, he did seem lighter, happier even. *Wonderful. At least he's managed to unburden himself from the untold secrets weighing him down.*

"When are you going to tell Grace?" she asked.

"Bloody hell, Anna. I've only just told you. Wouldn't it be better if I waited until after this trip, and we're back home?"

"No," she snapped. "I am not living with this until then. Do you have any idea how hard it is going to be for me to keep this from her?"

"Yes, as a matter of fact, I do. I've been keeping it from her for quite some time."

"Well, whose fault is that?" she hissed. "I am not living with your lie. You need to tell Grace before you go home. I'm not an idiot, I know why you're leaving early." Even she was surprised by the bitterness in her voice. "This has gone on long enough, it's not fair."

"Okay, okay, all right. I promise I'll do it." He held up his hands. "Can we just have tomorrow? It's an important day for Gran… for all of us. I don't want it to be about anything other than what we came here for. Is that okay?" He reached over and touched her arm.

She wanted to slap his hand away. Instead, she stared at it and inhaled loudly through her nose. "Yes, fine. Don't do it tomorrow… but you have to tell her before you go home. You're only making things worse by dragging it out."

He stared at her with a blank expression.

"I mean it, Rupert."

CHAPTER FIFTEEN

May 1988

News of her mother's sudden death blindsided Astrid. She had spoken to her on the phone only days before, updating her with the latest on the twins, which currently amounted to whichever Mutant Ninja Turtle or Australian pop star they most wanted to be.

"I can't keep up – one day it's Donatello, the next it's Donovan. At least with Kylie and Jason, they don't want to paint themselves green. But oh my goodness, the singing – *I Should Be So Lucky* with five minutes' peace!"

Her mother's hearty peals of laughter echoed in her mind.

Never before had she felt so far away from home, nor had she yearned this intensely to be back there, if only to confirm it was real. To confirm her mum, her dear mum, was really gone.

James had taken charge and organised things for the funeral, including their travel arrangements. He was her life raft in times of crisis, and right now Astrid was very grateful for this as she'd barely managed to keep her head above water since she'd received the terrible news.

James had offered, but she took it upon herself to tell the children. She sat them down and gently explained that her mum, their mormor, had died unexpectedly.

"Sometimes a heart just stops beating," she'd said to their confused little faces.

"But can't you get some new batteries for it?" asked Rupert.

Astrid laughed and then choked down a sob. "No, skatten min. I'm afraid not. Your heart will only beat so many times in your lifetime." She touched her palm to his chest. "Mormor's heart was very big, so it had to work extra hard."

Rupert bowed his head.

"Come on now, don't be sad." Astrid stroked his cheek and then Anna's.

Anna jumped up and threw her arms around her. Her reaction brought both comfort and pain. So serious and stoic for such a little one. So much like her mormor, but then she was her namesake after all.

James' wise words reassured her. "Death is a lot to process when you're not even six years old but they're more resilient than you think. They'll be fine," he'd said. "Besides, they have each other." He always knew what to say and when to say it.

After much deliberation, they'd decided not to bring the twins to Norway. Contrary to James's views on the matter, Astrid felt they were too young to attend a funeral, especially this one. She would struggle to get through it herself; she didn't have the strength to support them as well.

This was not only goodbye to her kind, gentle mother; it was a farewell to the last of her roots. Having lost her father when she was barely a teenager, her mother had been the only family member she remained close to. She felt adrift, untethered in internal chaos, as all of the parts that came before her, making her who she was, were gone. Now, there was only what lay ahead. The future in her small but perfectly formed world, made up of James, Rupert, and Anna.

Guilt swelled up in her like a wave when the time came to set off without the twins. Astrid squeezed them in the tightest of hugs. She hoped to squeeze away any pain they were feeling, and she selfishly hoped she could squeeze away some of her own pain too. Their sad little faces as they said goodbye almost floored her, but she reasoned that they were in the best place possible, in the care of James's mother, Edith. She was wise, pragmatic, and full of adventure; the kids adored her. Having her as a mother-in-law had made their recent move to England all the more bearable.

"Don't worry about Rupert and Anna. You know I'll take good care of them." Edith pulled her in close and Astrid smothered a sob on her shoulder.

"There are no words to heal this, my love. I know it's not the same, but I'm here for you, okay?" Edith said softly into her ear.

James's hand on her back told her it was time to go, and she extracted herself from the sanctuary of Edith's arms.

"We'll call you when we get there, Mum," he said.

* * *

After a short wait at Trondheim airport, an announcement called boarding for Widerøe flight 710. James and Astrid joined the huddle of passengers following the flight attendant out of the terminal and towards the small aircraft. As they waited in line to ascend the metal staircase, Astrid's teeth chattered in the bitter evening air. James pulled her into his broad chest and wrapped his strong arms around her. She buried her face into his thick wool jumper, inhaling his familiar smell – cedarwood, vanilla, and fabric softener.

James stowed their bags overhead and they settled into their seats. Against the pitch-black darkness outside, Astrid's reflection stared back at her in the window; her normally bright blue eyes looked dull and tired. She thought of her mum and longed to be enveloped in one of her warm hugs. Her heart squeezed at the thought of Rupert and Anna at home. She smiled, knowing that Edith would be reading them a bedtime story; some exciting adventure that would inspire their dreams.

As their twin-propeller plane taxied the runway for take-off, James gently held her hand. Astrid summoned a smile for him; he was sad too. He'd been very fond of her mother, but his sadness was mainly for her. He was such a good man, a good husband and father, she felt lucky and loved with him by her side. Fearing that she might cry again, Astrid closed her eyes and placed her head back on the headrest. Her tired body ached with grief. It wasn't long before she gave in to the overwhelming pull of a deep sleep.

She woke, startled by the noise of passengers disembarking the flight.

"Don't worry, it's just the first stop." James kissed her forehead and she smiled sleepily at him.

Once again, he took her hand into his own and rubbed her fingers with his thumb. Astrid allowed her tired eyes to close and surrendered to the darkness behind them.

CHAPTER SIXTEEN

January 2022

Torghatten

Anna's mind whirred all night, cycling through every possible outcome of Rupert telling Grace about his affair. She finally gave in and got up. She splashed some cold water on her face, brushed her teeth, and dressed in the dark, careful not to wake Lexi, who was sprawled out and sound asleep in the bed next to hers.

Edith was already in the hotel restaurant, tucking into her usual breakfast of boiled eggs and wholemeal toast, accompanied by a strong cup of tea. Anna helped herself to a small plate of gravlax and scrambled eggs from the buffet and set herself down opposite Edith.

"Morning, darling. Did you sleep well?" Edith's eyes smiled over the top of her varifocals and she turned her attention back to the folded newspaper in front of her.

"Not so good, you?"

"Mmm. Having a bit of trouble with ten down." Edith tapped her pen on the page. "Pining and then some. Eight letters."

"What have you got?"

"Starts with L, that's all I have."

Anna shrugged.

Edith sighed and put down her pen. She sipped from her cup, looking on as Anna ate. "How are you feeling about being back here?"

"I'm a bit sad, of course, but I'm pleased we're here."

"Me too." Edith smiled.

Anna finished her mouthful and scrunched up her napkin. "I think I'm going to head out for a walk and get some fresh air."

"Would you like some company?"

Anna shook her head and Edith looked into her face.

"Aha!" Edith's eyes widened and sparkled. "I've got it."

Anna raised her eyebrows.

"Lovesick." Edith grinned, snatched up her pen, and scribbled the letters into the grid.

* * *

Anna hoped the walk would clear her head of some of the less favourable outcomes she'd dreamed up during her restless night. She stepped outside, relishing the cold air on her face and breathing it into her lungs. The watery pink pre-dawn light started to creep in around the edges of the mountains, casting reflections in the inky waters of the harbour. The ground was slippery with ice and snow, and she was grateful for the ice grippers.

The walk along the harbour from the old town to the port didn't take long, so she sat on a bench and buried her hands deep into the pockets of her duck-down parka. As the light changed, it brought a renewed vibrancy to the iconic red-and-white framed houses set along the water's edge.

She wondered if her mum and dad had ever visited this tiny coastal town. They must have passed through Brønnøysund during their many trips here, but had they ever seen the same view she was looking at now? Perhaps they had sat on this very bench and watched the sunrise over the harbour. She smiled at the thought and a strong sense of them enveloped her like a hug.

Her mind turned to Grace, as it almost always did. She wished she was sitting with her now and that they could talk openly. There was so much she wanted to say. She stayed on the bench until the cold started to penetrate her layers and she meandered back to the hotel via the pretty stone Brønnøy church, the site of her parents' memorial service.

Anna arrived back just in time for Roy's briefing in the lobby. She shuffled up next to Gran and wrapped her arms around Toby to steal some of his body warmth.

"You're freezing, Banana," he protested but leaned back, accepting the hug anyway.

"Where have you been?" Grace whispered to her.

"Just getting some fresh air. I didn't sleep well," said Anna.

Grace frowned.

Roy cleared his throat. "Okay, everyone. Due to the icy conditions, the coach is going to take us over the Brønnøysund Bridge onto the island of Torget, dropping us off at the foot of Torghatten. From here, if you wish to do so, you can hike up the natural path on the eastern side of the mountain. I must warn you though, I'm told it is a fairly steep path and it'll be made even more challenging by the winter conditions." He raised his index finger into the air. "I urge you to only walk up if you are physically fit and able for it. You will need your ice grippers."

The shuffling and murmurs suggested most of the group had left them in their rooms.

Roy cleared his throat again. "It should take around thirty minutes to reach the infamous hole which goes right through the mountain. It looks small from far away but it's 160 metres long, around thirty-five metres high, and twenty metres wide, so there's plenty of room for everyone." He chuckled and nudged his glasses back up his nose. "Apparently the view is incredible."

Roy scanned over their faces and stopped when his gaze landed on Anna. "Ah, yes," he said, in a voice softer than before. "It's thanks to the Edwards party that we're here at all; this additional stop on the tour was at their special request. They lost some close family members in a tragic accident on Torghatten Mountain. I kindly ask that you give them the time and space that they need."

"Thanks, Roy," Rupert said with a solemn nod.

Anna stared at the floor to avoid having to return any of the sad sympathy smiles inevitably being thrown in their direction. A hand slipped into her own; she didn't have to look to know it belonged to Grace.

* * *

By the time the coach deposited them at the foot of Torghatten, the sun had fully risen in a cloudless sky. It seemed that the rest of the group had decided to give them a head start, as they set off on their ascent alone.

Edith led the charge, equipped with her well-worn hiking boots, ice grippers, and walking poles, "for a little extra stability." Although she was nearly eighty-three, they could barely keep her pace. The freezing air chafed Anna's throat and the pained expressions of the others suggested they were struggling too.

They reached the entrance of the hole and Toby gasped at the sheer vastness of the cathedral-sized crevice.

"Wow! It's ginormous," he said, eyes bulging.

They made their way down the wooden staircase and stood together, marvelling at the cavernous space.

"Hello," shouted Toby.

"Hello," his voice echoed.

"What's your name?"

His echo replied.

"I asked you first… I asked you first… No, I asked you first… No, I asked you first."

"Toby's an idiot," shouted Lexi, as did her echo. Toby hit her on the arm.

"Right then, now that we've got that out of the way," Edith chuckled, "shall we check out the view?"

They picked their way around the rocks of the cavern floor towards the light. The tunnel opened up into a panoramic view of the Helgeland archipelago and its hundreds of snow-crusted islands. Lexi took out her phone and snapped photo after photo, before organising them for a family shot.

Anna had visited Torghatten before with Gran, once when she and Rupert were far too young to remember it, and for a second time before they went to university. They came in summer on a Hurtigruten cruise, approaching Torghatten from the sea after an incredible journey through the fjords. It was hard to believe that this frozen landscape was the same lush green place they'd seen before. Anna's thoughts were interrupted by Rupert launching into storyteller mode.

"So, according to Norse legend the hole in the mountain was made by a troll who was chasing after a beautiful girl." Rupert seemed to have fully captured Toby's attention at the mention of a troll. Lexi zipped her phone back into her coat pocket and moved closer to listen.

"When the troll realised that he wouldn't get the girl he threw an arrow to kill her—"

"Typical," Lexi said. "If he can't have her, no one else can." She rolled her eyes and gestured with her hand for Rupert to continue.

"Anyway, the troll king saw what was happening and wanted to save the girl, so he threw his hat into the path of the arrow. When the sun came up everything was turned to stone, which means that right now, we are standing on the troll king's hat."

"Whoa," Toby mouthed.

"Or if you want the scientific version of events, this whole mountain used to be under the sea. The hole was a sea cave formed by erosion during the Scandinavian Ice Age," said Anna, throwing a glance at Grace, who was smirking.

"Do you think trolls still live here?" Toby asked, clearly more enthralled by the mythological version of events than what science had to say on the matter.

"As sure as there are leprechauns in Ireland, there are trolls in Norway," said Grace. "But don't worry, the little brutes only come out at night," she growled whilst tickling him.

"Mum, stop!" giggled Toby.

"Looks like the others have caught up to us. Shall we?" Edith said. She turned and took the lead again as they made their way along the rocky trail towards the western side of the mountain.

It was only midday, but the light was already fading, casting long shadows and a warm glow over the hillside. They reached the memorial plaque, a rectangular copper sign which had oxidised to green over time.

"What does it say?" Toby asked.

Rupert sighed. "The top line says, 'Thirty-six people perished here in the plane crash on 6th May 1988.' As for the rest, I'm afraid I can't remember."

"I can. I translated it a long time ago though," Anna said.

"Go on," said Rupert.

"It's something like, 'If you turn your face and keep looking back, it happens again and again. But when you let sorrow be your follower, your foot will be guided over the abyss, and in your trouble you will have peace.'"

Lexi wrinkled her nose. "Nice words, Banana, but what do they mean?"

"My translation is a bit ropey, but I always took it to mean that whilst you shouldn't forget the things that happened in your past, don't dwell on them too much or you'll be crushed by the weight of what was." Anna lifted her eyes from the plaque to Grace, who was looking right at her with an unreadable expression.

Silence settled around them like a blanket of snow. Edith rested her hand on the plaque, and so did Anna. Rupert wrapped his arms around their shoulders. Their pain may have dulled, and life had very much moved on, but despite the time that had passed, the loss of James and Astrid was still as cavernous as the hole that pierced through the mountain.

CHAPTER SEVENTEEN

May 1988

Waking daily around 6 a.m., Edith Edwards liked to get up and seize the day. She pulled on her pink dressing gown, slid into her slippers, and headed down to the kitchen. Switching on Radio 2, she hummed along with Rick Astley as she brewed her morning cup of tea, boiled some eggs, and popped two slices of wholemeal bread into the toaster.

Outside, the yew trees lining the end of her garden creaked and swayed in the wind. *What a shame*, she thought. She'd planned to take the twins to the park. Rain beat at the windows as Edith set down her breakfast and took her usual chair at the round oak table.

From the radio came the latest news roundup. "At approximately 8:30 p.m. last night, an aircraft operated by Widerøe Airlines crashed into Torghatten mountain on the western coast of central Norway."

Edith took a sip of tea and leaned across the table to turn up the volume.

"All thirty-three passengers and three crew who were on board are believed to be dead. Rescue attempts have been called off and an investigation into the cause of the crash is already underway. Norwegian Prime Minister, Gro Brundtland, has issued a statement offering her heartfelt condolences to the families of the victims and has said everything will be done to understand what caused this tragic accident."

Edith's china teacup fell from her hand and crashed onto its saucer, sending a teaspoon clattering across the table. James and Astrid had promised to phone home after arriving in Bodø. They hadn't phoned last night, but that was surely because they'd been delayed or were too tired from travelling.

The telephone's shrill ring shook Edith from her daze.

She floated into the hallway and lifted the receiver to her ear. "James? Is that you?"

"Hello. Is that Mrs Edith Edwards?"

"Speaking," she heard herself say.

"I'm afraid I have some bad news…"

The stranger's words hit her like a high-speed train. She crumpled to the floor and dropped the receiver. A once-familiar well of despair opened up inside her, and she sobbed until there were no tears left.

She had no idea how long she'd been there, in that hopeless heap of despair on the floor, but when she became aware of herself again, her first thought was *Thank goodness the twins didn't see me like this,* followed by, *How on earth am I going to break this to them?*

Delivering words that would change their lives forever was an unenviable task. Losing their mormor was merely a dress rehearsal for what was about to come. Edith stood up, smoothed down her dressing gown, and pulled the cord tight. She examined her reflection in the hallway mirror, wiped her eyes dry with her thumbs, and sniffed for good measure. *Now then, it's time to be strong; you have two little ones in your charge.*

She gently knocked on their bedroom door and edged it open. Sunlight from the hallway window danced across the forest-scape mural covering the wall behind their beds. In the corner stood a tipi, strung with fairy lights and decked out with cushions and blankets. It made for a great den and the frequent venue of their beloved story time.

"No wonder they love staying here. You spoil them, Mum," James often said to her.

"Well, it didn't spoil you, did it?" she'd always reply, recalling how she had tried to fill his childhood with wonderful adventures.

She shook the memory from her head and drew in a ragged breath, smothering the anguished sob that threatened to escape from her chest.

The twins stirred. Edith climbed into the bed alongside Anna and asked Rupert to jump in too, which he willingly did. It seemed he never wanted to miss out on any affection Anna was getting without him. Edith hugged them tightly, a twin under each arm.

"You're sad, Gran." Anna reached up and touched her pudgy little fingers to Edith's cheek.

"Yes, Anna, I am very sad and I'm about to tell you both something that is going to make you very sad too." Edith's throat wanted to close over in protest of the words she had to say.

Anna squeezed her tightly as if bracing herself for what was about to come.

"Your mum and dad love you very much, that will never change… but I'm so sorry to tell you that they won't ever be coming home. There was an accident in Norway and they…" Her voice cracked.

Tears flowed. Her well of despair wasn't empty after all.

"They died?" Rupert asked.

Edith nodded.

Anna drew in a deep, juddering breath that shook her small frame. Edith rocked her gently. "I'm here," she said through her tears. "You'll always have me… and you'll always have each other, from the first heartbeat to the last."

Rupert clung to them both, blinking back the heavy tears forming in his own eyes.

"It's okay, we'll be like the Three Musketeers," he said, inspired by the bedtime story Edith had most recently read with them. She tried to smile for him.

"Yes. Yes, I suppose we will," she said as the tears rolled down her cheeks.

CHAPTER EIGHTEEN

January 2022

Arctic Circle

"Come on, birthday girl. I left you as long as I could, but it's time to get up." Anna gently shook Lexi's shoulder.

"Ugh," Lexi groaned. She turned her face into the pillow, her wavy auburn hair fanned out around her head like a crown.

"I guess we'll leave without you then. There'll be no Arctic Circle crossing for you on your birthday." Anna laughed as she packed her washbag into the top of her backpack.

"Alright, I'm up," Lexi said, throwing back the duvet. "Happy now?"

* * *

The trip from Brønnøysund to Majavatn, via coach and a short ferry crossing, took a little over three hours. They arrived at Majavatn station before midday to pick up the Polar Express on its twice-daily route to Bodø.

As the train set out along the snowy track, Anna and Grace made their way to the restaurant car. Thanks to Roy, and his helpful coordination with the Nordland Railway, two booths had been reserved. The light of the short winter's day was already fading as they strung birthday bunting up over the windows.

"I can't believe she's eighteen," Grace said between puffs into a balloon.

"I know! It seems like it was only last week that you popped her out."

"You know full well that she didn't just *pop out*… eighteen years later and my woo-woo still hasn't forgiven me!" Grace laughed.

Anna raised an eyebrow. "I can't believe that eighteen years later you still call it a woo-woo!"

The smiley, round-faced lady from their last train ride gave them some Champagne glasses, and they unpacked a small buffet consisting of Lexi's favourites: party rings, cocktail sausages, and of course, Hawaiian pizza – a penchant for which she'd most definitely inherited from Rupert.

When everything was ready, Anna went to collect the others.

"Oh look, reindeer," she said pointing out of the window at nothing at all, distracting Lexi whilst Edith, Rupert, and Toby went on ahead to the restaurant car.

* * *

"Surprise!" they cheered as Lexi walked through the carriage door, and a smile cracked her face for the first time that day. They sang 'Happy Birthday' as Grace presented Lexi with a chocolate cake lit with eighteen candles. Lexi swept back her hair and blew them out.

"Let's get this party started!" Rupert slid into a booth and set to work on uncorking a bottle.

"Can I have some Champagne?" Toby asked.

"Just a sip," Grace said. "Only pour him a little bit, not like the last time, Ru."

Rupert nodded, and they exchanged a knowing glance. He passed out the fizz-filled glasses and raised his in the air. "Here's to you, Lexi, on your eighteenth birthday. May you live a long, happy life and get rich enough to take care of us all when we're old and decrepit. Cheers!"

They clinked their glasses together. "Also, I wanted to say thanks to Gran for arranging this trip and for taking us back to Torghatten. Yesterday was a really special day. Thank you, Gran."

The others murmured their thanks. Edith blushed and waved away the attention. "Not many people would be able to say they travelled across the Arctic Circle on their eighteenth birthday, Lexi. Hopefully, this is the first page in a life story full of many exciting adventures."

"Thanks, Gran. This is so cool. Most of my friends had lame parties and just got drunk on their eighteenths. At least we're doing something momentous."

"Ah now, my eighteenth was pretty momentous. Uncle Gene gave me my first taste of poitín. I broke the heel on my brand-new shoes, fell in a ditch and it took three fellas to pull me out. Howling like the banshee I was. Ma was raging at the state of me, as you can imagine," said Grace. Her story triggered a ripple of laughter. "I haven't touched a drop since," she added.

Rupert scoffed. "It's only poitín you discriminate against though, isn't it? You're not exactly teetotal."

"Ah well, you see it was the poitín that did the damage. Sure, there'd be no rhyme or reason for me to take it out on the other drinks, would there?" Grace grinned at Anna and took a sip from her glass.

"I don't remember our actual eighteenth birthday. Do you, Anna?" Rupert didn't wait for a response. "Probably because I was still hungover from Glastonbury the week before. The line-up that year was incredible... Counting Crows, Ocean Colour Scene, Moby. Not forgetting Bowie – the freaking legend, may he rest in peace!" He raised his glass skywards.

"Do you remember that random hippy girl who kept following us around? She tried to gnaw your face off during Fatboy Slim's set. She was so weird," said Anna.

"Yuck!" said Lexi, and Toby pretended to throw up.

"I barely remember her," said Rupert, "but I do remember you smoking a spliff and flashing your baps at Christina from the Wannadies when we saw her in the beer tent. You kept singing the *You & Me Song* at her. She looked terrified, the poor thing. Couldn't get away fast enough."

Feeling her cheeks flush, Anna covered her face as the others laughed.

"What's a spliff?" asked Toby.

"Tell you when you're older," Rupert and Anna said in unison. Toby stuck out his bottom lip.

"I tried a spliff once," Edith said.

Laughter erupted again and Rupert topped up their glasses with a new bottle. He winked at Anna as he poured Toby another little splash.

Lexi unwrapped her presents: jewellery, money, driving lessons;

then made a start on her pile of cards.

"Oh, that one's from me. Your present's in there too," Anna said when Lexi got to the yellow envelope.

Lexi opened the card. On the front was a chimpanzee holding a banana.

"If you're the banana, does that make me the chimp?" she laughed, and read aloud, "Happy 18th Birthday, Lexi, hope you're having an amazing Arctic adventure, here's something to look forward to later this year." Lexi unfolded the piece of paper inside the card. "OMG! How did you manage to get these? This is awesome!" she squealed. "Thanks so much, Banana."

"What have you got, Lex?" asked Grace.

"A ticket to Glastonbury! Four tickets actually." She held up the placeholder tickets Anna had made in place of the real deal arriving.

"Oh, that's amazing! Who are you going to take with you?" Grace asked.

"You and Banana obviously, and maybe Alice or Switch. Possibly Ed." Lexi shrugged. "Whichever of them is annoying me least at the time, I guess."

"Aw, you don't have to take us, Lex. They're your tickets. Take your friends, you don't want us cramping your style," Anna said.

"I want you both to come with me, I always have the best fun with you two. Besides Mum, I'll need you to bring the poitín and Banana, you can source the spliffs." Lexi laughed.

"Well, break it gently to your dad that we'll be going to Glasto without him," Anna whispered. She glanced over at Rupert; he was busy thumb-wrestling Toby.

The party was interrupted by the rest of their tour group entering the carriage.

"Gather in, gather in," Roy said as the group filled the remaining seats in the restaurant car. "We'll shortly be crossing over the Arctic Circle, so I wanted to bring you all together with a little bubbly to mark the occasion. Especially now there isn't anything to see."

Everyone laughed, but Roy was right; all that could be seen through the windows was the occasional puff of white, as a snowdrift got whipped up by the force of the train, against the darkness that had enveloped the landscape.

Lexi pulled out her phone and they looked at her map app. The GPS tracking showed a flashing blue dot rapidly approaching the dotted line which marked the Arctic Circle.

Glasses were handed out and filled with Champagne. Roy raised a glass to Lexi and Rupert initiated another raucous round of 'Happy Birthday'. Lexi groaned and tried to sink down in her seat as much as the table would allow. Shortly after, Roy announced that they had now crossed the Arctic Circle, prompting whoops and cheers from the merry passengers, some more merry than others.

With still another two hours to go until they reached Bodø, gradually members of the group made their way back to their carriage. Grace took charge of Toby, who was feeling sick after too much chocolate cake, the Champagne probably not helping much either. Phone in hand, mumbling something about Alice and Switch, the birthday girl excused herself. Edith yawned and returned to her seat for an afternoon nap, leaving Rupert and Anna to tidy up.

"I have news," Rupert announced when the others had left. "I made a couple of calls earlier and with the help of our chum Roy, I've managed to change my plans."

"What do you mean?" Anna asked as she removed the bunting from the windows.

"I mean, I'm not going home tomorrow, I'm going to stay for the rest of the trip. I realised yesterday that I was making a mistake." Rupert looked pleased with himself, but his face fell when Anna didn't return his smile. "Aren't you happy I'm staying?"

"Yes. No." She shook her head. "I don't know. What do you mean, you realised you're making a mistake?"

"I'd be making a mistake leaving early, and I'd regret it." He shrugged. "Yesterday reminded me that we'd have given anything to have had more time with Mum and Dad, so I'm going to be better for Lexi and Toby. I owe them the best version of me, like who I used to be before the guilt started eating me up and stressing me out all the time."

Anna frowned. "Right, but you're still going to tell Grace about Nicole, aren't you?"

"Yes, I told you I'd do it on this trip, and I will… but as I'm staying until the end, I'll wait and find the right moment to tell her that I'm in love with someone else." His eyes bulged and he puffed out his cheeks. "Wow, saying that out loud feels so weird. I need time to prepare saying it to Grace."

"Right, okay then. That's good, I guess." Anna suppressed the urge to say more. As much as she usually loved having him around, she was still angry with him. On top of that, she would have to continue living with his lie and feeling awkward around Grace.

"I don't think there's ever a right moment to tell your wife that you're in love with someone else." She popped one of the balloons.

"I know, I know, but I'm trying to do the right thing," he replied, seemingly oblivious to her tone.

"Maybe that's what got us into this mess in the first place," she muttered.

"What do you mean?" He manhandled another of the balloons until it popped.

"Never mind. It doesn't matter."

CHAPTER NINETEEN

January 2004

Anna's bashed-up Nokia 3310 vibrated across her bedside table. She prised her eyes open a sliver to squint at the tiny phone screen. *Rupert.* The red digits of her alarm clock blinked 03:09.

A call from him at this time meant one thing.

She sat bolt upright and grabbed at the phone. "Grace – is she okay?"

"Hey, yeah, we're at the hospital." His voice sounded tight and breathless. "Her waters broke at home, and I think she's in labour."

"Shit. How's she doing?"

"She's fine… at least she was when I left her. I had to come outside for some air. It was really hot in there, although I seemed to be the only one who thought so."

"Is she in pain?"

"They've given her some drugs, so she's all doped up… she keeps asking for you, Anna. Do you think…? I mean, would you mind coming to the hospital? I know it's late or early or whatever bloody time it is, but I'd like it if you were here too. I'm a bit freaked out, to be honest. It's all so—"

"I'm on my way!" Anna didn't need to be asked twice; there was nowhere else she'd rather be.

After fishing yesterday's clothes out of her wash basket and hopping into her jeans, she ran her fingers through her hair, not caring what it looked like. Outside, she clipped on her helmet, jumped on her bike, and cycled from her uni halls to the hospital as fast as her legs would take her. The bitter night air whipped around her face and made her eyes water.

Rupert stood out the front, his shoulders hunched and hands stuffed into his pockets, shivering in just a thin blue Oxford shirt, half tucked into his jeans.

"Where's your coat?" she asked.

He shrugged.

"Please tell me you went back inside to Grace after you called me?"

"No, I waited here. Anna… I'm not ready to be a dad," he said through chattering teeth.

Anna pulled off her coat, threw it over his back and it hung around his shoulders like a capelet.

"C'mon," she said, puffing out a misty breath of laughter. With her arm around him, they walked through the sliding doors into the strip-lit hallway. Her trainers squeaked as they moved along the empty corridor. Anna's burning desire to get to Grace was stymied by Rupert's pace, slower and stiffer with every step closer to the maternity unit. Anna stopped and turned to face him.

"I know you're scared, Ru, but imagine how Grace must be feeling right now." She squeezed his shoulder and looked into his face. "She's effectively got to push a whole watermelon out of her woo-woo, or whatever it is she calls it."

Rupert sniffed out a laugh.

Anna smiled. "There's no going back. This baby is ready to be born whether you like it or not." She nodded towards the dark blue double doors. "Shall we?"

"Maybe you should go in on your own?" Rupert backed away.

"No. You've done all of the antenatal work with her. I don't have a clue. I've seen the movies – it should be your hand she breaks when she's squeezing out that watermelon, not mine." Anna chuckled. "C'mon Team Edwards!" She softly punched his arm.

With a closed-lip smile and a nod, Rupert resigned himself to the inevitable. Anna followed as he pushed through the heavy doors and swung a left into the delivery room.

"Where the feckin' hell have you — ah feckin' feckety fuck," Grace moaned. Her face screwed up with the pain of a contraction.

"Sorry, Grace," he said, his voice unusually small. "I went to get someone for you."

Anna stepped out from behind him. Grace beamed and then her face contorted as she was pummelled by another contraction.

"Hey, you." Anna walked around to the other side of the bed and took Grace's hand. "How are you doing?"

"I can't lie, I've been better." Grace smiled up at Anna. Her eyebrows knitted together in confusion. "Is that a bra?"

Anna peered over her shoulder; a hot pink bra was twisted in her hoodie. "Yeah, I got dressed quickly, and in the dark… at least it's my own," she muttered and flushed with embarrassment.

Rupert laughed as she retrieved the bra and stuffed it in her pocket.

A nurse, dressed in pale blue scrubs, moved efficiently around the room. Rupert helped Grace to concentrate on her breathing, whilst

Anna held her hand and stroked her hair. For almost five hours, the clock above the door ticked out the rhythm of their pacing, breathing, squeezing, screaming, and finally, the "Push. Push. Push."

"One more big push for me now, Grace," said the midwife. The room blurred around them like a long exposure shot and snapped back into focus with the wail of a newborn.

Collectively, it seemed, they released a breath.

Perspiration dripped from the forehead of the smiling midwife as she looked from Grace to Rupert. "Congratulations, you have a daughter." She swaddled the baby in a yellow blanket and placed her in Grace's arms. Rupert and Anna stood on either side of the bed.

The intensity of love Anna felt for the tiny pink and yellow bundle in Grace's arms astounded her. The expressions on the faces of Grace and Rupert told her they felt the same. Yet with everything gained, everything lost came into sharper focus – how all at once, Anna was both part of this new dynamic and superfluous; an extra in their new family cast of three. *It's time to move on.*

"Alexandra. I think we should call her Alexandra," said Grace, looking up at Rupert.

"Yeah, I really like that." He smiled and ruffled his fingers through his hair. "How about Alexandra Astrid?"

Grace smiled into the sleeping face of her little girl. "Alexandra Astrid Edwards. It's perfect!"

"Our little Lexi," said Anna as she stroked the wispy red hairs on Lexi's head.

CHAPTER TWENTY

January 2022

Bodø

"With its positioning in southern Arctic Norway, Bodø is one of the top spots to get a great celestial sky show," Roy said into the microphone as the coach pulled into a dark mountainside spot. He warned them against looking at phone screens, as it would 'ruin their eyes', making it harder to adjust to the darkness and see the northern lights, should they appear.

Rupert snatched away Lexi and Toby's devices. Lexi protested that she was now officially an adult, so she could 'ruin her eyes' if she wanted to. She backed down when Rupert reminded her that it would limit her chances of getting any good photos.

Anna peered out of the coach window at a ceiling of clouds, backlit by the moon. According to the aurora app she'd downloaded, the forecast was poor.

"And now we wait for Mother Nature to put on her show," said Roy.

The driver cut the engine and the interior lights faded to darkness. In anticipation, the group's chatter hushed to near silence, as if awaiting the appearance of a rare bird that would flit away at the slightest noise. After forty-five minutes, the increased shuffles and murmurs suggested a collective resignation to Mother Nature's no-show. Lexi groaned, zipping and unzipping her coat. Toby entertained himself by fogging up the coach window with his breath and drawing what he claimed were mountain trolls.

"They look like deformed broccoli," Lexi said.

Toby gasped. "Mum, Lexi's being a b—"

"Mind your mouth, Toby." Grace stretched up and out of her seat. "Come on, you lot. Let's get some air."

They stood in the dark, icy car park, looking hopefully to the skies, but observing only clouds. It was late, they'd had an early start and travelled all day, so at Roy's suggestion the group agreed to give up their northern lights hunt for the evening.

* * *

"Nightcap?" Rupert suggested when they arrived back at the hotel.

Edith declined and offered to get the very sleepy Toby to bed. Anna, Grace, and Lexi went to their rooms to shed some of their excess clothing. On their return, Rupert beckoned them over to the seats he'd commandeered by the fire.

Sinking into the sofa next to Anna, Lexi yawned, triggering Grace to do the same.

"Blimey, you lot, where's your party spirit? The night is young, it's only quarter to eleven," said Rupert. "Lexi, it's your eighteenth birthday. You are squandering the gift of youth, my girl!"

Lexi yawned again and rested her head on Anna's shoulder.

"I'll enjoy the gift of youth tomorrow, Dad."

"I've just been looking at the aurora app." Anna held up her phone. "The forecast is pretty strong; it gets up to a KP5 at midnight. It was only a KP2 when we were on the coach. Providing the sky is clear enough, which the weather app reckons it will be, there's a good chance of seeing something. Does anyone fancy going out for another look? We could try the harbour along the back of the hotel."

"No thanks, Banana, not tonight. I need some sleep," Lexi mumbled with her head still resting on Anna's shoulder.

"I'm not sure I've got it in me, Anna. I'll be out like a light when my head hits the pillow," said Grace.

Rupert rubbed his hands together. "Count me in. The night is young."

They finished their drinks and returned to their rooms. Lexi was sound asleep within seconds of getting into bed.

Rock on, Lex. Anna chuckled to herself.

Just before midnight, Anna pulled on her snow boots and coat, stuffed her gloves and hat into her pockets, and closed the door quietly behind her. As it clicked shut, the door of the room opposite opened and Grace walked out.

"Hey, I thought you were going to bed?" Anna whispered.

"Ha, I was. Got a second wind. I felt shattered before, but I'm wide awake now so I may as well go gallivanting with you."

Anna nodded towards the door. "Is Ru coming?"

"Is he shite! He's still fully clothed, face down and drooling onto the pillow. I can guarantee you he'll still be exactly like that in the morning." Grace laughed.

"Fair enough. Shall we, then?" Anxiety twisted Anna's stomach; she hoped Grace didn't probe her further about the conversation she'd had with Rupert.

"Yep, let's go." Grace marched on ahead. "With you dragging me out at all hours of the night in the freezing cold, I'm telling you that sky better be lit up with all the glories of nature, or else!"

"Or else what?"

Grace looked back over her shoulder and answered with a grin.

* * *

The Arctic cold hit them as they stepped outside. Grace shivered and hugged herself into Anna's arm. They walked around the back of the hotel and along the wooden boardwalk. Icy water lapped the hulls of moored fishing boats and fierce-looking sea vessels. The lights on the boats cast enough of a glow to cut through the darkness. With no one else around, Anna would usually be a bit unnerved. But in the dead of night, in an Arctic town, in the middle of winter, there was a perfectly rational explanation for the eerie lack of people.

The breaks in the clouds were bigger than they'd been earlier, with glimpses of the sky beyond but still no sign of aurora. They walked the length of the boardwalk until they reached a bench overlooking the harbour.

Grace's breath misted the air. "Shall we sit for a while?"

"Sure. Are you warm enough?"

"Yeah. Besides, this will help." Grace reached inside her jacket and pulled out a small silver hip flask.

Anna flung back her head and laughed. "Please tell me that's not poitín in there?"

"Hell, no! Do you take me for some kind of a masochist?" Grace giggled and offered the hip flask to Anna.

Anna took a sip and passed it back.

Out ahead, boats bobbed in the sea against the backdrop of a snow-covered island. Above them, the clouds drifted further apart, revealing vast patches of starry sky. Aside from the far-off chiming of a buoy, they sat in comfortable silence, looking up at the stars. Grace rested her head on Anna's shoulder and huddled in close. Their breath clouded together in the frigid air.

Possibly aided by whatever firewater Grace had plied her with, Anna realised she'd let go of her earlier anxieties. She usually tensed up when alone with Grace like this, but instead she reached for Grace's gloved hand and pulled it into her pocket with her own. Grace didn't resist; she snuggled in closer and nuzzled Anna's neck. Anna could feel the cold tip of Grace's nose, her warm breath on her skin. She'd spent so long resisting intimacy with Grace that she'd forgotten how good it felt to have her this close.

"Oh wow. Look!" Anna pointed out in front of them. A faint green light danced across the sky, unmistakably an aurora.

Grace gasped. "Wow! It's incredible."

The wispy green light grew brighter and more striations appeared, rippling in a mesmerising palette of greens and faint purple hues.

"It's so beautiful," said Grace.

"Truly beautiful," said Anna, except she wasn't looking at the sky any more. She took Grace's face in her hands and looked into her eyes, *green like the aurora.*

Grace's breath hitched. "Anna, what are you—"

"Shh." Anna's gaze dropped to Grace's lips, those soft pink lips, still parted in an unfinished question, and she leaned in and met them with her own. Their cold breath mingled in a long, lingering kiss. The aurora swirled above them with growing fervour, as if the electricity between them was adding to the charge of the particles dancing in the sky.

Eyes closed, they rested their foreheads together, gloved fingers entwined.

"That felt… amazing. But our pact? I mean, we don't do *that* any more, do we, Anna?"

Anna spoke softly, afraid to shatter the moment. "I know we don't… but for once, I'm not sorry."

"Okay, I just…" Grace stepped back, breaking away from their embrace. "I don't understand why now, after all this time?"

Anna looked at her, brain buzzing with Rupert's secret – *no, not now.* "Perhaps it was a natural phenomenon, like the aurora."

Grace narrowed her eyes.

"I don't know, Grace." She shrugged. "I wanted to kiss you, so I did. Stop asking questions or I'll do it again."

"Maybe you should."

So Anna kissed her again and they stayed out by the harbourside until even Grace's firewater could no longer keep them warm, then they walked back to the hotel, hand in hand. With Grace leaning in so close, Anna's senses were alive, yet the edges of her vision blurred and the air felt heavy as if she were intoxicated.

* * *

They kissed again in the hallway outside their rooms. Their bodies pressed together and electricity charged between them, awakening an urgent, aching need. Anna extracted herself and pushed Grace away. It was all she could do not to just have her there and then.

"Get away from me, you wicked woman," she whispered.

Grace giggled and it was contagious. They covered their mouths to mute their laughter.

Breathless, Grace leaned back against the wall. She licked her tongue along her front teeth, looking Anna up and down, sizing her up like a devilish dessert. "Goodnight then, you. Sweet dreams," she said.

Tearing her eyes away, Anna dashed inside her room. She bolted the door and slumped against it, breathing deeply, trying to compose herself. Knowing that Grace still stood on the other side, probably doing the same thing, it took all her resolve not to throw open the door and go back for more.

"Fuck," she mouthed, her stomach flipping somersaults.

Lexi stirred. "Banana, is that you?"

Anna crashed back down to Earth. "Yeah, it's me, Lex."

"Did you see the lights?"

Anna touched her finger to her lips where she could still feel Grace. "We did… it was magical."

CHAPTER TWENTY-ONE

September 2004

Out of breath from the ride, Anna unclipped her helmet and lugged her bike up the steps. She pressed the doorbell with her usual three short rings and caught sight of her reflection in the door's glass panel.

"Shit," she said to the hot mess looking back at her. She touched her sweaty hairline and looked down at the dark patches blotting her pale green scrubs. "Come on, come on, come on," she muttered and pressed the doorbell again, this time holding it down.

"Alright, alright, I'm coming." The door swung open.

Grace looked at Anna and laughed.

Anna glared at her. "Don't say a thing." She wheeled her bike inside, propped it against the radiator and clipped her helmet to the handlebar.

Grace leaned in and kissed her on the cheek. "Ooh, you're all sweaty."

"I know! Nightmare! Clinical practice ran over so I didn't get a chance to clean up and change."

Grace grinned. "I'd figured as much with the state of you."

Anna looked at her watch. "Shit, she'll be here soon. Do you mind if I run upstairs and freshen up?"

"Help yourself. You know where everything is. Do you need a change of clothes?"

"I'm all good." Anna patted her backpack and smiled. "Hey, Ru. Something smells delicious, I'm starving," she called out as she ran up the stairs and into the bathroom.

Anna washed and changed into light denim jeans and a loose-fitting white shirt. After brushing her hair, she hunted in the bathroom cabinet for Grace's perfume. She sprayed a little on herself and closed her eyes as she inhaled the musky sweetness.

"Okay. You'll have to do," she said with a nod at her reflection.

* * *

In the small kitchen, Lexi kicked and cooed in her highchair as Grace sat feeding her at the breakfast bench. An apron-clad Rupert halved cherry tomatoes and tossed them into a salad bowl.

Anna kissed the top of Lexi's head, taking a moment to breathe in the baby-powder scent of her. She moved behind Rupert and squeezed his shoulders. "Thank you so much for this. Is there anything I can do?"

"All under control, Sis. Grab yourself a drink, there's beer in the fridge… or is it strictly red wine these days?" He looked around and gave her a wink.

"Beer is fine. I'm parched." Anna helped herself to a bottle and popped off the cap. She exhaled a shaky breath before taking a long swig.

"Are you okay?" Grace asked, her voice laced with laughter.

"Yeah, I think so… I guess it's a big deal to introduce someone to you guys." Anna cupped her once-again-sweaty palms around the bottle.

"If you like her, we'll like her." Rupert peered into the oven at a bubbling cheese-topped dish. "It's pretty much ready. I'll turn it down until she gets here."

The doorbell chimed. Anna blew out her cheeks and exhaled loudly.

"Go on, answer it." Grace chuckled and wiped a bib over Lexi's apple-puree-smeared face.

Anna opened the door to a tall brunette in her mid-thirties, who was brandishing an expensive-looking bottle of red wine and a huge bouquet of fresh lilies.

"Hey, gorgeous." She beamed at Anna, leaned in and kissed her on the lips.

Anna hugged her.

"Mmm, you smell divine. Sorry I'm a few minutes late. Got stuck in a meeting. Bloody bore of a day, but don't get me started on that." She widened her chestnut eyes. "Anyway, here I am. Will my car be okay?" She gestured to where she'd snugly parked her shiny Audi TT, next to a grubby Corsa missing a hubcap.

"Yeah, I'm sure it'll be fine." Anna shrugged. "You could try parking in the hallway next to my wheels but I'm not sure we'll both fit." She gestured to her bike, then cringed. *Seriously, Anna?*

"You're so funny." She gave a throaty laugh and snatched another kiss. "Can I come in then?"

"Yeah, of course, sorry." Anna turned to see Grace and Rupert in the kitchen doorway, spluttering with laughter. "Shut up," she mouthed and they cracked up even more. "Rupert, Grace. This is Toni."

"It's Toni with an i," said Toni. "Ah, Rupert, yes I can see the resemblance. Lovely to meet you." She handed him the flowers and turned to Grace.

"Hi. It's Grace with a G," said Grace.

Anna glared at her, prompting both Grace and Rupert to giggle again.

"*Enchantée*, Grace." Toni air-kissed her and smiled down at the sleepy bundle in Grace's arms. "Ah, and this must be the darling little Lexi whom I've heard so much about. Oh, she's quite simply angelic."

"She's not so angelic when she's screaming the house down at 2 a.m.," said Grace.

"Shall we go through to the dining room?" Rupert gestured off to the right of the hallway.

They walked through to the modestly furnished room, dressed with a plethora of plants, cushions and throws. One end of the room was home to a beaten-up leather Chesterfield facing an original cast-iron fireplace, with a flat-screen TV mounted above it. A chunky pine dining table and its four chairs mostly filled the other end of the room. Dust motes floated in the early evening sunlight streaming through the sash window.

"Wow! What a beautiful home you have, it's very... on trend," said Toni.

"Ah, it's all thanks to Grace. If it were left up to me it'd just be the sofa and the TV. I believe the style is 'shabby chic', is that right?" Rupert looked to Grace.

"Yeah, something like that." Grace pulled her lips into a flat smile. "Now that she's had her feed, I'm going to put this one down. I shouldn't be too long, she's pretty tired."

"Toni, can I get you a drink?" Anna asked.

"May I have a glass of this please, Anna?" She handed over the bottle of red. "I'll just have the one since I'm driving."

"Great, yeah. I'll just…" Anna nodded towards the kitchen. "Grab a seat." She glanced at Rupert, who was staring at Toni with a weird grin plastered on his face. "Ru?"

"Hmm?" He tore his eyes away and looked at Anna. "Yes. I, er, need to get back to dinner, the salad won't make itself." Rupert smiled at Toni again and followed Anna into the kitchen.

"Wow, she's really hot," he whispered.

Anna laughed nervously. "I know, but shh! She'll hear you."

"No, I mean it. Wow!" Rupert's eyes bulged and he turned back to the salad. "Ding dong! You have outdone yourself, Skywalker." He whistled, picked up his knife and deftly diced some spring onions.

"Stop it!" Anna said, suppressing a smirk. She uncorked the bottle of wine, poured out a glass for Toni, and grabbed another bottle of beer for herself.

Grace returned and lit the candles on the table already set for dinner. She pressed play on the CD player and Norah Jones sang softly from the speakers.

"There, we're almost sophisticated." Grace winked at Anna.

"Almost." Anna laughed.

"Voilà! My very first attempt at moussaka." Rupert brought in a steaming oven dish. They took their seats, and he served up. "Help yourselves to salad. Bon appétit!"

"Mmm, delicious," Toni said, taking her first mouthful. "I've eaten a lot of moussaka on my various trips around the Med. Of course, in Kefalonia, there's no cheese on top, just béchamel. Oh, and there's a delectable Levantine version with chickpeas, which is…" she kissed her fingers like a chef. "But this, mmm… it's up there with the very best. Are you sure you haven't made it before?"

Rupert beamed. "No, genuinely my first time."

"Well, I hadn't even heard of it before yesterday. He sent me out for the ingredients and there was me looking for eggplants in the aisle with the eggs," said Grace.

Toni released a howl of laughter.

"Surely you'd heard of an aubergine before?" Anna giggled.

"Yeah, I'm not a heathen, I've heard of *aubergine*. But like I said, he put *eggplants* on the shopping list. How was I supposed to know he was using an American recipe? He could've at least translated it for me." Shaking her head, she scooped up another forkful.

"Well, it all worked out. This moussaka is a triumph." Toni tipped her wine glass to Rupert. "So, anyway, tell me, how did you two meet?"

Anna coughed, choking on a mouthful of salad leaves. Toni put an arm around her and rubbed her back, whilst continuing to hold her gaze on Rupert and Grace.

"At uni. Rupert got lost on his way to the bar one day and found himself in the library, where I was *actually* studying. The rest is history." Grace shrugged and shot a glance at Anna.

"Gosh, so it all moved pretty fast… wedding, baby, house?"

"Ha, yeah you could say that. Finding out Grace was pregnant was a bit of an unexpected plot twist." Rupert laughed.

Grace shifted in her seat, and Anna pushed her remaining moussaka around the plate with her fork.

"As for this place, we're renting for now. I've just started a graduate placement at a marketing firm in the city, which is going really well." Rupert grinned and took a swig of his beer. "Then after Grace does her PGCE next year, we'll see where the wind blows us. Perhaps we'll move out to the suburbs, live around some proper green spaces for Lexi."

"Sounds great." Toni nodded and looked at Grace. "What do you plan to teach, Grace?"

"English or drama, hopefully a bit of both. That's what my degree is in. The timing worked perfectly; I managed to finish my course and graduate before Lexi was born."

"Almost like you planned it," said Toni.

"Well, that we most definitely did not!" said Grace.

Anna stared at her plate.

Rupert cleared his throat. "So, er, how about you two?"

"Oh, I'm sure Anna must have already told you?" Toni chuckled. Anna smiled and shook her head. "No? Oh, okay, well it was at a veterinary conference. I'm in sales for veterinary pharmaceuticals. We bumped into one another at the conference and hit it off right away, didn't we?" Toni smiled at Anna and touched her cheek.

"Yeah, we did." Anna blushed and smiled back. She stole a glance at Grace, who was stabbing at a cherry tomato on her plate.

When they finished their meal, Rupert and Grace cleared the

dishes from the table and brought out dessert. Grace poured coffee from a cafetière, and Rupert cut and plated slices of lemon cheesecake.

"I must confess, I'm more of a savoury chef. This next course was prepared by my good friend, Mr Sainsbury."

The conversation continued to flow, thanks to Rupert and Toni and their in-depth discussion on the fast-paced world of sales and marketing. The topic moved onto rugby, Rupert and Toni's increased animation underscored by their shared passion for the sport. *At least someone is taken with Toni*, thought Anna. Grace's yawns and eye-rolls suggested any hope of glowing feedback from her was dwindling.

* * *

Toni air-kissed Rupert and Grace. "Thank you again for a delightful meal. Anna is a closed book, so it's been wonderful getting to know you both a bit more. My place next time?"

They nodded, Rupert far more enthusiastically than Grace.

"Anna, are you sure I can't give you a lift home? You can pick up your bike some other time."

"Thanks, but I need it to get to uni in the morning and then I have to be at the surgery in the afternoon."

"You can stay at my place again." Toni gave an unsubtle wink and Anna's cheeks burned. "I can drop you off in the morning on my way to the office."

"No, really, thank you. My place isn't too far from here, I'll be fine." Anna smiled and leaned in to kiss her cheek.

The three of them stood on the doorstep and waved as Toni got into her car.

Rupert draped his arm around Anna's shoulder. "She's fantastic, Anna. I really like her."

As the front door closed, the baby monitor crackled and Lexi wailed.

"It must be me this time. You two can do the dishes," Rupert called over his shoulder as he took the stairs three at a time.

"Good to see he's pulling his weight with Lexi," Anna said as she and Grace returned to clear the dessert plates and coffee cups from the table.

"He's been fantastic actually. It's like he can't get enough of her. He's smitten… almost as smitten as he was with Toni. You better watch him with her." Grace's laugh sounded forced.

"Well, she's gay, so I'm pretty sure he's not her type." Anna's words came out harsher than intended and she winced.

Grace sniffed.

They continued to move around in silence. Anna snapped on a pair of yellow washing-up gloves and got to work on the dishes stacked in the soapy water.

"*Toni with an i. Hi, I'm Toni with an i,*" Grace muttered. "*Ooh, you should taste the chickpeas in the Levantine moussaka…* I mean, what a pretentious twat!" She imitated Toni's air-kisses with the plate she was drying.

Anna stopped and looked at her. "Oh my God. You're jealous."

Grace took a breath, opened her mouth, and said nothing.

Anna sighed and returned her attention to the dishes.

"Of course I'm jealous," blurted Grace. "I feel terrible about Rupert,

I do… but my feelings for you didn't just disappear when I married him. It's agony seeing you with someone else."

"How the fuck do you think I feel?" The cup in Anna's hand splashed back into the sink. Her jaw clenched as she stared at Grace.

Through tear-filled eyes, Grace stared back.

Anna breathed heavily through her nose.

The intense silence gave way to a surge between them and their bodies pulled together like magnets. In the sudden unleashing of an almost animalistic desire, their lips locked and tongues swirled in a frenzied kiss. Grace's fingers tangled in Anna's hair as Anna's rubber-gloved hands dripped soapy dishwater down Grace's back. The insistent press of Grace's hips reciprocated Anna's own carnal ache.

"Fuck." Anna broke away, panting and breathless. "What are we doing? We can't do this."

Grace stared at her. "Are you going to punish me forever?"

"What? What's that supposed to mean?" Anna narrowed her eyes. "I'm not punishing you. You're married to my brother. You can't have your cake and eat it, Grace."

"I thought…" Grace touched a finger to her lips, tracing where Anna's had been seconds before. "I thought you still felt the same way I feel about you." Her shoulders slumped and tears welled in her eyes. "*She's* not right for you, you know?"

"Well, *she's* not married to Rupert, so that's a good start." Anna instantly regretted her bitterness as Grace's tears started to fall. "Look, I like her. She's mature," she added in a softer voice.

"Right, *mature*." Grace sniffed and curled her lip. "You mean she's up her own arse? Is she *mature* in bed?"

"I am not having this conversation with you, Grace. I'm trying to move on. I suggest you do the same."

Anna yanked at the washing-up gloves until the rubber snapped away from her fingers and, without another glance at Grace, she stormed out.

CHAPTER TWENTY-TWO

January 2022

The Lofoten Islands

Anna woke and glanced across at the unmade bed next to hers; Lexi must have gone down to breakfast already. She stretched out her arms and grinned at the ceiling, her head swimming with Grace.

Up until now, she'd tried to resist the magnetism between them, for the good of the family and the sake of her sanity. Years ago, they made a pact to never again discuss how they *really* felt; when they did, it always ended up with them screaming at each other, or worse, entwined. So sparks were ignored and feelings went unspoken – the elephant in the corner of every room they were ever in together.

To calm the whirlwind within, Anna made a mental list of the status quo: *Rupert still hasn't told Grace about his affair. Grace will be furious when she finds out that I knew and didn't tell her… especially after last night. Of course, there are the kids to think about. Not to mention Grace's family. We'll hardly be able to just sail off into the sunset together; people would be scandalised. Grace cares far too much about what people think. Besides, we only kissed… oh my God, we kissed.*

"Get a grip, Anna," she said aloud, then screamed into her pillow.

That smile crept across her lips again, the lips Grace kissed only hours ago; and for the first time in a very long time, it felt so right. It seemed that whatever it was they had uncorked quite simply wasn't going back in the bottle.

* * *

Nerves fluttered in her stomach as she made her way down to breakfast, but they quickly abated when she locked eyes with Grace across the buffet. *Mutual permission to stare.*

A cheeky smile played on Grace's lips as she poured herself an orange juice. "Morning, you," she said. "Did you sleep well?"

"Yeah, you?"

"I had the sweetest dream." Grace grinned.

Anna's stomach flipped. She poured a cup of coffee and sat next to Lexi. Toby was at the next table telling Roy and some of the others that his mum and Auntie Banana had seen the northern lights. Brandishing Grace's phone, he showed them the photos Grace had managed to capture.

Rupert loudly huffed before shovelling another spoonful of muesli into his mouth.

"What's up with you, grumpy?" Anna dared to ask.

"I'm gutted I missed it. I still don't know why you didn't wake me up, Grace." He threw a dirty side glance at her.

"How many times, Ru? I tried but you were dead to the world. You hadn't so much as moved by the time we got back."

"Never mind," said Edith. "We'll get another chance to see them on the Lofoten Islands. I was far too tired last night. You two did well to stay awake. What time did you get in?"

"No idea but I was feckin' freezing," said Grace.

"It was after 3 a.m.," Lexi said without looking up from her phone.

"How do you know? You were asleep," said Anna.

"I heard you come in and I looked at my phone. I spoke to you, didn't I? You said something about it being magical, then I must have drifted off again." Lexi shrugged.

Anna's heart stopped for a second. *Did we really stay out for so long?* They had three photos to show for it at the most; surely that looked suspicious. She glanced at Grace, who didn't seem bothered in the slightest, and neither did anyone else.

Roy clinked the side of his coffee mug with a teaspoon. "Can I have everyone's attention please? In an hour, we need to be all packed up and back on the coach. We're heading to the spectacular archipelago of the Lofoten Islands. The journey will take around seven hours, including a couple of stops along the way. It's a scenic drive and most of it will be in daylight, so you'll get some wonderful views from the coach and, later on, the ferry. Any questions?" Roy paused. "No? Great. See you on the coach at 10 a.m."

Lexi groaned. "Oh seriously, another seven hours on a coach?"

"Seven hours of *amazing views*. Remember, it's about the journey, not just the destination." Grace flashed Anna a heart-stopping smile.

"It's a coach *and a ferry,* Lexi," said Toby as he bounced back over to their table.

Lexi pulled a face at him.

* * *

Anna settled into a window seat at the back and pulled on her headphones to listen to the indie-pop playlist she'd made for the trip. Right from the off, Roy's promise of amazing views delivered. The winding roads hugged huge frozen waterfalls on one side and steep cliffs dropped off the other. Snow-crested mountains rose from the sea and were lapped by the icy waters of the fjords. Photos through a coach window wouldn't do the view justice, so Anna sat back and took it all in, occasionally touching her fingers to her lips and grinning.

After a while, Rupert made his way down the aisle and shuffled into the seat next to her. She pulled down her headphones.

"What's up?" he said.

"Nothing, just enjoying the scenery." Anna smiled at him.

"Good, yeah, me too." He nodded. "Our motherland is a beauty, isn't she?"

"She sure is." Anna fixed her gaze out of the window. Her mind flashed back to her liaison with Grace, just hours ago. She still didn't feel guilty about it, making it distinct from other encounters they'd had in the past. Emboldened, she challenged Rupert again. "So, have you come any closer to telling Grace about Nicole yet?"

"Yeah, that's what I wanted to talk to you about. I was thinking of doing it tonight. Perhaps I'll suggest a walk after dinner, and I'll tell her then. What do you think?"

"Okay, sounds like a plan. It's best to get it out of the way, Ru. Have you thought about what you're going to say?"

"I don't think I've thought about anything else. I spoke to Nicole and she—"

"Fuck's sake, Ru!" Anna gritted her teeth. "You shouldn't be getting her involved in it."

"Well, she is involved. That's the point, isn't it?" He spoke a little too loudly, then lowered his voice. "Look, I want to be sensitive about it and I thought Nicole would be able to help. She's good with this sort of thing—"

"What? Wrecking homes?"

"No, that's not what I meant. She does feel terrible about all of this." His eyes glazed and a grin spread over his lips; an odd saccharine smile Anna hadn't ever seen on his face before. "You're really going to like her," he said.

"Focus," Anna hissed and punched his arm.

"Ouch!" He frowned at her. "Okay, so I think I'm just going to tell Grace that we've had a lot of great years together. We've raised two amazing kids and we've had a lot of good times. There have also been some difficult times, which is usual in a marriage… but the bad times have outweighed the good for a long while now—"

"Maybe don't go on about the bad times so much, it'll sound like you're making excuses."

"Right, okay. Good point. Then, I was going to say something like, 'I've met someone. I like her, a lot… and I want to be with her. As a couple. So… I think we should get a divorce.' How's that?" He stretched his lips into a grimace.

"Wow, yeah. Gosh, the 'D' word, it sounds so final, doesn't it?" Anna inhaled sharply. "Are you prepared for questions? She's going to ask you what 'I've met someone else' means and you're going to need to be honest about that. Even if she doesn't ask, Ru. You have to tell her that it's been going on for two years."

"I know. I don't want her to hate me. We have Lexi and Toby; I want us to be friends for their sake if nothing else. We're going to be in each other's lives for a long time."

A surge of sympathy compelled her to take his hand in hers. "It's going to be okay," she said.

"She probably won't want to sleep in the same room as me after I tell her. Would you mind asking Lexi if she'll share with Gran tonight? If Toby's with you it'll be easier for us to switch and he'll ask fewer questions. You don't mind sharing with Grace, do you?"

"Er, yeah, sure. That's fine," Anna said, but her thoughts spiralled. Until now, the sleeping arrangements hadn't even crossed her mind. Her stomach somersaulted at the thought of sharing a room with Grace. All of that energy charging between them, and not to have to worry about trusting themselves alone together.

Stop it, Anna.

In reality, Rupert's revelation was about to change everything. She needed to brace herself for the fallout as she'd have to be there to support them all. A wave of sadness hit her with the realisation that it wasn't the right time to start something with Grace. *Somehow, it's never the right time.*

CHAPTER TWENTY-THREE

October 2004

Sunlight burst through the gaps in the Venetian blinds; after a week of early autumn rain, some sunshine was very welcome. The crisp white bed-sheets stirred behind her. Fingers ran softly down her back and she arched in response. A naked body drew close and soft breasts pressed into her shoulder blades. Warm kisses, starting behind her ear, traced the length of her neck and down her spine, continuing south to her ankles.

A growing need swelled within her and she softly moaned as she rolled onto her back and parted her legs. An eager tongue licked its way up her inner thigh until reaching the desired destination. A lingering pause, followed by a sharp intake of breath, and her lover dived inside her.

Anna closed her eyes to the image of Grace. Their recent kiss had been so intense, so loaded with pent-up frustration. She'd wanted so much more in that moment. She wished she'd ripped off those washing-up gloves and lifted Grace onto the sink. With Grace's legs wrapped around her waist, she would've fucked her right there in the kitchen then carried her to the bedroom for more.

Her moans grew louder. She bucked her hips and her lover responded with more vigour.

"Fuck!" she cried out.

The tension subsided and, breathless, she relaxed back onto the plush, white pillow behind her.

"Morning, gorgeous. Goodness, that was quick this time! You must have been thinking nice thoughts," Toni's husky voice purred as she fought her way out from under the duvet. She surfaced, rising above Anna, her face flushed and her long brown hair dishevelled. She looked into Anna's eyes and gave her a long, hard kiss before collapsing onto the pillow next to her.

"Morning." Anna grinned at her.

Toni traced her fingertips around Anna's nipple; it didn't seem to mind. A sudden rush of guilt hit her. Here she was, being adored by this wonderful woman, but she was thinking about Grace. *Fucking Grace,* she thought, then she smiled again at the thought of just that.

"What are you thinking about?" Toni stared into her face.

"I was thinking… that was a nice way to be woken up. Thank you."

"You can thank me later," Toni said with a sultry laugh. "It's Saturday, the sun is shining, and we both have the day off. Let's do something."

"Mmm. What do you have in mind?" Anna smiled and closed her eyes.

"Well, I was thinking I'll bring you breakfast in bed, then maybe we can drive into the countryside and take a long walk. We could have a nice pub lunch before coming back here and soaking our achy muscles in a hot bath. Then, once we've worked up an appetite… we'll order a takeaway. Your choice. How does that sound?" She squeezed Anna's erect nipple a little too hard.

"Ouch!"

"Oh, I'm sorry. Let me kiss it better." Toni enthusiastically administered first aid to the wounded area with her tongue.

"It sounds like the perfect day, it really does." Anna sighed. "But I promised I'd meet Gran and Rupert at midday. I'm sorry to let you down… again."

Toni's smile fell away, but her cheerfulness didn't wane. "Oh well. A promise is a promise, I suppose. I still have plenty of time to make you breakfast. Maybe you could come back here later on? You do have a little unfinished business to attend to after all." Her full, red lips twisted into a half-grin.

"If you don't mind, that would be great actually," Anna responded to Toni's seemingly endless kindness with a long kiss.

"Right," Toni said, "before you start something you're not going to finish, go and jump in the shower and I'll fix us breakfast. Coffee and croissants okay?"

Anna nodded. "I don't deserve you," she said, gratitude spilling into her voice. She climbed out of bed and let the sheet fall away from her naked body. Aware of Toni watching her with hungry eyes, Anna gave her butt a little wiggle on her way to the en-suite.

Toni growled. "Don't tempt me to come in there with you. You won't get your breakfast."

Anna giggled and closed the door to the en-suite, which was all glass, steel, and clean white lines, like everything in Toni's immaculate apartment.

* * *

The sun hung low in a cloudless sky but a chill in the air hinted at frosty days to come. Anna turned her collar up against the cold and walked up the hill to the bench where Edith and Rupert were already sitting looking out over the city. Highrise buildings rose like jagged teeth on the horizon, their sharp edges tempered by a blanket of trees; a patchwork quilt sewn in browns, greens, and yellows. Edith used to bring them here when they were young; this particular spot was one of her favourites.

Perhaps sensing she was near, Rupert turned around. "Well, hello hello. If it isn't my long-lost twin, finally returning to the family fold."

Anna hugged and kissed them both, then sandwiched herself between them on the bench.

"How's Toni?" Rupert asked, nudging her with his elbow.

"She's good. How's Lexi?"

"She's a little angel. She's growing so quickly. I was just telling Gran, she started crawling the other day, it's utter madness!" He beamed.

"Wow!" Anna swallowed, steeling herself from the unexpected pang of regret that she'd missed out on a milestone.

"We haven't seen or heard from you since you had dinner at ours. That must have been, what… three, four weeks ago? Grace keeps asking me to text you to check if you're still alive… but I didn't want to interrupt anything." He laughed. "I bet Toni's been keeping you busy!" He elbowed her again, and Anna blushed.

"Oh, Rupert, give the girl a break." Edith chuckled. "I think it's nice that you're seeing someone, Anna. I look forward to meeting her."

"Yeah, I look forward to meeting her again too. Forget Tony the Tiger, she's *Toni the Cougar*… and there ain't nothing frosty about her!"

Rupert laughed at his own joke.

Anna shot him a dirty look, but she couldn't resist a smile. *We really do share the same taste in women.*

"Thank you for meeting me here today. You know this is one of my favourite places." Edith closed her eyes and raised her face to the sky as if letting the sunlight kiss her. She took a breath and spoke again. "I'm afraid I don't have the best of news. I'd been having quite a bit of pain, so I went to the doctor to get myself checked over. She found a lump, in my breast." She closed her eyes again.

Anna exchanged a worried look with Rupert. "It could be nothing, Gran. Is the doctor referring you to the hospital for some tests?"

"I'm sorry to say they've already done their tests, my darling." Edith took Anna's hand. "It's a spot of cancer. In short, I need to have a procedure. It's called a mastectomy and I'll have to have some treatment afterwards. Chemo or radiotherapy, I'm not sure which. Maybe both."

Rupert turned away.

The floor of Anna's stomach dropped. "Oh, Gran. I'm so sorry. Why didn't you say you were having tests? I would've come with you." She put an arm around her and noticed the bones in her shoulders. Until now, it always seemed like Gran had been made of stronger stuff than the brittle and breakable bones of mere mortals.

"Oh, darling, you're so busy with your studies, you wouldn't have had time for all of that. Besides, like you said, it could have been nothing. You know I don't like a fuss." She patted Anna's hand.

Rupert sniffed.

"Are you okay, Rupert?" Edith asked.

"Yeah, fine. Sorry, I'm just…" his voice frayed.

"Look, I don't want you both getting upset. There is plenty they can do for me. I am fit, well and ready for them to do their worst. Don't be getting your funeral umbrellas out. It's not raining yet, my loves." She chuckled.

"We'll be with you all the way, Gran. Whatever you need, we're there. Don't worry about a thing. I'll see if I can suspend my course for a while and I'll move back home whilst you're getting better," said Anna.

"No, no. That won't be necessary. I have good friends, they'll rally around. Anna, you must finish your course, you're so near to the end. And Rupert, you have Grace and little Lexi to take care of, so don't you start getting any ideas either. All I ask is that you visit and keep me well stocked in grapes."

Eyes red with tears, Rupert turned around and faced them again. "Whatever you need, Gran, we'll be there. The Three Musketeers, that's us." His worry-furrowed forehead betrayed his attempt at light-heartedness. He enveloped them both in a bear hug with Anna squashed in the middle.

"All for one and one for all," Edith chuckled, holding them both close.

CHAPTER TWENTY-FOUR

January 2022

Svolvær

As the ferry approached the Lofoten Islands, the Edwardses huddled close and braced themselves against the freezing Arctic air to take in the view from the front deck. They chugged towards a chain of rock formations protruding from the water, which from a distance looked like the rounded backs of huge frozen hippos, but up close were towering ice-encrusted skerries.

Anna tensed when Grace's hand slipped into her pocket. She glanced across at the faces of the others, all of them oblivious. She relaxed and squeezed the hand that had been searching for her own. The pink light of the sunset faded and the sky turned to blue, then black.

* * *

Back on the coach, they drove through the mountains, along winding roads and headlong into a thick snowstorm. The wipers were barely able to keep up with the massive white flakes flurrying into the windscreen. Toby spent the entire journey hanging from his seat into the aisle to get a better look.

The coach pulled up to their hotel, an impressive glass and chrome building in an attractive square. A huge Christmas tree stood in the centre, simply decorated with warm white bulbs. Ahead of them was the harbour, mooring fishing boats and luxury yachts.

Toby jumped off the coach like an uncoiled spring.

"Anyone would think you'd never seen snow before." Lexi laughed as he ran around trying to catch snowflakes on his tongue.

"Please, please can we make a snowman?" he asked.

"Later, Tobes. Let's get checked in and have some dinner first," said Grace, picking up their bags as they were unloaded from the coach. "I hear you're in with Banana and Lexi is with Gran, is that right?"

"Yes! Banana, can we jump on the bed?"

"Er, no. Just because we're sharing a room it doesn't mean I'm going to let you act like a hooligan." Anna shouldered her backpack and took Toby's suitcase from Grace.

Toby frowned. "Gran lets me."

Anna laughed. "Well, Gran's a rebel."

* * *

The hotel was the fanciest they'd stayed in so far; its opulent, plush decoration made a change from the contemporary Scandinavian style. Large chandeliers adorned the ceiling of the entranceway, accentuating the black and gold colour scheme, which continued into the bedrooms.

After dropping their bags, they met for dinner in the hotel restaurant. Roy stood up and read from his clipboard that there would be, "three courses, starting with butternut squash soup, a main course of roasted pollock—"

"Roasted what?" Rupert asked, smirking at the sniggers in the room.

"Roasted pollock," Roy replied. "I believe it's locally caught." He frowned and nudged his glasses up his nose. "And there'll be a chocolate lava cake for dessert."

* * *

Once they'd finished their meal, Anna conceded to make a snowman with Toby. Lexi reluctantly agreed to join them. Dense cloud cover ruled out any chance of aurora sightings, so most of the tour group were socialising at the hotel bar, including Edith, who had settled by the fire with a sherry in hand.

This gives Rupert the perfect opportunity to speak with Grace, she thought as she pulled on her coat and snow boots.

The snowstorm had passed, but a thick blanket had settled on the ground. The ploughs set to work, scooping snow off the road and dumping it into the harbour. Anna, Lexi, and Toby crunched their way along the boardwalk and over a bridge that connected a tiny island to the harbour. Dotted along the water's edge were dozens of traditional red fishing huts in striking contrast to the backdrop of white mountains in the distance.

Anna and Lexi helped Toby roll three big balls of snow and they stacked them on top of one another. Toby scavenged around and found some twigs for arms. He crafted a face out of things he pulled out of his pockets: a bottle top, a coin, and a red string of strawberry liquorice for the mouth.

"Very creative, Tobes. What are you going to call it?" asked Anna.

"Mr Snowman," said Toby as he stood back to survey his work.

Anna laughed. "Okay, I take back my praise for your creativity."

Toby shrugged and gave Mr Snowman his hat and scarf, and, as always, Lexi captured the moment on camera.

Anna sat on a bench and watched Toby and Lexi giggle as they made snow angels. Despite their age gap, they sometimes reminded her of when she and Rupert were young, especially when Lexi stopped trying to grow up so fast and remembered to have fun. Even with the tragic loss of their parents at such a young age, Gran had always been great at reminding them not to take life too seriously.

Thinking of Rupert, her stomach knotted. She checked her phone. No notifications, so she jumped up to join in with the snow angels.

* * *

After hot chocolate in the bar, Anna took Toby back to their room. It didn't take him long to drift off to sleep.

She made herself a cup of tea and sat in the comfy armchair next to the lamp to read an online article about animals that mate for life. This list included wolves, beavers, and surprisingly, shingleback lizards. She must have nodded off as she was awoken by a light but persistent tapping. She answered the door to Rupert.

He stood hunched with his bag slung over his shoulder. In barely a whisper, he said, "It's done." He dropped his bag onto the floor and bear-hugged her; she could feel the weight of sadness in his arms.

"That was so much harder than I thought it was going to be," he said.

"How did she take it?"

"She wasn't angry. She was just so… disappointed. I think it would've been easier if she'd shouted and raged, but she didn't." His Adam's apple bobbed in his throat. "She was so quiet and cold with me. She didn't even tell me to leave, but I think it was for the best."

Anna nodded slowly but her mind raced.

"Will you go to her?" asked Rupert. "Make sure she's okay. Please tell her again how sorry I am. I never meant to hurt her like this."

Anna rubbed his arm and tried to offer a reassuring smile. She felt for him, she really did. But right now… *Grace*.

Rupert kicked off his shoes and eased himself down onto the bed next to Toby. Anna gathered up the few things she'd pulled out and stuffed them back into her backpack.

Her stomach knotted again as she made her way along the corridor towards Grace's room. She knocked and Grace answered almost immediately, as if she'd been waiting by the door.

She didn't look at Anna. Without a word, she walked back into the room and sat in the chair. She drew up her knees and hugged them to her chest. Anna put her backpack down in the small hallway and followed Grace into the room. She looked around, then perched on the edge of the bed.

"Are you okay?" she asked.

"What do you think?" Grace stared ahead into the void.

Anna took a deep breath. "Well, I guess that you're shocked by what Rupert told you. I'm sure you must feel angry and upset but—"

"I'm not shocked. I already knew." Grace looked into her eyes.

Anna stared back, open-mouthed. "What? …what do you mean? You knew Rupert was—"

"Jesus, what kind of eejit do you take me for? He's been seeing her for over two years and you think I didn't suspect anything?" Grace scoffed. "Of course I did. Not the exact details. The ins and outs, as it were. But I knew there was someone else. I suppose I wanted to see how long it would take for him to tell me. Or for him to tell you."

"I've only known for a couple of days. Rupert told me on the train to Brønnøysund and I demanded that he tell you. Before that, I honestly had no idea." She held up her hands. "Well, I suspected something was going on with him, but I didn't know that it was *someone else*."

"I knew that you knew last night. That's why you kissed me like you did," Grace blurted.

"Hold on, that's not fair. It wasn't like that… and you kissed me too."

Grace looked down and picked at her fingernail.

"Why didn't you tell me, Grace? All this time. You could've spoken to me." Anna examined her face, hoping she'd find the answers there.

Grace sighed and let go of her knees. She rested her hands in her lap. "I knew everything would have to change when it all came out."

"Well, yeah, of course, but why would you want it to stay as it was? You've both been unhappy."

"Truth is, Anna, I've been scared that losing him would mean losing you."

"Why would you lose me?"

"Well, until you kissed me like you did last night, I didn't know you still even felt *that* way about me. Sometimes I dared to hope that you did, but we had our pact… and I was afraid the only reason you continued to put up with me, after everything I've put you through over the years, was for the sake of Rupert and the kids."

Anna opened her mouth to speak. "Oh," was all that came out as her brain jammed with everything from confusion to relief. She slid off the edge of the bed and knelt before Grace.

"For the first time in forever, I feel like it's okay that I love you in the way that I do." Anna took Grace's hands and looked up into her face. "That's why I kissed you. I've spent so many years trying not to feel the things I feel for you. Then we were alone… and it felt so right…" Her voice cracked, and before she had the chance to blink them back, hot tears fell.

Grace tilted Anna's chin towards her. She kissed Anna's closed eyes and then she found her lips and covered them with slow, soft kisses that became more urgent when Anna surrendered and kissed her back. They stood and stepped towards the bed, arms and legs entangled as they frantically undressed.

Anna's hands felt their way over the soft curve of Grace's hips – fuller than the last time her hands had had free rein over Grace's body. Her fingers traced over the blemishes that rippled across Grace's abdomen – the lifelines that had taken Grace from her, but at the same time bound them closer together.

"Oh." Grace shrunk away from Anna's touch. "I hate those—"

Anna hushed her with a kiss and pulled her onto the bed.

CHAPTER TWENTY-FIVE

December 2004

"Merry Christmas, Gran." Anna bustled through the front door, laden with bags.

"Merry Christmas, darling." Edith leaned in and kissed Anna's cheek.

"You look fantastic." Anna stepped back to fully take her in. *She's responding well to the treatment.* "I'm loving the festive headscarf."

"Well, I thought I'd make an effort." Edith smiled and did a little twirl.

Anna laughed and hugged her. "It's actually freezing. I just heard on the radio that we might get snow today. It's snowing up north already."

"A white Christmas! Wouldn't that be lovely?" Edith clapped her hands and craned her neck to look outside. Toni's gleaming Audi kicked up the gravel as it sped out of the driveway. "I take it Toni isn't coming in?"

"No, it was a drop and dash. She's off to see her family. To be honest, she's still a bit upset with me because we're not spending the day together, but I didn't want to miss Lexi's first Christmas," Anna said, hanging up her coat and scarf.

"Well, she'd have been more than welcome to join us, darling.

Although I do understand how that's a bit tricky for you too." Edith smiled and a glint sparkled in her eye.

Anna cocked her head and narrowed her eyes. "What makes you say that?"

A loud clatter from the kitchen snatched away their attention.

"Come on, we better go through. The aspiring MasterChef is dying for you to taste his Christmas cocktails. It's some unholy concoction of cranberries, orange juice and way too much gin for my liking." Edith stuck out her tongue.

"Sounds like my kind of cocktail." Anna followed her through to the kitchen. If the smell was anything to go by, Rupert had outdone himself.

"Skywalker!" He dropped his oven mitts on the sideboard and threw his arms around her. "What time do you call this? You're late. And where's that bloody gorgeous girlfriend of yours? I thought she'd at least have a drink with me... I mean us." He winked at her and laughed.

"Perhaps for the best that she didn't see you dressed like this." Anna gestured to his Santa hat and matching apron. His cheeks were flushed, suggesting he'd been doing a fair bit of cocktail taste-testing already.

"Humbug!" He handed her a sugar-rimmed glass and clinked it with his own. "Merry Christmas. Cheers."

"Mmm, delicious, Ru," she said, taking a sip. "Lunch smells incredible, I'm starving."

"It's about twenty minutes away so get that down you whilst you wait." He spun around to deal with a spluttering pot.

"Well, look who finally showed up." Grace's voice came from the hallway. Anna turned and watched as she shuffled through the doorway with Lexi holding onto her fingers and toddling along in front of her. Lexi beamed when she saw Anna. She let go of Grace and made the final few tentative steps into Anna's open arms.

"Banna, Banna," she garbled.

"Look at you all dressed up as a little elf." Anna tickled Lexi's tummy, making her giggle. She scooped her up and jangled the little bell on the end of Lexi's hat. "Was this Mummy or Daddy's idea?"

"Whose do you think?" Grace nodded towards their very own Santa. "Anyway, Merry Christmas, you." She brushed a kiss past Anna's cheek. "You came without your bodyguard today then?"

Anna scoffed. "Toni is spending the day with her family."

"I'm surprised she took her claws out of you long enough for you to get away."

Before Anna could respond, Grace sauntered over to Rupert.

"Mmm, it smells so good." She squeezed him from behind whilst he stirred the gravy.

"So do you, my sexy little Christmas elf." He turned and pecked her on the lips. Grace cupped his face, reciprocating with a long, lingering kiss.

Anna's heart lurched. *What the—?*

She'd never seen them being affectionate with each other like this before, even on their wedding day. She caught herself staring and quickly looked away. Acidity rose from her stomach and burned in her throat. She gulped down the last of the pink liquid in her glass and turned her full attention to making Lexi giggle.

* * *

"Jamie Oliver, eat your heart out! Rupert, that turkey was worth the five hundred and fifty-two hours you put into preparing it." Grace pushed back from the table and patted her full stomach. "Like the turkey, I am now stuffed!"

"Hear, hear!" said Edith. "I couldn't eat another bite. Rupert, what a wonderful meal."

"Yeah, delicious. Thank you." Anna raised her glass to him.

Rupert beamed. "Well, chef's privilege… I get to go put my feet up in front of the TV and you two get to do the dishes." He pointed at Grace and Anna.

Edith excused herself to take a much-needed afternoon nap and Rupert carried a very sleepy Lexi into the lounge. Anna and Grace cleared the table and took the dishes through to the kitchen.

Anna puffed out her cheeks as she surveyed the chaos. "You fancy another drink to get us through this?"

"Yeah, go on then. But only if you promise not to get all amorous with those gloves again." Grace grinned.

Anna laughed, relieved that the mood between them had lightened. She popped the cork of a bottle of Prosecco and poured out two glasses.

Grace flicked on the radio and the latest Band Aid Christmas number one played. She turned it up and they sang along as they stacked the dishes by the sink and cleaned up Rupert's mess.

"I mean, these aren't anywhere near as sexy as yours…" Anna said as she pulled on Edith's flowery washing-up gloves and wiggled her fingers at Grace, "…and at least I was wearing protection," she muttered and smirked to herself.

Grace gasped. "As if you actually just said that!" She playfully hit Anna with the tea towel.

Laughing, they got to work on the dishes.

"You and Ru seem to be getting along well." Anna took care to steady her voice.

"Yeah, things have been really good lately. We've been making a lot more effort with each other. We may as well." Grace grinned at the plate she was drying.

Despite a bite of jealousy, Anna felt glad that they seemed to be genuinely happy.

"I'm sorry I've been a bit of a dick about Toni," Grace said, breaking off Anna's train of thought.

"What do you mean, *a bit of a dick*?" Anna laughed. "You've been a massive knob!"

"Yeah, I know and I'm sorry. She's not so bad, and I know you're into her. I just had to get used to seeing you with someone, but I think I'm after turning a corner with all of that now. I'd love for us to be able to spend time together again. I've missed you."

Anna stopped and stared into the soapy water. "I'm going to break up with Toni."

"Oh."

Silence would have fallen between them had Aled Jones not been walking in the air.

When Anna didn't offer up any further information, Grace probed. "I thought you liked her; I mean I thought you were—"

"I do like her. Quite a lot, actually. But I don't think I want what she wants."

Grace looked at her and frowned.

"She wants me to move in with her."

The glass Grace was drying almost slipped from her hand, but she caught it.

"It's a big step and I'm not ready for that. She's so intense… I can't imagine living with her. I've been thinking for a while that I need to end it, but it'd be cruel to do it at Christmas. She's put a lot of effort into gifts, she must have spent a fortune on me." Anna sighed.

Grace cleared her throat.

"She keeps making all these plans for us, so it never feels like a good time. I need to stop being such a coward and just get it over with."

"I don't know what to say, Anna." Grace picked up her half-full glass and gulped down the Prosecco in one go. "I'm sorry again for being like I was. If that's made it harder for you, I mean, if this is because of me or anything like that, you shouldn't—"

"No, it's not because of you… You were right though."

Grace raised an eyebrow. "How so?"

"When you said she's not right for me."

Grace put down the tea towel and wrapped her arms around Anna's waist from behind and squeezed. Anna closed her eyes as Grace pecked a kiss on her shoulder.

"Rupert is going to be gutted," she said and Anna snorted a laugh.

As Grace refilled their glasses, the intro to *All I Want for Christmas Is You* chimed out of the speakers. "Tune!" she gargled through a mouthful of Prosecco and cranked the volume up another notch.

CHAPTER TWENTY-SIX

January 2022

Svolvær

Anna woke with her limbs entwined with Grace's. For a brief moment, she could've tricked her brain into believing the last two decades had been a dream and she'd woken in her room at uni, where they'd last been together like this.

Grace stirred.

"Morning," said Anna.

"Morning, you." Grace stretched and snuggled her head back into place on Anna's shoulder. "Mmm, this is nice," she said as she rubbed her naked legs against Anna's.

"Nice is one word for it." Anna giggled. "Naughty is another. I can't believe we let this happen." She traced her fingertips in lazy circles over Grace's bare back.

"I was bound to get lucky sooner or later."

Anna smiled and exhaled a big breath. "Yeah, but what now?"

"Sure, haven't we got a lot of lost time to make up for?" She squeezed Anna's thigh between her own.

Anna tensed.

"Ah now, you're not going to go all moralistic again on me, are you?"

Grace lifted her head to look at Anna's face.

"No, it's not that." She shook her head and chewed her lip, aware of Grace waiting for her to say more. "Well, it is a bit. I was thinking about Rupert and I wondered whether we should speak to him first before we start anything."

"Yeah, sure. I'll get him on the phone, shall I?" Grace rolled onto her stomach. With her pinkie and thumb, she mimed a phone call. "'Hi, Ru. Yeah, it's me. I shagged your sister last night and we were about to go at it again, but she wanted to check in with you first.' For feck's sake, Anna, he's been getting his rocks off with someone else, hasn't he?"

"You know I didn't mean it like that. I don't want to keep this from him. It's not fair. You saw him last night. He's gutted that he's hurt you… and here I am jumping straight into bed with you… to lick your wounds, so to speak." She grimaced at her turn of phrase.

Grace buried her head into the pillow and released a muffled scream. "I don't feel like I owe him an explanation. At least not when it's taken him two feckin' years to tell me he's been having an affair."

"I see your point, but I'd argue that we've been much worse." Anna looked at her through wide eyes. "Seriously, over the years. In thought, if not in deed. Actually, even in deed. You can't pretend we didn't cross the line way too many times."

Grace shrugged. "But haven't we also been very good girls for the longest time? I gave you my Brownie's honour – and I stuck to it… until now." Her green eyes sparkled and Anna had to look away to hide her grin.

"Look, what Rupert has done is shit but it doesn't absolve us of anything. It doesn't automatically make this okay and I want this to be more than just a sordid little secret. I don't just want to be your rebound."

"How could you possibly be my rebound?" Grace stared at her, open-mouthed. "It was *you* I never got over, Anna."

Anna examined her face and read the sincerity of her words. Disarmed by those sparkling green eyes, a smile erupted on her lips. After all this time, Grace was all hers, with no complications. Well, admittedly there were a few, but for now, she pushed all of that out of her mind and ravished every inch of the delicious, naked woman next to her.

* * *

As outlined by Roy, the tour agenda for the day involved a visit to one of Norway's oldest fishing villages, Nusfjord, followed by a chartered boat trip to observe sea eagles. As much as Anna wanted to see the eagles, she'd rather spend the day alone with Grace, so she was delighted with the plan they'd concocted.

Leaving Grace in the room, Anna went down to breakfast. The sight of Rupert shuffling around the breakfast buffet with his hands stuffed in his pockets triggered a tidal wave of guilt. Anna avoided him, poured herself a coffee and sat at the table with Lexi, Toby, and Gran.

"How's Grace?" Edith asked. "Rupert said she was unwell last night, and you stayed with her. That was kind of you, darling."

Was that the hint of a grin? Anna avoided eye contact and sipped her coffee. "She's feeling a bit better, but she's not really up to the trip today. I'm going to hang back here and make sure she's okay."

Lexi raised an eyebrow but didn't look up from her phone.

"Can't Dad stay here and look after her? I want you to come with us, Banana," Toby whined.

Anna smiled and stroked his hair. "You should spend some time with your dad. He remembers all of the cool stories about these islands. I only know the boring science stuff."

Toby shrugged and stuck out his bottom lip.

"I'll let Roy know we're not coming, and we'll see you back here later for dinner." Anna finished her coffee and walked over to Rupert, who stood staring at the muesli like it was a puzzle he was struggling to solve. She rested her hand on his hunched shoulder and he turned to look at her with bloodshot eyes.

"Hey. How's Grace doing?"

"She's okay. She just needs some time. Go out today with Gran and the kids and I'll stay with her." Anna forced a smile, hoping her face didn't betray her wringing insides.

"Shit. Yeah, alright. I'm so sorry, Anna."

"For what?"

"For ruining your trip. You've got to stay back here and deal with my mess whilst I go out on a jolly day trip. It's shit… I'm shit."

"Stop it. I'm happy to stay here. All of this travelling around is exhausting; I could do with a day off." She stacked a plate with pastries and fruit. "Honestly, please stop beating yourself up. You've done the right thing. This is all for the best. Go, have fun, and make sure you get some good photos of the sea eagles for me, okay?"

Rupert smiled sadly and another wave of guilt crashed over her. But she shook it off because right now... *Grace.*

CHAPTER TWENTY-SEVEN

July 2005

Rupert clinked a teaspoon on the side of his glass. The chatter of the thirty-or-so guests seated around the long makeshift table died down and Craig stopped strumming his guitar.

"Hey, everyone. Sorry to interrupt," said Rupert. "I just wanted to say a couple of things. Firstly, thanks for coming along today. We couldn't have asked for better weather. Usually, you only have to think about hosting a barbecue and the heavens open." He glanced up at the clear blue sky.

"For once, sunny skies have prevailed. Anyway, as well as today being my birthday, and of course Anna's too…" Rupert smiled and nodded over at her. "We're gathered to celebrate something far more important – the wonderful news that Gran is now officially cancer-free."

Anna cheered, and Jen, the pretty brunette sitting next to her, touched her arm and smiled.

"We're so proud of you, Gran. You kicked cancer in the balls like an absolute *badass*."

"Rupert!" Edith shouted through a shocked laugh.

Rupert raised his glass. "To the invincible Edith Edwards, our wonderful Gran."

"To Edith," the group chorused.

Edith swatted away the compliment as if it were a midge and blushed as she looked over the smiling faces of their friends. "Thank you all for being here today and for supporting me throughout my… little ordeal. I couldn't have gotten through it without all of your love and care. Mostly, thank you to Rupert, Anna, and of course the wonderful Grace. You three are my angels."

A round of applause ensued and the chatter of the group picked up. Craig resumed his guitar set with his rendition of James Blunt's *You're Beautiful*, which he dedicated to the two girls gushing in front of him.

Anna beamed at Rupert as he bounded over.

"Was that okay?" he asked, pulling up a chair. "I didn't know what else to say."

"It was perfect, Ru." Anna smiled. "What else is there to say? She is a *badass*."

Jen giggled. "I could never get away with calling my Granny that."

Anna glanced over at Edith, who was holding court in an animated conversation. She looked radiant wearing a flowing summer dress; her rapidly growing-back hair was styled into a trendy pixie cut.

Rupert swigged from his bottle of beer. "So, Jen, I hope Anna hasn't been telling you too many embarrassing stories about me."

Jen giggled. "Ah, that would be telling. You'll have to wait and see what juicy gossip I spread around the office, won't you?"

"Believe it or not, we have got more interesting things to talk about than you, Rupert," said Anna.

"Ha, what could possibly be more interesting than me?"

"Wouldn't you like to know?" Anna said.

"Like to know what?" Grace's voice came from behind. She leaned over Anna with a bottle of Prosecco and topped up her glass. Her sweet, musky perfume lingered in the air as she rested a hand on Anna's shoulder.

"Grace! Come and sit with us. I haven't had a chance to properly introduce you to Jen yet," said Rupert.

Grace moved around the table and sat next to Rupert.

"Remember, Jen is the one I told you about from work?" Wide-eyed, he looked at Grace and jerked his chin towards Anna.

Grace smiled at Jen. "Sorry, I must've been putting Lexi down when you arrived. It's nice to meet someone Rupert works with, at last."

"Thank you for inviting me," said Jen, her pale cheeks glowing red. "Rupert has told me about you all. It's lovely to put faces to names. I'm still quite new in town so it's good to interact with people outside of work." Jen glanced at Anna and quickly looked away.

Anna smiled and then looked at Grace, whose grip had tightened around the neck of the Prosecco bottle she was still clutching.

"Having got to know Jen a bit, I thought that Jen and Anna would, you know… get along." Rupert winked at Grace.

As subtle as a brick, thought Anna.

"Well, it certainly seems like they've had plenty to talk about all afternoon." Grace's smile didn't reach her eyes and the muscles in her jaw tensed.

Anna shifted in her seat. It seemed neither Jen nor Rupert had sensed the undercurrent, but she was feeling its heavy pull.

"Cool, maybe we should leave them to it then, Grace?" Rupert raised his eyebrows and patted Grace's knee.

Jen looked at her watch and stood up. "Oh, sorry. I actually need to be heading off. I have an early start tomorrow so I don't want to miss my bus. Thank you again for inviting me." She smiled at Rupert and Grace. "Anna, it was really lovely to meet you. You have my number, text me if you still want to go out next week. I'd like that. Oh, and happy birthday again, both of you."

Acutely aware of Grace's watchful glare, Anna stood and hugged Jen.

"Lovely to meet you too. I hope everything goes well tomorrow… and yes, I'll text you about next week," said Anna.

"I'll see you out." Rupert put his arm around Jen and escorted her away.

Grace emptied the remaining Prosecco into her glass and leaned back into the chair. "She seems nice." She took a long sip and kicked her heels off under the table.

Anna stared at her, literally biting her tongue with the indecision of whether or not to say something. When she spoke, she was surprised by the calmness of her voice, even-toned and at odds with the frustration inside her.

"Are you going to be like this every time I meet someone, Grace?"

Grace stared back with a blank expression. "Like what?"

"You know *exactly* what I'm talking about."

"Well, she doesn't strike me as your type… a bit too mousy perhaps?"

Anna frowned.

Grace tutted. "I'm not sure what Rupert was thinking, the big eejit… and being so blatant about it too. 'Oh, look, Anna, I found you a girl who likes girls, she'll be your type.' He doesn't get it that you won't be into every other lesbian you meet. Jeez, that must have made you feel pretty awkward."

"No, Grace. It didn't. *You* made me feel awkward. Just like you always did with Toni. Seriously, you have to let me go. You and me, we're never going to happen. Not now, not ever. So, what do you expect me to do?"

"So you're going to go out with her then?" Grace narrowed her eyes.

"You're completely missing the point." Anna looked at her hands; they were shaking. "Yeah, maybe I will go out with her. You're right, she does seem nice, and we have quite a lot in common. Regardless of whether it's her or someone else. Whether it's just one date, five dates and a shag, or happy ever after… you have no right to be like this and I can't keep letting you hold that power over me." She threw up her arms. "I want you to be happy for me like I'm trying to be happy for you."

Grace stared at her, looking like she'd just been slapped. Her eyes were big, and when she spoke her voice was small. "I know I'm out of line, I'm sorry. I don't mean to be like this, it's as if something possesses me. For what it's worth, I hate myself for it."

Red blotches spread from Grace's neck to her cheeks and she blinked rapidly, trying to fight back tears. "I'd just about got used to the idea of you being with Toni and now… the thought of seeing you loved up with someone else has me raging. I want to be the one who makes you happy, Anna." She hiccupped a sob. "And I know it's not fair on you…" she paused and shook her head. "I'll try harder, I'm sorry."

An inexplicable surge of affection caused Anna's resolve to melt away. She got up, walked around the table and wrapped her arms around Grace's shoulders. She kissed her cheek and held her lips there. Holding her, breathing her in.

"It's okay," she said into Grace's ear.

In a change of tempo, Craig switched from strumming an upbeat Franz Ferdinand song to softly picking the chords of *Wonderwall.* In a heart-stopping moment, it transported Anna to summer three years ago and a life much less complicated. She stood, clutching Grace, rocking her in a gentle sway until Rupert bounced back over to them, smiling like a smug twat.

"Sounds like you've scored there, Sis! Jen is *very* keen to see you again. What do you think? She cute, eh?"

"Sorry, Cupid. She's not my type. A bit too mousy."

Rupert frowned.

Anna held up her hands. "Don't worry, I'll let her down gently."

"Really? Huh. I don't get it, I thought you two were getting along so well." He shrugged. "Jen is lovely. *I would.* I totally would..." His eyes flicked to Grace. "If I were Anna, I mean."

* * *

Anna opened her front door and stepped into the stuffy hallway. She didn't bother to turn on the light and cursed when she tripped over a box on her way to the kitchen. She'd moved in nearly three weeks ago and still hadn't got around to unpacking.

Compared with the buzz of the party at Grace and Rupert's, her flat was so quiet. As nice as it was to have finally graduated from student digs to a place of her own, she still had to get used to the sometimes deafening silence of living alone.

She poured herself a glass of cold water from the kitchen tap and took it into her bedroom, which was also still strewn with boxes and a half-emptied suitcase.

I really must sort my shit out, she thought as she looked over her stuff.

She opened the sash window as far as it would go, allowing the cooler night air to breathe into the room. She peeled off her top and flung herself back onto her bed. The cool breeze kissed her sticky skin. She thought of Grace's proprietary hand resting on her shoulder at the party. She'd wanted to lift it to her mouth and kiss it; to take each of Grace's fingers between her lips and—

"Argh, Grace, what are you doing to me?" she said aloud.

As if on cue, her phone lit up. She couldn't help but smile at the name illuminated on the screen.

'Hey you. I'm sorry about earlier. I can't promise I won't do it again, but I will try my utmost to be less of a twat. I love you xxxx'.

Anna responded with, 'I love you too x'.

She read and re-read Grace's message. Grace meant those last three words, just as she meant them back, and not in the way sisters-in-law should.

Her chest ached with desperate longing, the yearning for an impossible thing. More than anything she wished Grace was lying next to her now. She'd kiss her perfect lips and pull her close, Grace's hot, sticky skin pressed against her own. She ached to be touched by her, to touch her, to taste her sweetness again.

Her thoughts pushed the yearning down from her chest to between her legs. She slipped a hand past her waistband and into her pants, imagining that her fingers belonged to Grace. *Does she think about me like this? Does she ache for me?*

Amidst a frenzy of fantasies about Grace, Jen flashed into her mind. Jen and her cute, shy smile. Cute, *mousy* Jen, oblivious to the smouldering fire between her and Grace. As was Rupert. *Fuck, Rupert.* She yanked her hand out of her jeans as if burned by her own heat. Pressing her palms into her eyes, she breathed heavily until her pounding pulse slowed.

The stillness of her small, empty flat and the impossibility of her situation with Grace suddenly struck her. She was teetering on the edge of a precipice, a yawning canyon of emptiness below, threatening to engulf her. She curled into a ball and sobbed. The one person she wished was there to comfort her was the source of both her pain and her joy. She didn't want her life to be like this.

As hard as it would be, she had to get away from Grace. As far away as possible.

CHAPTER TWENTY-EIGHT

January 2022

Narvik

Anna zipped up her coat against the bite of the blizzard which hit her as soon as she stepped outside the hotel. She trudged through the deep snow on the pavement and hauled her backpack into the open luggage compartment of the coach. On board, she settled into her usual seat at the back and watched snowflakes swish and flick around in the light of a streetlamp.

She caught sight of her smiling reflection in the window. She hadn't been able to wipe the ridiculous smile from her face since she'd woken up for a second morning entangled with Grace. She'd have to tone down her mood; there was no excuse she could think of to explain why she was this high. Gran, Rupert, and the kids knew her too well to see through anything she could think up.

If nothing else, we'll always have Svolvær. Beautiful Svolvær. Anna closed her eyes and retraced the day they'd spent together.

* * *

She'd returned to their room with the fruit and pastries acquired from the buffet and delivered breakfast in bed to Grace. There they remained until their hunger for more food surpassed their hunger for each other. Free and uninhibited, they went out and explored the small island.

When they were together for that short time at university, Grace had been too shy and unsure of herself to be affectionate in public. Yet it was Grace who suddenly stopped as they were walking along the snowy street. She spun Anna around and kissed her in broad daylight. Anna was in awe of the woman Grace had become; afraid of nothing, at least not in this little Arctic town in northern Norway, where nobody knew her.

They came across a little Italian café and feasted on a massive pepperoni pizza, so big they'd taken leftovers back to the hotel. They lay together in a steaming bubble bath, belly-laughing as they sipped red wine straight from the bottle. It was as if a fog had lifted, revealing the horizon within touching distance; the horizon being the naked woman lying between Anna's legs in a hotel bathtub.

Grace's ocean-green eyes stared into her own with an intensity that could only mean one thing. She traced the tip of her tongue up Anna's neck and met her lips with a silky kiss. A gentle tide of soapy water lapped the edges of the tub as their bodies slipped together.

Come dinner time, the tour group returned. Anna answered a knock on the door to Lexi and Toby and she stepped into the hallway, pulling the door closed behind her. She told them Grace was sleeping and they wouldn't be joining them for dinner as they'd had a late lunch; at least that bit was true.

Alone again, they drank more wine, ate cold pizza in bed, and talked until the early hours. At some point, they drifted off to sleep in each other's arms, and that was where they'd woken just over an hour ago to the unrelenting chime of Anna's alarm.

* * *

Anna grinned at a flashback of Grace stretched out across their hotel room bed, covered in nothing but the warm light from the pastel-coloured sunset.

Grace's voice jolted Anna from her daydream. "Is this seat taken?"

Anna beamed up at her and scooped her coat onto her lap. "For you, it isn't."

"What were you grinning about?"

"Just thinking about yesterday."

"Mm-hmm, what about it?" Grace grinned.

"Well, I was mainly thinking about the risqué woman who kept taking her clothes off in my hotel room," Anna whispered.

"Oh, you had one of those in your room too?"

Anna laughed. "Are the others on their way?"

"Yep. Rupert seems to have Toby organised and Lexi was helping Gran with something, so I left them to it. They're all treating me like the walking wounded. Rupert's steering well clear, which is probably for the best."

She nodded and studied Grace's face, her lightly freckled cheeks still rosy from the cold. "Can't we stay here forever? Just you and me. We could live out the rest of our days with yesterday's agenda on repeat."

"Sounds divine, but we'd get fat if we drank wine and ate all that pizza every day... even with all the sex." Grace sat tall and looked around, then she ducked down and kissed Anna on the lips.

This is so wrong, but at last, it feels so right. A fizz of excitement pulsed through her as she pulled Grace's hand under the coat on her lap and squeezed it in her own. "I've been thinking that we probably shouldn't share a room in Narvik."

"Why not? Don't tell me you're worried about Rupert again?"

"No, it's not that. Well, it is a bit, but I was more worried about how we explain it to Lexi and Toby. Won't they think it's strange? It made sense here because they thought you were ill, but what reason would we have now?"

Grace sighed. "Yeah, I suppose you're right. I guess it would be a bit of a shock if we just came out with it. 'Hey kids, your dad is after leaving me for another woman but it's okay, I'm replacing him with your aunt.' Jesus, how Jeremy Kyle does that sound?"

It does sound all kinds of wrong when put like that. Rupert's side of the bed isn't even cold yet and I'm in it. She must have been frowning as Grace squeezed her hand.

"What's wrong?" she asked softly.

"Perhaps we should've taken things a bit slower."

Grace exhaled a laugh. "Ah now, it wasn't as if we planned it."

"I know, but we need to be careful. Take our time and make sure we're doing the right thing. It's going to be hard enough for Lexi and Toby with you and Ru. This, on top of that... I don't want to damage them any more than—"

"I can't bring myself to think about any of that yet." Grace waved away Anna's words and rested her head on her shoulder. "I'll share a room with Lexi in Narvik, and you can share with Gran. All good?"

"Yeah, that makes sense." Anna swallowed. "I'll miss waking up with you though."

* * *

As they journeyed from the Lofoten Islands to Narvik, the sky lightened and, like a developing photograph, slowly revealed the view of the immense fjords surrounding the archipelago. They crossed the impressive suspension bridge stretching over the Tjeldsundet strait between the mainland and the island of Hinnøya.

Out of the window, sea eagles circled and swooped into the fjords. Anna craned her neck to get a better look. *I'd miss the eagles all over again to have another day like yesterday.* She smiled as the thought elicited another flashback of Grace arching her back and moaning in pleasure.

The coach snaked its way along the road that skirted the shores of the Ofotfjorden, arriving in Narvik a little before lunchtime. Colossal cargo ships, stacked high with sea containers, dwarfed smaller vessels in the vast expanse of water; even the industrial juggernauts somehow looked beautiful in the polar pink daylight.

They checked into their hotel, a rustic lodge nestled into the side of the mountain. Lexi and Toby shrugged off the change in sleeping arrangements, both far too excited about tomorrow's ski day to care about the trivialities of who slept where.

Around half the group opted to ski, so they followed Roy's

instructions on how to collect their rental gear. The other half planned to explore the town of Narvik, including Edith. Despite being a very good skier, a few years ago she'd decided to give her octogenarian knees a well-earned rest and hang up her ski poles for good.

* * *

In the deep pink and orange shades of sunset, the view of the fjord below became more impressive with each turn of the winding road up to the rental shop. Lexi and Toby marched on ahead, leaving deep footwells in the snow. Rupert, Grace, and Anna trailed behind, their conversation stilted and awkward. So much had shifted in the last forty-eight hours, Anna worried that at any moment she might slip and fall, and it had nothing to do with the snowy path beneath her feet.

As they neared the shop, Rupert held out his arms and brought them to a halt. He stepped forward and turned to face them. Grace huffed and angled her body away from him.

"Look, I had a lot of thinking time yesterday and there are some things I need to say to you both." He placed his hands on top of his beanie-covered head. "I know I've fucked up; I really have. I get it... Grace, look at me. Please."

Grace turned towards him, her expression hard like steel. Rupert showed his palms in surrender.

"I should've been honest with you a long time ago. You're a wonderful mother to our kids and we've had so much fun together over the years. I'm beyond sorry that I betrayed your trust and I've hurt you."

Grace stared at him, and he stared back with his hands still held up. Eventually, her gaze softened and she nodded. Rupert puffed out a breath and he looked to Anna.

"I've asked too much of you. I don't deserve such a wonderful sister, you've always—"

"Ru—" Anna reached out to touch his arm, but he stepped back and held up his hands again.

"No, I need to say this. Please."

Fuck. Anna stared down at her snow boots, willing this excruciating conversation to be over. A sickening cocktail of guilt and frustration curdled in her stomach.

"You two are my best friends. I know this is going to be hard and it will take time, but I am going to make it up to you. I need you both in my life. I won't have it any other way. Fuck it." He threw his arms out and pulled them into one of his bear hugs.

Anna released a shuddering breath into Rupert's puffa-coated chest and squeezed her eyes tight against her tears. The three of them stood as one sniffling, complicated mess, hugging in the snow.

Rupert loudly exhaled and patted their backs. "We'll have an awesome ski day tomorrow with the kids. Let's enjoy the rest of this trip and we'll figure out all of the tough stuff when we get home, okay?"

"Come on, you lot," Toby shouted from outside the shop. "All of the good skis will be gone."

CHAPTER TWENTY-NINE

February 2006

Anna jumped at the chance of an overseas secondment when it came up. She'd been employed as a junior vet for less than a year and, being so fresh out of university, she was keen to get all the experience she could. An international placement would look great on her résumé, at least that's what she told herself. If this wasn't a gift from the universe, giving her a chance for a clean break, she didn't know what was.

Tensions between her and Grace ebbed and flowed. Some occasions were more bearable than others, but more often than not, she came away from time with Grace feeling as dark as she had last summer.

Whenever she thought about Rupert, guilt consumed her. He was trying so hard, completely focused on being a good dad to Lexi and taking care of his little family. He appeared oblivious to the unrelenting undercurrent between her and Grace. He even encouraged them to spend time together, which made Anna feel terrible. It was driving a wedge between them; they'd always been so close, but she'd felt herself pulling away from him, which added to the depths of her loneliness.

The only way to resolve things was to put distance between them. And lots of it.

It hadn't taken long to put things in place. She easily managed to sublet her flat to a friend from university, relieved that he hadn't minded her things being stored in boxes and stacked in a corner. Over an afternoon tea, Anna broke the news of her imminent departure to Gran. Gran had been delighted for her, as was Rupert when she told him.

Predictably, Grace had not reacted so well. They sat side by side at a sushi train, picking colourful plates off the conveyor belt. When Anna dropped her bombshell, Grace speared a California roll with a chopstick. She said she'd read a study about how, statistically, career-focused women end up alone. When Anna laughed, Grace cried.

Big round tears rolled down her cheeks and plopped into her miso soup. Anna put an arm around her shoulder. Grace shrugged it off and told her she was selfish for leaving. Anna said it would be more selfish if she stayed.

Grace chugged down her glass of Pinot Grigio and pleaded, "If not for me, then stay for Lexi. Think of everything you'll miss out on. And what about Gran? She's only after just getting better. She needs you… we all do."

Anna shook her head and swallowed the lump in her throat. Grace's reaction only affirmed that she was doing the right thing, for both of them. Like the unstoppable force paradox, something had to give.

A clean break and a fresh start became her mantra. She said it aloud every time she wavered; every time Grace's beautiful tear-stained face popped into her head and all she wanted to do was kiss her and tell her how much she still loved her.

* * *

Weary from the first flight of her long journey, Anna arrived at the departure gate, grateful that it was air-conditioned, unlike other parts of the hot and humid terminal. Boarding wasn't for another thirty minutes, so she relaxed into a seat on an empty row and pulled her laptop out of her bag.

She'd had a good twelve hours to think about what she wanted to say, so the words flowed quickly from her fingers and onto the screen.

To: gracey_ryan81@hotmail.com
From: A.Edwards@yahoo.co.uk
Subject: Sorry

Hey you,

I know you're going to be angry that I didn't come over to say goodbye. I know you wanted me to come by when we'd have been alone, but I couldn't. I knew I'd lose my resolve if I saw you again. To be completely honest, I don't trust myself when I'm alone with you. I hope you'll understand, and I hope you can forgive me.

I want us to be able to be in each other's lives, to be close to each other without the risk of tearing everything apart. Putting myself 10,000 miles away might seem a bit extreme but it'll give us both some space and time to figure this all out. I know it's not what you want but you can't focus on building a life with Rupert if I'm there as a constant reminder of a very different time between us.

You have to put me out of your mind, Grace, or you'll be crushed by the unbearable weight of everything we were. Everything we can never be.

That chapter is over; we need to move on.

Rupert was talking about all of you coming to visit me in a few months. In the nicest possible way, please don't. I'm sure over time I'll change my mind, I'll be desperate to see you but no, whatever I say, remind me of this. Cold turkey – let's be strong. If you don't want to slip over, then you should avoid slippery places.

Give that gorgeous baby girl a million and one kisses from me. Tell her that her Auntie Banana will be back one day with as many koalas as she can carry! Please don't let her forget me, I love her so much.

Look after Ru, I know he can be an insensitive pain in the arse, but he has a big heart. You've got a good one there, you really have. Please give Gran an extra big hug from me every time you see her, she needs them more than she lets on.

Grace, I can't tell you how much I'm going to miss you. There aren't any words big enough for it. You know though, I know you know.

Be strong, be brave.

I love you x.

Anna hit send. She blinked back her tears and closed her laptop. If she could just get through the next twelve months and have a full Grace 'detox', then perhaps she could come home and reset. They could be a normal family without all of this weird tension bubbling away under the surface.

An announcement scratched out from the tinny speakers above her. "Calling all passengers for Flight QF-001 to Sydney. The aircraft is now ready for boarding. Please have your passports and boarding cards to hand."

Anna stood, stretched, and joined the queue. Her stomach knotted as her mind snagged on the mental image of Grace opening the email and being crushed by her words. She exhaled a deep breath and pushed the thought away.

"A clean break and a fresh start," she said under her breath as she handed her travel documents over.

"Have a nice flight, Miss Edwards," said the impossibly attractive air hostess with the flash of a flawless smile.

CHAPTER THIRTY

January 2022

Narvik

As they waited first in line for the lift to open, Toby bounced around with the infectious excitement of a cocker spaniel. The Narvikfjellet gondola propelled them 650 metres up the mountainside, depositing them outside the restaurant. They stopped to admire the breathtaking view of Narvik from above. Fresh snow etched the outline of the craggy land against the dark icy waters of the Ofotfjorden, monochromatic in the dull, pre-dawn light.

Since their conversation with Rupert, Anna hadn't found a moment alone with Grace. An awkwardness had descended between them and Grace had barely even looked at her since yesterday afternoon. The thrill and excitement had shifted to embarrassment and shame. However, when it came to Grace, she was far more acquainted with feelings at this end of the spectrum. After a restless night, she resolved to put it out of her mind. There was no remedy as good as a ski day to lift her spirits.

Anna took a deep breath of the icy mountain air and exhaled. "Come on, you lot. This mountain won't ski itself."

Despite Rupert and Toby insisting they should go straight to the top, they reluctantly agreed to let everyone get their ski legs back first on a couple of easy green runs and moderate blues. Rupert led the charge, with Toby and Lexi following close behind. They darted in and out of the fluffy powder along the edges of the piste and competed to jump as high as they could over any little kickers they could find.

"Take it steady," Grace shouted after them. Despite being a competent skier, she was the least confident of their group, her unfounded worries about Lexi and Toby a projection of her own nerves.

Unlike Rupert, Anna didn't mind which runs they did, how fast they went or where they ended up. She just enjoyed being in the mountains, preferably on skis. When Lexi and Toby were younger, she'd always been the one to hang back and collect up the debris from their frequent falls. She would reunite them with their kit as Grace picked them up and dusted them down; then off they'd whizz, like nothing had happened. Anna had always marvelled at their resilience and fearlessness.

Their first run was a wide, easy green which meandered spectacularly through the snow-burdened trees down to the gondola they'd arrived on. Grace insisted they do another easy run before taking the chairlift to the top, so Rupert picked one of the blues and challenged Lexi and Toby to a race. Howling like wolves, the three of them darted off.

Anna waited as Grace connected a string of turns down one side of the piste, leaving fresh tracks in the snow. Grace stopped and looked back up as Anna dropped and made a helix out of Grace's line with a few quick turns.

"Show-off!" Grace smiled as Anna slid to a halt next to her.

Anna grinned and looked back up the hill at the pattern they'd made.

They both went to speak at the same time, laughed, and did it again, underscoring their new-found awkwardness.

"Sorry," Anna said. "Are you okay? You know, after yesterday and our chat with Rupert."

"It made me feel rotten, it did. I thought after what he's done I wouldn't care. Turns out I care more about the great eejit than I thought I did."

"He really meant all of that stuff he said. I gave him such a hard time and I had no right to."

Grace took a deep breath. "I haven't been fair on you, I'm sorry. I shouldn't have put you in this position. I just wanted you so much but I've no excuse, I should've listened to your reservations."

"We did what we did *together* and for what it's worth, I'd do it all over again. I just wish this wasn't so complicated." Anna sighed, reacquainted with the impossibility of their situation, a familiar ache weighing heavy in her chest.

Grace poked at the snow between them with her ski pole. "When has it ever not been complicated with us?"

"I don't know… for about six months, back in 2002?" Anna smirked.

"Right," said Grace. "We better catch them up, or else they'll think I've taken a tumble."

* * *

The sunrise threw out glorious orange hues as they ascended on the chairlift to the top of the Narvikfjellet. At just over 1,000 metres, the peak offered a panoramic view of vast fjords and mountains that serrated the horizon. They were at the top of the largest drop in Scandinavia, a steep red run cascading ahead of them.

"Awesome," said Toby.

The look on Grace's face said the opposite.

"Last one down buys the drinks." Rupert flicked around on his skis and whizzed past them.

"Rupert! Don't encourage them to go so fast," Grace yelled after him. It was too late, the three of them were gone and clouds of powder puffed up in their wake.

Anna shook her head and laughed as she sidled up next to Grace.

"Quick photo before we go?" They leaned in with the majestic view behind them, and she snapped a rare shot of just the two of them. Anna pecked her on the cheek. "Go on, you go ahead. I'll catch you up."

"Sure, you always do." Grace laughed and tentatively took off on the steepest part of the run.

Any piste-bashing efforts on the peak had been in vain, as a thick layer of powdery snow had settled on top overnight. The soft powder beneath her skis gave Anna a weightless floating sensation as she glided effortlessly into her turns. She quickly caught up to Grace but stayed back, giving her plenty of space to pick her way down without feeling pressured.

After less than two hours of daylight, the sun started its descent behind the mountains, casting a whole new palette of colours across the magnificent landscape.

"I could literally look at this forever," Rupert said, before kicking the snow off his boots and heading into the mountain restaurant. Anna laughed and lingered outside a little longer.

As they waited for their food, Rupert spread the piste map across the table, smoothing it flat with his palms. He, Lexi and Toby studied it and planned their afternoon, eager to squeeze out every last run they could. Their agenda involved some of the area's renowned off-piste terrain as well as time in the snow park.

"Now do you remember what happened last time you made me go off-piste?" asked Grace.

Lexi giggled. "It's a good job Dad had that little shovel with him."

"And to think your mother mocked me for buying it." Rupert cleared his throat and slipped into a falsetto impression of Grace. "What the feckin' hell have you bought that for, you eejit? Are you thinking that you're Bear Grylls now?"

Laughter erupted from their little corner of the restaurant. Grace tried to hide her smile behind her hand. Rupert winked at her.

"If it's all the same, I'd rather stick to the greens and blues," she said.

Toby whined but Rupert held up his hand. "We're Team Edwards. We stick together—"

"No, it's okay, Ru. Why don't you three go off and enjoy your afternoon? I'm sure Banana won't mind hanging out with me." Grace rubbed Anna's thigh under the table. A mischievous grin played over her lips as her hand edged higher. "You don't mind do you, Anna?"

Anna shook her head and grinned, despite herself. Any guilt concerning Rupert was quashed by the joyous prospect of an afternoon alone with Grace.

* * *

After four more runs, Grace suggested they have a drink before riding the gondola down.

Anna sat in one of the two leather hide seats placed side by side next to the fire. Grace returned from the bar with two steaming mugs of hot chocolate, piled high with whipped cream.

"Who are you and what have you done with Grace?" Anna asked upon seeing Grace's drink selection.

"Ah, come on now, would I let you down?"

Anna tentatively took a sip and was hit with the booziness of rum cutting through the hot chocolate. "That's my girl." She grinned.

"Ah now, look at the state of you." Grace pulled her sleeve over her hand and wiped the cream off Anna's nose. She rested her hand on Anna's cheek.

Anna smiled. "You skied well today."

Grace waved away the compliment. "Sure, you're just being kind. I felt as stiff as a plank."

"No really, you looked great out there. I was watching you."

"I bet you were, pervert." Grace smirked.

Anna laughed. The fire crackled, and they sipped their drinks.

"What are we going to do?" Anna said, staring into the flames.

Grace stirred her drink and Anna's eyes traced over the soft curve of her neck, the glow of the fire on her face and her lightly freckled cheeks, rosy from the heat, her normally perfect auburn curls tousled by her ski helmet.

"You look beautiful," Anna said, and she meant it.

Grace laughed. "I bet I look an absolute fright… but thank you, I'm pleased you think so. You're not so bad-looking yourself, you know."

They smiled at each other.

"In answer to your question, I don't know." Grace turned her attention back to the flames. "I think all we can do is get through these next few days on this trip and we'll figure it all out when we get home." Tears glistened in her eyes. "I can't even begin to think about what it all means yet, with Rupert, the kids… my family. Fuck, my family."

Anna reached over, took Grace's hand and held it to her lips.

CHAPTER THIRTY-ONE

February 2007

A persistent tapping roused Anna from a deep sleep; she groaned and rolled out of bed. Her body lagged with tiredness as she stepped over the luggage strewn across the bedroom floor and through to the hallway. She yawned and squinted against the daylight as she opened the front door. A gust of cold, damp air hit her, and she regretted not grabbing a cardigan.

"Grace! What are you doing here? I thought we weren't catching up until tomorrow." Anna folded her goose-bumped arms over her chest, acutely aware that her T-shirt offered little modesty.

"Surprise!" Grace said with an uncertain smile. Rain dripped off the hood of her yellow raincoat and trickled down her nose and chin. Tendrils of wet hair stuck to her face like tentacles.

Anna stared at her through wide eyes.

Grace frowned. "Can I come in or are you gonna leave me out here to drown?"

"Yeah, sorry. I'm not really awake yet." Arms still folded tightly across her chest, Anna stood aside.

Grace stepped over the threshold and held out a sopping-wet bouquet of red roses. "I got you these. I saw them on my way here, and I thought they'd be nice… to welcome you home."

Anna focused on the flowers as they dripped all over the floor. Grace removed her wet coat and hung it on the hook by the door.

"There, that's grand." She rubbed her hands together. "I bet you've not seen rain like this for a while?"

Anna shook her head, her eyes still trained on the bouquet.

"I'm sorry for just showing up, unannounced like. I didn't think you'd mind. I was on my way to work but I had to see you. I couldn't go the whole day knowing you were back here, and I hadn't seen you yet."

"Grace, I…" Anna strained for words, gave up and sighed. "Sorry, I'm still half asleep. Can I make you a drink?" Not waiting for an answer, she walked through to the kitchen, placed the flowers in the sink and flicked the kettle on. When she turned around Grace embraced her.

Anna's heart raced at the perfect fit of Grace's body pressed into her own. Grace's hands on her back, pulling her close. She breathed in the sweet, musky scent of her and for a moment nothing had changed. *But no—*

Anna opened her eyes and stepped back. Grace reached out and touched her cheek.

"It's so good to see your face. You're so tanned, look at you… and you've cut your hair. It suits you. God, I've missed you so much."

Anna swallowed, her mouth suddenly dry. She tucked some loose strands of hair behind her ear. "I've missed you too, Grace, but there's—"

"Before you say anything, I have to say a few things. You know how you said we needed space and time to figure things out?"

Anna looked at her and nodded.

"Well, you were right. My mind is clearer than ever. All of this time you've been away, you're all I've thought about. I'm leaving Rupert. I want us to be together. There's no other way. I have to be with you."

Panic gripped Anna's throat. She opened her mouth and closed it again when no words came out.

"Hey, hon, was that the kettle I heard? I could murder a cuppa if you're making one," the see-saw song of an Australian accent called out from the bedroom.

"Who's that?" Grace whispered.

"That's Mel… my girlfriend," Anna said softly. She lowered her eyes from Grace to her bare feet and wished they were anywhere but here. Her and Grace. Her and Mel. Or even better, just her and her feet.

Grace's smile melted into a frown.

Anna muttered, "I was going to introduce her to everyone tomorrow at Gran's."

"You didn't mention a girlfriend when we spoke." Redness blotched up Grace's neck to her cheeks and she narrowed her eyes. "I thought she might've come up, especially seeing as you've brought her back with you. Most people bring back a feckin' didgeridoo from Australia, but you… you go and bring back a *girlfriend*."

"I didn't know she'd be coming back with me."

Grace narrowed her eyes. "Oh, she just popped out of your suitcase, did she?"

"No, obviously not. I meant that this hasn't been planned for long. It just worked out this way and… here we are." Anna took a deep breath. "She's going to be staying here with me."

"Right. I see. Okay. Well, that changes things then."

They stared at each other.

Grace shook her head and backed away. "I better be off."

Anna followed her into the hallway. "Grace, wait. We need to talk about what you said before. Let me just get dressed and we'll go to a coffee shop. I'll tell Mel it's a family emergency."

Rainwater showered the floor as Grace shrugged on her coat.

"Please. Slow down for a minute. We have to talk about this," Anna whispered.

"No. Just pretend I never came here. Forget I ever said what I said."

Anna took hold of her arm. "Grace, I can't just pretend—"

"Oh, so this is the amazing Grace!" Mel padded into the hallway, wearing nothing but Anna's oversized Oasis T-shirt. It barely skimmed the top of her long, tanned thighs. "Lovely to meet you at last. I've heard a lot about you." She pulled Grace into an involuntary hug.

"And I have heard *nothing at all* about you," said Grace, unsmiling.

Mel laughed. "Ah well, plenty of time for us to all get to know each other, hey?" She draped an arm around Anna.

"I have to be getting off now. I'll be late for work." Grace turned and fumbled with the lock.

"Here, let me." Mel leaned over and unlatched the door.

Grace shot Anna a look.

Mel smirked. "Well, you have a good day at work, Grace. We'll be seeing you tomorrow, I suppose?"

Grace pulled her lips into a tight smile. "Yes, I suppose you will." She didn't look back as she walked off into the rain.

Mel closed the door and chuckled. "Wow! She's as intense as you said she'd be."

Anna stared into the middle distance and chewed her lip.

"You look pale, hon. Are you alright?"

"Yeah. I think it's the jet lag kicking in." She faked a yawn.

Mel wrapped her arms around her. "I'll make us that cuppa. We can have it in bed, then I guess we better unpack." Mel kissed her forehead and walked through to the kitchen. "Where the hell am I going to put all my stuff? This place is tiny."

Anna leaned against the wall, her head spinning. It'd been a whole year since she'd seen her. Even soaked right through with mascara smudged around her eyes, Grace still had the same effect. All of that 'detoxing' and yet here she was, completely intoxicated again.

The air fizzed and the edges faded out as the words Grace said repeated in her head. *'I'm leaving Rupert... I have to be with you.'*

Anna raised a hand to her mouth and clutched her stomach. Eyes watering, she darted into the bathroom and threw up.

"You okay, hon?" Mel shouted through the door.

"Yeah, I'll be fine in a minute," Anna lied and chundered again.

She was the opposite of fine. She was totally fucked.

* * *

The words 'Welcome Home Banana' adorned a colourful hand-painted banner strung across the porch of Edith's house. Unmistakably the handiwork of Grace, with what appeared to be some scribbled assistance from Lexi. The banner flapped in the wind as their taxi crunched to a stop on the gravel driveway. Mel paid the driver and took Anna's hand as they exited the cab.

"Are you sure you're feeling up to this, hon? I'm sure your family wouldn't mind if you took a rain check."

"No, really. I want to see everyone. Besides, I'm fine now, I think it was my body rejecting all of that nasty plane food." Anna squeezed Mel's hand. "Are *you* feeling up to it? That's the real question."

Mel grinned. "I'm hoping I might get a warmer reception from Grace today, but I'm not holding my breath."

As they stepped towards the house the lead weight in Anna's stomach sunk deeper. She took a breath and puffed out her cheeks. The front door was flung open, and Rupert piled out with Lexi in his arms.

"Skywalker!" Rupert bellowed. His blue eyes sparkled as he rushed over.

"Skywalker?" asked Mel.

"Oh, it's Rupert's lame *Star Wars* joke, which he should have left in the eighties… along with this jumper. What on earth are you wearing, Ru?" Anna hugged him and took Lexi from his arms.

"Hello, my gorgeous little monster." Anna squeezed Lexi and planted kisses all over her face. "My goodness, I can't believe how much you've grown. What have you been feeding her, Ru? Bricks? She's so heavy!"

Lexi wriggled in Anna's arms and covered her face. Anna put her down and she darted behind Rupert's legs.

"I don't know why she's being all shy now, she hasn't shut up about you all morning." Rupert laughed and reached down to stroke Lexi's mass of curly red hair.

Edith appeared, beaming with arms outstretched as she folded Anna into a hug. Emotion choked in Anna's throat as she breathed in her scent, the woody fragrance of patchouli. *Home.*

"I've missed you so much, Gran." She stood back to survey her and smiled. "You look so well."

"As do you, my darling. I love your new hairdo." Edith grinned and nodded towards Mel. "Are you going to introduce your friend?"

"Oh, sorry. Yes, this is Mel. Fellow vet. We met at work, obviously. Mel has taken a secondment over here, and she's going to be staying with me. At my place."

"Nice… Anna finally moves a girl in. It must be serious," said Rupert.

Mel laughed and Anna shot him a dirty look.

"Mel, tell me, is that short for Melissa or Melanie?" Rupert asked as he put his arm around her and shepherded her towards the house. Lexi still clung to his leg and glanced back at Anna.

"It's Melanie." She gestured to her chest. "And yes, before you say it, I know I am rather."

Rupert laughed. "Ha, Melanie, melon-y!" He looked back over his shoulder at Anna and mouthed, "I like her."

Anna smiled and shook her head.

"Where's Grace?" she asked Edith as they followed on.

"She went upstairs for a little lie-down. She's a bit out of sorts and says she's not feeling too well." Edith stopped and looked at her.

"I think she missed you, darling."

Anna swallowed. "I imagine you all did," she muttered, looking down at her scuffed Blundstone boots.

Edith chuckled. "Well, yes. But you know what I mean."

They stepped into the hallway and Anna's heart lurched as Grace descended the stairs, her loose auburn curls cascading over the shoulders of a faded green sweatshirt. Anna's sweatshirt. Grace stood on the bottom step, her hand resting on the newel post. They stared at each other. Only when Edith cleared her throat did Anna remember she was still beside her.

"I'll er… go and give Rupert a hand." Edith shuffled off towards the kitchen.

"Oh, sure. Sorry, Gran. I'll be there in a minute."

Grace stepped down and embraced her. "I'm sorry," she whispered into her ear.

Anna moved to release herself, but Grace pulled her closer.

"Can we just pretend yesterday didn't happen? Pretend I didn't say the things I said. Please?"

"I've been worried sick, Grace. Don't leave us – Rupert, I mean. Don't leave Rupert." Anna tightened her arms around Grace's waist.

A ragged breath escaped from Grace as she released her grip and held Anna out at arm's length.

"I won't. I promise I'll stay… but only if you promise you won't leave me again."

Anna flung back her head and exhaled.

Grace tried and failed to blink back tears. "It was the worst year of my life. I know you thought it would make things better, but it made them worse. I couldn't stop thinking about you the whole time."

"Okay, I promise. I won't go away like that again." Anna pulled her into another hug. "God, I missed you so much."

Rupert stuck his head around the doorway. "Come on, you two. The drinks are ready." He frowned when his gaze settled on Grace's face.

She sniffed and dabbed her fingers underneath her eyes.

"Seriously, Anna, she's been moping around the whole time you've been gone. She better cheer up now that you're back."

CHAPTER THIRTY-TWO

January 2022

Narvik

"Where the fuck have you two been?" Rupert rushed over as they stepped out of the gondola.

Anna quickly dropped her hand from Grace's waist.

"What's up, Ru?" Her silly grin fell away as she registered Rupert's worry-creased brow.

He brandished his phone at them. "I've been trying to call you. Why didn't either of you answer, for fuck's sake?"

Anna unzipped her phone from her pocket; notifications crowded the screen. Nine voice mails, fourteen missed calls and even more messages. "Shit. I'm sorry, it must be on silent. What's wrong?"

"Roy called. It's Gran." His voice was tight and breathless. "She collapsed earlier when they were in town. They rushed her to the hospital. Roy is with her but he told me to wait for you, so I did. You were ages. I was so worried when I couldn't get through to you."

"Oh my God. Is she okay?"

"I don't know anything. I was trying to call you both and you weren't answering."

"We're here now. Come on, let's go." Anna linked her arm through his.

"Ru, where are the kids?" Grace asked.

"We returned our ski gear and Lexi offered to take Toby back to the hotel. I thought it was a good idea. I haven't told Toby about Gran, but Lexi knows."

"Okay. Go on, you two get to Edith, I'll sort the kids out." Grace pulled them both into a hug. "She'll be alright. She's a tough old nut." She threaded her fingers with Anna's and squeezed.

* * *

Anna and Rupert sprang out of the taxi as they pulled up to the hospital. Squeaks from their shoes echoed down the long corridor as they power-walked to the A&E department.

"Edith Edwards," they said in unison at the desk. Unsmiling, the nurse looked over the top of her reading glasses. She raised a chubby arm and pointed at bay six.

Anna turned to a tap on her shoulder. Roy stood there with a newspaper folded under his arm.

"Thank goodness, I was hoping to catch you two before you saw Edith. Can I have a word?"

"Can't it wait, Roy?" asked Rupert.

"No, sorry. I really do need to speak to you both."

Anna exchanged a confused look with Rupert as they followed Roy over to a row of shiny blue plastic chairs in the empty waiting room. It reeked of disinfectant. Anna perched on the edge of the seat next to Roy. Rupert stood next to her, breathing heavily through his nose.

"Can I get you a drink? It's vending machine coffee but it's not too bad." Roy gestured to the machine in the corner of the starkly lit room.

"No thanks, Roy, we just want to see our gran." Rupert shifted his weight and crossed his arms.

"Yes, of course, of course. Well, the thing is…" Roy shuffled on the plastic seat and tugged at the collar of his checked shirt.

"What is it, Roy?" Anna asked.

Rupert rolled his eyes.

"Well, you see, the thing is. I've been here with Edith all day. I even stayed with her when she was speaking to the doctors."

"Yes, thanks, Roy," said Rupert, thinly disguising his impatience. "We appreciate it, but please can we just—"

"It has come to my attention that Edith is terminally ill," Roy blurted.

"She's what?" Rupert asked.

"Whilst they were examining her, Edith informed the doctors that she has a type of blood cancer and it's terminal."

Anna and Rupert stared at him.

"You see, none of this was disclosed to Great Arctic Adventures. It would've caused all sorts of complications for the trip. We really should have been informed." Roy tutted and pushed his glasses up his nose.

Anna covered her mouth with her hand.

"Oh my goodness! You didn't know?" Roy shook his head. "I'm so sorry. I just… well, I assumed you were already aware."

Rupert stood up and rubbed his hands through his hair.

"I'm going to have to make a few calls to the office to sort things out. I'm afraid it most likely means that Edith won't be able to continue onwards to Sweden tomorrow." Roy's eyes followed Rupert, who was pacing the room with his hands on his head. "I'll recommend that she fly back from Narvik once she is discharged from hospital. We can help to make those arrangements, but I think it would make sense for one of you to travel home with her." He looked at Anna and she nodded.

"Again, I'm so sorry that this has happened. It's such a shame." Roy arranged his lips into a sad smile. "Right, well, I best be getting back to the hotel now. I will leave you to see your gran. Please do call if there's anything at all you need." He patted Anna's shoulder as he passed her.

* * *

Anna pulled back the pale green curtain to reveal Edith sitting up in bed, wearing a hospital gown and sipping a cup of tea.

"Hello, my darlings. I wish you hadn't come. I did tell Roy not to make a fuss and disturb you." She shook her head. "How was the skiing? What were the conditions like? And most importantly, did you have fun?"

Anna wasn't sure what she'd been expecting behind the hospital curtain, but it wasn't this. She smiled and gently squeezed Edith's hand.

Rupert stood sentinel at the end of the bed, his face like thunder. "Why didn't you tell us that you're dying, Gran?"

Edith chuckled. "We're all dying, my love. From the moment we're born, we're dying."

Rupert threw his hands up into the air. "You know what I mean,

Gran. You're actually dying. Like, *imminently*."

"Well yes, I am aware of that, Rupert. It's one of the reasons I wanted us to take this trip. One last big adventure as a family. You know I don't like a fuss. I didn't want you both worrying about me. You have so much going on in your lives."

Eyebrows raised, Anna and Rupert glanced at each other.

"My levels ran a little low, that's all. This is a whole lot of fuss over nothing." She smoothed the palm of her hand over the blanket and flicked away some invisible crumbs. "I did ask Roy not to call an ambulance. There's not much they can do for me anyway." Her eyes creased as she laughed.

Neither Anna nor Rupert laughed with her.

"Look, when I get out of here, tomorrow at the latest, we can get on with our trip. Let's enjoy the time we have left, okay?"

"How long is that exactly, Gran?" Anna asked gently.

"I don't know *exactly*, my love. None of us ever do really, do we?"

Anna tilted her head.

"I'm told that, optimistically, it'll be a few months. But remember what I said about those funeral umbrellas before? It's not raining yet. I want to enjoy the time I have left and not be looking at sad, moping faces all the time."

Rupert sniffed and wiped his nose on his sleeve. He sat on the edge of the bed and took Edith's other hand in his own.

"Are you in a lot of pain, Gran?" Anna asked.

"No, it's not too bad. There are good days and bad days but all in all, I'm comfortable. It's nothing I can't handle."

"Okay then, Gran, how do we break you out of here?" Rupert

whispered.

Edith and Anna laughed, but Rupert didn't.

"Well, I have a plan." Edith's eyes danced with excitement. The twins smiled at each other and leaned in close to listen to her, just like they had when they were children.

CHAPTER THIRTY-THREE

May 2007

"Hey, Gran. Slow down," Anna called out.

Edith stopped, her hands on her waist as she surveyed the view and waited for Anna to catch up to her. She inhaled a deep breath. "I could never get tired of this. Beautiful, isn't it?"

The early morning mist shrouded a vista of rolling green hills. A honey buzzard cawed and swooped into the valley, diving towards the lake, its surface so still and shiny it looked like glass.

Anna stood alongside her, panting. "I think I'd appreciate it more if you weren't making me run up this hill." She laughed and doubled over at the increased intensity of the pain in her abdomen.

"A positive mindset, that's all it takes. My knees will give up before my mind does."

Anna grimaced. "I don't think a positive mindset will get rid of my stitch."

Edith chuckled and took off again, striding ahead.

At the summit, jagged peaks jutted out of the clouds, which were stuffed into the valley like a thick blanket of cotton wool. Edith removed her light jacket and set it down on a grassy bank. From her bag, she pulled out a flask and poured two cups of coffee into plastic mugs. Anna flopped down next to her.

"I don't know how you do it, Gran. You're a force of nature. You haven't even broken a sweat," Anna said between breaths. She took off her jacket and pulled out a packet of biscuits from her backpack. Edith grinned; fig rolls – her favourite. "I thought they'd go nicely with our coffee. Plus, I think I need some sugar." Anna held out her shaky hands in front of her.

Edith took a biscuit and dunked it in her mug. "So, you wanted to talk to me, darling?"

Anna bit her lip and nodded.

"Sorry to make you hike all this way for our chat, but you know me, I do like a scenic spot for important conversations."

Anna grinned. "You've made me hike up a mountain, we could've gone to the park for the scenery."

"After some fresh air and a good, long walk, I often find that my perspective has completely changed. I see things in a different light and I'm able to find a new solution for the problem that was troubling me."

"I know, you're right. You're always right." Anna smiled and sipped her coffee. "I've been feeling a bit run-down lately, which I guess explains my lack of energy today. Work has been busier than ever, and things haven't been great with Mel. You don't really know someone until you live with them, I suppose."

"I don't necessarily think that's what it takes to *know* someone. But I'm sure living with them must make it harder if they're not the right person to begin with."

Anna sighed. "I guess it was never going to work out with Mel… because I'm in love with someone else." She shot a sideways glance at

Edith to gauge her reaction. *Not even a raised eyebrow.*

Edith helped herself to another fig roll. "And how does this other person feel about you?" She dunked her biscuit and squinted at the view.

"I think she feels the same… but it's complicated. I mean it's *really fucking complicated.*" Anna checked herself. "Sorry, Gran. I'm so frustrated. It all feels impossible. I don't know what to do any more." She put her cup down and lay back. Tears prickled in her eyes, and she closed them to the pale blue sky.

"Maybe she's just not ready to love you in the way that you want her to. Otherwise, I presume it wouldn't be so complicated, would it?"

Anna propped herself up on her elbows and looked at Edith. "What do you mean?"

"What I mean is that if you love her, and she feels entirely the same way, you would move heaven and earth to be together." Edith sharply inhaled. "I don't think for one second that Mel would be an issue if you knew you could be with Grace."

Anna sat bolt upright, her heart pounding.

"And neither would Rupert be an issue if Grace were ready to love you in the way that you want her to. She's holding onto him for a reason, darling. You're right, it is very complicated." Edith shook her head.

Blood rushed in Anna's ears. "You… you know it's Grace?" Her mouth was suddenly dry, and her voice came out sounding strangled, but all of her questions poured out at once. "How? How do you know? How long have you known? Has Grace said something to you?"

"It's okay, Anna. Calm down." She rubbed Anna's back and smiled at her. "I've always known. Since the day you and Rupert introduced me to Grace. I saw the spark between you two. It's never gone out. I wondered if it would with time, but no, it still burns as bright."

"Oh my God!" Anna put her head between her knees and breathed rapidly. "Does Rupert know?"

"No, I'm pretty sure he doesn't know anything. He's certainly never let on if he does."

"Why didn't you ever say anything to me?"

Edith smiled wistfully. "Would it have changed anything if I did?"

"No, no it wouldn't." Anna shook her head. "Nothing has ever changed the way I feel about her. But I could've talked to you about it, rather than struggling alone for all this time."

"You could've spoken to me at any time, darling. I've always been ready to listen to you."

"How do you know she's not ready to love me?"

"Oh, don't get me wrong. She loves you fiercely, I don't doubt that. What I said is that 'she's not ready to love you – *in the way that you want her to*.' She's not able to give you her everything, which is no less than you deserve, and she knows that."

Edith closed her eyes and inhaled deeply before speaking again. "I was once like Grace. I loved someone like she loves you, but it wasn't enough. I couldn't give enough because I was afraid of it. I was terrified of the intensity of my feelings. I didn't come to terms with any of that until it was too late."

"When was this, Gran? Before you were married to Dad's dad?"

"No, no, it was a few years after James Senior had left. Your dad was maybe around six or seven years old, still at primary school anyway. I hadn't been looking for it, so I wasn't expecting it. If anything, after James left us, I was broken. I didn't think I could love again. So when it hit me, it knocked me over completely. It was like nothing I'd ever felt before or since."

"Who was he? What happened?" Anna asked.

Edith looked right at her – eyes twinkling, eyebrows raised. "*Her* name was Helene."

"Oh!" Shock gripped Anna for the second time in as many minutes. She shook her head. "Gran, you never said. Even when I came out, you never said anything about this. Maybe it would've helped me, knowing that you were like me."

Edith chuckled. "You didn't need my help, darling. You've always known who you are; all I had to do was give you the space to be yourself. You were so comfortable in your own skin; you were able to shrug off other people's assumptions and opinions like a coat you didn't need to wear." She sighed. "Unfortunately, Grace and I… we haven't been gifted with the same certainty of self."

Anna cocked her head. "How so?"

"Perhaps we've let ourselves be too burdened by the weight of other people's expectations. We put on that uncomfortable coat and didn't quite know how to take it off again." Edith paused and chuckled again. "Do you remember when you first told me you liked girls?"

"Yeah, I must have only been about ten years old. All of the girls I liked were only hanging out with me to get closer to Rupert though." Anna laughed. Her gaze settled on Edith's face; she'd closed her eyes and angled her face towards the sun. "You can't leave me hanging, Gran. What happened to Helene?"

"I've never talked about this before. I just preserved her memory in here." She touched her hand to her heart. "Over time, I became worried that if I spoke about her it would dilute the memory somehow. It would vaporise, and she'd disappear altogether. On reflection, that's a bit silly, I suppose."

Anna put an arm around her and squeezed. "You don't have to talk about it if you don't want to."

"No. I want to tell you about her." Edith poured the remaining coffee into their cups and began. "As I said, James was still at primary school. There was a sudden death in his teacher's family towards the end of the school year. They struggled to find someone with availability at such short notice, but they did… they found Helene." She smiled as the name passed her lips.

"She'd just come back from overseas where she'd been teaching English as a foreign language. Some of the parents were concerned that she was too young and inexperienced, but she quickly won everyone over. She was so charming and confident. The kids adored her… and we clicked right away." Eyes wide, she looked at Anna. "I've never clicked with anyone in an instant like I did with her. I couldn't stop thinking about her. It was constant." She rested her hand on top of Anna's. "You know exactly what I'm talking about, don't you?"

Anna smiled and nodded.

"I made excuses to talk to her when I collected James from school. She was new to the area and didn't have any friends, so I invited her over for dinner. After that, we started spending a lot of time together. All our time, in fact. At first, I thought I was just enjoying the company of a new friend, but I soon realised it was more than that. The butterflies in my tummy when she looked at me. *The way she looked at me.*"

Edith stared off into the distance. Anna looked at her, still trying to get her head around the revelation that her gran had once been in love with a woman.

"Like you, Anna – she was comfortable with who she was and she'd always known what she wanted. When she told me about herself, I was shocked… but I have to admit that I was also thrilled. I was excited by everything she was, and I think I knew right then that what we had between us was more than platonic. When we kissed for the first time, it felt so right." Edith closed her eyes and again lifted her face towards the sky as if remembering the feel of Helene's lips on her own.

"When it was just us, alone together, I didn't care. It was the sixties, however, and things were very different then." Edith frowned. "I worried about James and what people might say to him. I worried what people would say about me, what it meant I was or wasn't. The way she made me feel when we were together, most of those worries went away but I could never put it out of my mind altogether." She picked at a loose thread on her fleecy top.

"What happened?" Anna asked gently.

Edith looked at her, her pale blue eyes brimming with sadness. "I'd let her get close, and then I'd push her away. One day, I pushed too hard, and she left altogether. We had a terrible quarrel; she packed all of her things that had accumulated around my house over the months, and then she was gone. It was too late when I realised that it didn't matter whether she was a man or a woman – she was my soulmate, my missing piece, and I'd let that go."

"Oh, Gran."

"I was too worried about what other people would think, what other people might say. None of that really mattered. I let true happiness with Helene slip through my fingers." Edith's voice snagged and she blinked back tears. "It was all such a long time ago; I don't know why I'm getting upset now." She sniffed.

"I can't believe you've never talked to anyone about this before. It must have been so hard for you."

Edith pressed her lips into a thin line. "I'm sorry, my darling. I didn't mean to burden you with my sadness. I was supposed to be helping you."

Anna put her arm around her again and squeezed. "Believe it or not, you have. I'm so happy you told me about Helene. I'm only sorry that it didn't work out. I'd have loved to have had two awesome grandmas, instead of just the one."

CHAPTER THIRTY-FOUR

January 2022

The Arctic Express

Anna and Rupert spoke to the medical team and, as per Edith's instructions, they insisted she be discharged into their care. The duty doctor and nurses checked Edith over again and reluctantly said she was free to go once the paperwork was signed.

With the excitement of their plan falling into place, Edith sprung up out of the hospital bed. Waving away Rupert's protests, she attempted to remove her cannula rather than wait for a nurse. She tugged at the small tube in the back of her hand and blood pooled under the surface of her papery skin. Conceding defeat, she allowed Anna to assist her.

They hailed a taxi, driven by a bearded giant called Aksel, who cornered the icy bends of the mountainside road at inadvisable speeds. The headlights flashed through the darkness, illuminating a blur of rocks and snow. Anna squeezed her eyes shut but in the front seat, Edith squealed, giddier with each turn.

"I wouldn't mind some of whatever it was they gave her," Rupert said in a loud whisper.

A dim light emanating from the hotel lobby welcomed them home.

The early hour meant there was little risk of seeing anyone from their tour group; nonetheless, Edith made Rupert go ahead to check the coast was clear. With a finger held to her grinning lips, she then insisted that they tip-toe to their rooms.

* * *

Anna and Edith rose early to go to Narvik station and board the Arctic Express ahead of the rest of the tour group. Edith reasoned there was very little Roy would be able to do if they were already on the train to Sweden once it had departed.

At least a metre of snow had fallen overnight, and large flakes were still flurrying down. Anna struggled out of the taxi and trudged her way around to help Edith. They passed through the station and onto the platform, where the train was ready for passengers to board.

A thick blanket of snow buried the track, which would have been the cause of travel chaos in many places, but not above the Arctic Circle. The departure boards indicated that the train was scheduled to depart on time. Anna stowed their bags and returned to the station to fetch some breakfast.

"I can't wait to see Roy's face when he realises," Edith chuckled as she bit into a bacon roll.

"You are a rebel, aren't you, Edith Edwards?" Anna smiled and shook her head at her gran's childlike glee. Her smile faded and a weight dropped in her stomach as her thoughts turned to how sick Gran was, her remaining days numbered.

"I wish I'd been more of a rebel when it mattered," Edith said out loud, but as if to herself.

"How so?" Anna asked.

"I wish I'd been braver."

"Do you mean with Helene?"

Edith nodded. "I've been thinking about her a lot of late."

Anna stroked Edith's arm, but she couldn't think of anything to say. With a mountain of her own regrets to contend with, she didn't feel qualified to offer any words of comfort.

* * *

Big clouds of powder puffed up as the train ploughed along the track. After about an hour into the three-hour journey, the snowstorm ceased and the sky cleared, giving way to pastel-pink daylight. Beyond the barely-defrosted train windows, they caught glimpses of frozen forests and vast lakes.

The Edwardses reunited on board, and Edith filled in Grace, Lexi, and Toby on her great escape. Her watery blue eyes sparkled as she recounted how she and Anna had given Roy the slip so they could continue the trip.

The train had already crossed the Swedish border by the time Roy was alerted to the two stowaways. Flustered, he bumbled into their carriage, tutting and shaking his head. "This is highly irregular for Great Arctic Adventures. Of course, Edith, you have my deepest sympathies—"

"I'm not dead yet, Roy, but thank you." Edith grinned and clasped her hands together in her lap.

"I, erm, I'm just…" he stuttered, "…I'm just very concerned that I am now responsible for escorting a *very* sick woman to yet another country. How am I going to explain this to the—"

"Calm yourself now, Roy. What is it… three nights we have left? We'll take care of the invalid, don't you worry." Grace winked theatrically at Edith.

Rupert stood and patted Roy firmly on the back. "We'll keep a more watchful eye on Gran from now on. I can assure you, there will be no more antics ending up with her in hospital."

Roy glared at them and exited. Their laughter exploded before the carriage door had time to fully slide shut.

* * *

As they journeyed into Kiruna, the sky burned in a fiery, blood-orange sunset.

"Whoa, what are they?" Toby pointed out of the window at a spectacular display of pearly iridescent clouds diffracting the light in a spectrum of luminous colours. "They look like rainbow clouds."

"You're not wrong, Tobes, that's what people call them. They're stratospheric clouds and you can only see them in the polar regions. They're pretty rare. They look like rainbows because of the way the ice particles scatter the light," said Anna.

"I love that you know that, Banana. You're such a geek." Lexi laughed and snapped dozens of photos on her phone.

"Phenomenal. It's almost like a daytime aurora," said Edith.

Rupert huffed and crossed his arms. "Well, I wouldn't know. I've never seen the aurora."

"Oh, get over it, grumpy. It was you who fell asleep." Grace laughed and shot a smile at Anna, which sent a charge pulsing through her.

* * *

More rustic than the hotels they'd stayed at in Norway, Camp Norden comprised rows of wooden cabins sprawling out in all directions from a main lodge. They looked like gingerbread houses, iced with thick wedges of snowy white fondant.

After checking in, they dragged their luggage through the snow to their respective huts. Anna suggested that she stay with Gran, and Lexi quickly commandeered her own room in their cabin, leaving Rupert, Grace, and Toby to argue over their sleeping arrangements.

Once again drawing the short straw, Anna was last to shower. Edith and Lexi went on ahead to the main lodge to join the group for pre-dinner drinks. Anna tugged on her coat and snow boots, required even for the short walk to the lodge. She shivered as she stepped out into the sub-zero night air and smiled to see Grace had just left the cabin next door.

Anna approached her from behind. "Hello, you," she said and squeezed Grace's waist.

Grace startled and let out a yelp. "Oh, you frit the bejesus out of me." She exhaled a puff of white air with her laughter.

"Sorry, I didn't mean to scare you." Anna pulled her into a hug. "Have Rupert and Toby gone on ahead?"

Grace nodded. "I *really* missed you today. I missed you last night too."

"I could've done with a hug after everything with Gran. I almost knocked on your door when we got back, but it was late and I didn't want to wake you."

"There's no one else I'd rather be woken by." Grace giggled. "But Gran, though. I can't believe she didn't tell us how poorly she is. What was she thinking?"

"She says she doesn't want everyone to be sad because she's not dead yet. I suppose I can understand that but yeah… it was a shock alright. Rupert didn't take it too well. He was so angry with her at first."

"There are going to be some tough times ahead and we're all going to have to look after each other, aren't we?" Grace touched Anna's face and stroked her hair, tucking a few loose strands behind her ear. "Right now, we're here, under the stars in Sweden and I have you in my arms."

Grace's gaze drifted from Anna's eyes to her mouth. The space between them dissolved as their lips met; their hot breath misting in the freezing night air as they kissed.

"What the actual fuck?" Rupert's voice hammered out of nowhere.

Anna and Grace stopped dead and pulled away from each other. Neither of them said anything; they just stared at him.

"I mean, seriously, what the fuck is going on?" Rupert clenched his fists and breathed heavily. Misty breath puffed from his nostrils like a raging bull.

Anna's pulse thumped violently in her ears as Rupert's shouting rattled through her.

"Rupert, come on now." Grace stepped towards him and reached to touch his arm, but he snatched it away.

"I wasn't talking to you." He threw Grace a filthy look and then glared at Anna. "I'm talking to *you*, Anna. What the fuck are you doing? She is still my wife."

Grace scoffed. "I don't think you're really in a position to say anything about—"

"Oh, this is all a bit too convenient, isn't it? You made me feel like an absolute bastard for what I did, but I bet this is what you wanted all along." He paced back and forth with his hands on his head, puffing air in and out. "You never really moved on from her, did you? After all this time, you're still chasing after the one that got away. You're pathetic, Anna."

"Ru, please. It's not like that..." Anna tried to speak, but her voice sounded small and weak.

"What is it fucking like then? How long has this been going on behind my back?" Rupert fronted up to her. She stared down at his boots, almost touching hers.

"Rupert, you need to calm the fuck down. Don't speak to her like that." Grace squeezed between them. "It was me. I started this, not Anna. You have no right to stand there saying '*she's still my wife*,' like that means something. It didn't mean anything when you were bollock-deep in your little French tart, did it?" Grace shoved him, but to little effect. He towered above her, staring down, his jaw clenched as well as his fists.

He stepped back, looking from Anna to Grace. "You're fucking welcome to each other." He turned and stormed off. In his wake, Anna doubled over, gasping for air as if she'd been holding her breath the whole time.

"He's a real feckin' nerve," Grace muttered. She rubbed Anna's back and glared after him.

Anna rushed over to the bank of snow opposite their cabins and vomited.

CHAPTER THIRTY-FIVE

June 2008

Through the crowds of the Arrivals hall, Grace's Uncle Gene stood tall in a three-piece tweed suit and matching flat cap. When he caught sight of them his ruddy face beamed a smile of pristine false teeth.

"Ah now, if it isn't my favourite girl," he said, scooping up Lexi and spinning her around, before throwing his arms around Grace. "Ah, the lovely Anna too." He shook Anna's hand with both of his big warm hands, then, apparently deciding this was too formal, he embraced her instead. "Now let me see, I haven't seen you since Grace and Rupert tied the knot, have I?"

Anna smiled and shook her head.

"Must be, let me see…" He looked at his wristwatch, "…five years ago?"

"Wow, yeah… something like that."

"Ah, such a happy day. Wasn't it grand?"

Grace winked at Anna. "Yeah, something like that."

"Well, c'mon you three, your chariot awaits. Your ma has been like a cat on hot bricks waiting to get you home, Gracey, so we better be on our way or else there'll be trouble." Waving away their protests, Gene loaded himself up with their bags like a packhorse and led the way to his immaculate old car.

With Gene's overly cautious driving, the one-hour trip took two; with his singing, it felt like four. He warbled along with Daniel O'Donnell as the Virgin Mary rocked back and forth on his dashboard like a pious metronome. Mary only ceased her relentless sway when they pulled up in front of Heaney's.

"You girls go on in now. I'll fetch the bags," said Gene.

They surveyed the old pub from the kerbside. Grace exhaled a controlled breath and linked her arm through Anna's. They ducked under the wooden door lintel, etched with the words, 'Céad Míle Fáilte', and entered into a heady haze of furniture polish and stale beer. The bar buzzed in a hive of activity: bunting was being strung, glasses were being polished, and orders were being barked by Grace's mum. Even at five foot nothing, Mary Ryan was formidable, with wild green eyes, a shock of flaming red hair and the temper to match.

Mary spotted them and screamed. She dropped the bunting she was holding and dashed over, embracing the three of them and smothering Lexi in kisses. Lexi giggled and squirmed.

"Now where's that husband of yours, Gracey?" Mary tutted and held Grace out at arm's length.

"He sends his apologies, Mammy, I told you this already. He had some work stuff he couldn't get out of. Sure I went one better and brought Anna with me." Grace grinned at Anna.

Mary's thin-lipped smile did little to hide her disappointment at the poor substitution for her beloved son-in-law. Grace's family loved Rupert, as he did them; his rowdiness was a good match for their own.

"Just let me know if there's anything I can do to help, Mary," said

Anna.

"An extra pair of hands will not go amiss. There's much to do. But first, get yourself a drink and have a little sit-down, you must be done in after all that travelling."

"Where's Da?" Grace looked around.

"He's outside dealing with the whatchamacallit-tent-thing and sorting out your man with the hog roast. Best to leave him to it for now, you know he doesn't fare too well with distractions."

Grace and Mary exchanged a knowing look.

"And where's the bride-to-be?" asked Grace.

As if on cue, Roisin, the eldest of Grace's two younger sisters, appeared in the doorway behind the bar. A mass of dishevelled red hair flowed down past her shoulders to where her low-cut lacy top was fighting a losing battle to contain her ample breasts.

"Ah now, here we have the long lost, prodigal…" Roisin slurred and swigged from a half-empty pint glass, "…black sheep of the family." She hiccupped and came at Grace with open arms, but tripped over the step from the bar. Grace and Anna caught her between them.

"Jesus, Ros, look at the state of you," said Grace. "You should be taking it easy; you're getting married in the morning."

Grace's words triggered a raucous burst of song from the patrons and helpers. "*She's getting married in the morning, ding-dong the bells are gonna chime—*" Roisin flailed her arms, conducting the choir; she stumbled forward again, only to be caught by Anna. A burst of laughter followed and the verse tailed off.

"Raving mad, the lot of you! But that's enough now… back to work," ordered Mary.

Grace tried to prop her inebriated sister up against a bar stool.

"That'll be your da and Uncle Genie responsible for the state of it." Mary shook her head and tutted at her drunken daughter. "She's easily led astray, but as of tomorrow, she'll be someone else's liability. Young Danny Hannigan is going to have his hands full with this one, that's for sure."

Roisin groaned and took another swig. "At least I can have a drink on my wedding eve. You couldn't, could you, Gracey?" Roisin smirked and gestured her pint glass towards Lexi.

"Right, well, thanks for reminding us of that," Grace said flatly. She turned to Anna and rolled her eyes. "Let's go and chuck our stuff in my room and then we can muck in. Looks like the first job will be sobering this one up." Grace nodded towards Roisin, who was now slumped across the bar. Anna grabbed her bag and followed Grace, leaving Lexi with her Nanna.

Grace flung open the door to her old bedroom. "Christ, they preserve it like a feckin' shrine." The springs creaked as she flopped back onto her old bed.

Anna inhaled the musty, sweet smell of Grace's childhood room. She wasn't sure what she'd been expecting; perhaps not quite as much pink or quite so many Boyzone posters. She dropped her bag on the window seat and sat on the edge of the bed.

"I feel like I'm being watched," she said.

"How so?" Grace asked. She rolled onto her side and propped her head up with her elbow.

"By them." Anna pointed at the posters. "Particularly him." She gestured to the sparkly-eyed Stephen Gately, his floppy, curtained hair falling boyishly onto his smiling face.

"Well, he is my favourite so that's probably why he's keeping an eye on you. He's making sure you don't corrupt me." Grace leaned forward and poked Anna's side.

Anna laughed and swatted Grace's hand away. She stretched her arms up and then flopped back on the bed. Side by side, they stared up at the yellowing wood-chipped ceiling.

"Are you happy to be home?" Anna asked, breaking their easy silence.

"It doesn't really feel like *home* any more. I appreciate you coming with me, you know. I love them all to bits, but they drive me mad."

"Are you talking about Boyzone or your family?" Anna grinned.

Grace playfully poked her again. "Seriously, I feel like I lose myself if I spend too much time here with them. It's like I get sucked back into the world I used to live in." She sighed. "Don't get me wrong, it wasn't a bad childhood, it was just… small… sheltered. Do you know what I mean?"

Anna nodded.

"When Rupert comes here with me, he gets carried away with them all. I mean, it's grand that he fits in, but he's more like them than I am. Having you here, it's like you're an anchor, tethering me to the person I've become."

"I've never been called an anchor before… something that rhymes with it though."

Grace laughed. "Wow, that was *almost* as bad as one of Rupert's jokes."

Anna rolled onto her side and studied Grace's profile, as she had done a thousand times before. The smooth curve of her jaw. The soft arch of her cheekbone. Her pale skin, alabaster except for her nose, peppered with freckles after being kissed by the sun.

Grace looked at her and grinned. "What?"

"Nothing." Anna smiled. "I was just thinking how far we've come since last year. I feel like we're properly friends now, like we've moved on and left the past behind us. It feels different, doesn't it?"

"Mm-hmm." Grace nodded.

"It's nice being able to spend time with you," said Anna. "I don't feel like I'm doing something wrong just by being with you. Maybe we're growing up?"

"Ha, speak for yourself. Here I am in my pink Boyzone shrine of a bedroom feeling like I'm about thirteen again."

* * *

Anna sat amongst Grace's family in one of the pews of the quaint little Catholic church where Rupert and Grace were married on that blustery day. Today, much like Anna's mood, the weather was more clement and sunlight poured in through the stained glass windows.

Despite her drunken state the day before, Roisin looked stunning as she walked down the aisle in a flowing white dress. Two bridesmaids walked in her wake – her younger sister, Shona, holding the silky train of Roisin's dress, and Grace, holding the hand of the four-year-old flower girl. Lexi smiled from ear to ear, lapping up the attention from the cheerful faces craning from the pews to get a better look at her.

Anna beamed at the sight of Grace and Lexi, her girls. Not that they were *hers* exactly, but she was here with them. As Anna caught her eye, Grace smiled and mouthed, "Hi."

Fizz, fade… *focus, Anna.* She shook herself to avoid falling down that familiar hole. *Look how far we've come… we're properly friends now.*

The long, traditional ceremony, including a full Catholic mass, was followed by photographs in front of the church. A horse and cart transported Roisin and Danny the short distance back to the pub, followed by a walking convoy of their wedding guests. After a drink in the bar, the guests were invited through to the marquee for the wedding breakfast. Anna was seated with Grace and Lexi, along with Uncle Gene, Grace's cousin, Sean, and his wife, as well as their six-year-old son, Callum. Within minutes Lexi and Callum were firm friends, entertaining each other in an animated conversation.

"Where's that husband of yours, Gracey? He always loves a good party, does he not?" asked Sean, whilst tearing into a dinner roll.

"Indeed, that he does. But I'm afraid he's after getting caught up with work," said Grace.

"Ah well, can't be helped. He's a busy man no doubt. Instead, we have the lovely Anna." Sean smiled and raised his glass to her. Anna reciprocated the gesture.

Gene wiped his chin with a napkin. "So, tell me, Anna, do you have a fella?"

Grace coughed, choking on her wine.

"No, there's no fella. Not for me," said Anna.

"Ah now, that's a crying shame, a lovely girl like you. Sure the fellas must be falling over themselves to court you." Gene shook his head.

Anna shrugged. Catching Grace's eye, she grinned.

The speeches commenced as they tucked into their main course. Danny's best man regaled them with a few sanitised tales of their youthful misadventures, including the time they kidnapped a goat, dressed it in a nightie and gave it a full face of makeup before putting it back where they'd found it.

"Upon finding the goat, the farmer contacted the local rag. And would you believe it, his cross-dressing goat only went and got front-page coverage?" He held up a yellowing newspaper. "Our proudest achievement," he said, slapping Danny on the back.

Thomas Ryan followed. Choking back tears, he said, "It's two daughters down and only the one to go. Nonetheless, I am delighted to have another fella in the family, to even the odds, like." He raised his glass. "To Danny and Roisin, may the road rise up to meet yous."

Danny stood to applause when Thomas passed him the microphone. "I'm not usually very good with this sort of, er…" His eyes flitted around the room and then down at the cue cards in his shaking hand. "Roisin and I, we met on holiday in Ayia Napa. It was a bit of a holiday romance—"

"Oi oi," cheered the best man, to a ripple of laughter.

"Shut up, Gary," hissed Roisin. "Go on, Danny." She smiled up at him.

"Er, we didn't know it was meant to be. We'd had our bit of fun and said our goodbyes, and that was that. At least until I heard her voice on the plane. I'd know that voice anywhere. We were on the very same flight home. She was just two rows back, and that's when I realised… destiny."

Grace leaned towards Anna and muttered into her ear. "It's a shame destiny didn't splash out on the Ryanair upgrade to get them seats next to each other."

Anna released a whoop of laughter and clapped her hand over her mouth, sinking into her seat to avoid Mary's death stare. Grace grinned and sat back, her green eyes dancing with amusement.

Danny looked down at Roisin and picked up his flute of Champagne. "To my gorgeous bride, the new Mrs Hannigan."

The new Mrs Hannigan beamed.

The tables were pushed back to make a dance floor and the band got down to business, warming the crowd up with a few classic Irish numbers. Grace danced with her sisters and gestured for Anna to join them. Anna laughed and waved her away. She couldn't match their moves and she'd only embarrass herself. She sat back and looked on, keeping half an eye on Lexi, who was busy with Callum hoarding the unclaimed boxes of sugared almonds from the tables.

After a dozen songs, an out-of-breath Grace slumped down in the seat next to Anna. "My feet are feckin' killing me," she said and kicked off her heels.

"You have given them a battering," Anna chuckled and poured Grace a glass of wine from one of the bottles on the table.

"Why wouldn't you dance with me?" Grace pouted.

"You know I can't dance," Anna laughed.

"You don't seem to care when it's *Mr. Brightside*."

"Ha, true, but they haven't played *Mr. Brightside*. Besides, I don't really dance to that. I just jump about a bit and wave my arms around."

"Girls, girls. Have you enough to drink here?" said Mary as she checked the wine bottles on the table.

Grace held up the full glass in her hand. "Yeah, we're fine thanks, Mammy."

Mary exhaled loudly as if deflating, and sank into an empty seat next to them.

"Ah, she looks so happy." Mary watched Roisin dance with Danny to the band's rendition of *Girls Just Want to Have Fun.*

Mary turned her attention to Anna. "Now then, Genie has been telling us that you're on the lookout for a fella. Thomas and I know a lovely young lad. Aidan." She tapped Grace's knee. "I think you know him, Gracey? He works alongside your man with the gimpy leg. Well anyway, he'll be coming along shortly for the hog roast and whatnot so we'll introduce you." Mary sat back and looked delighted with herself.

Anna opened her mouth to respond but Grace beat her to it. "Mammy, what do you think you're doing? People don't want you interfering with their lives."

"We thought maybe Anna might like to meet a nice Irish fella whilst she's here. You can't beat the Irish lads. No offence intended, Anna, but you're not getting any younger. You wouldn't want to be leaving it much longer before you settle down."

"I appreciate the concern, Mary, thank you… but I'm pretty sure Aidan won't be my type," Anna said.

"Ah now. You don't know that until you've met him. Look at our Roisin and Danny. Destiny, or as I like to call it – God's good planning. Go on, have a drink with the fella and see what you think." Mary nodded in conclusion.

Anna sat forward. "Okay. Well, the thing is, Mary, I know I won't like Aidan because I don't like men, not in that way at least. Never have, never will. I'm gay. So again, thank you for the thought, but I'm fine as I am." Anna looked her in the eye and smiled.

Mary stared back, her open mouth bobbing like a fish's. Anna glanced at Grace, whose eyes were wide and her cheeks burning red. The band struck up the opening chords of *Mr. Brightside*. Anna stood, downed the remaining wine in her glass and took Grace's hand.

"*Now* it's time to dance," she said.

Grace happily obliged, perhaps grateful for any excuse to move on from that conversation. Mary looked on, her mouth still agape, as Grace and Anna jumped around together on the dance-floor.

* * *

Anna gently pulled back the duvet and climbed into bed, trying not to disturb the sleeping Lexi, who was sprawled out in the middle, hardly leaving any room either side for her or Grace.

"I think she had a great time," Anna whispered.

"She sure did. She's shattered, she was out like a light. Hopefully, she'll let us have a lie-in, although I won't be holding my breath." Grace switched off the lamp on her bedside table, plunging the room into darkness.

Anna lay there for a while, staring into the dark and wrestling with herself about whether or not to mention what had happened with Mary. Grace must have been doing the same as she spoke first.

"I'm sorry about my ma and how she was. That must have made you feel pretty awkward."

"It's not the first time I've come out and it won't be the last," Anna said softly.

"Well, still, people shouldn't make assumptions. I'm sorry they were like that with you."

"I was a bit surprised they didn't already know to be honest. I thought it might have come up before now. I mean, we've been in each other's lives for a long time." Anna paused but Grace offered no response. "Can I ask you something?"

"Sure." Grace exhaled as if she'd been holding her breath.

"Are you embarrassed by me?"

"What? No, of course, I'm not. Why do you ask that?"

"It's just when I told your mum, you looked really uncomfortable."

"It was uncomfortable. It definitely made her feel uncomfortable; you saw her face. She knows that we're close, so I suppose I wondered whether it'd make her think certain things about me."

Anna laughed. "You think that she might think you're a lesbian because you hang out with one? Imagine what she'd think if she found out we used to sleep together." Anna gasped mockingly. "Seeing as you're a married woman, I'm fairly sure my gayness doesn't reflect on you."

"Please don't make fun of me." Grace's voice was taut, like she was trying not to get upset. "You know it's different here. It's a small place, they don't get exposed to a lot of unfamiliar things. They're not bad people, really, they're not. They go to church, and the church teaches that it's wrong, so that's what they believe. I wish they were more open-minded… I wish they were more like how Gran is, but they're not."

"I'm sorry. I get it, I do," said Anna.

"I'm not embarrassed by you. I'm embarrassed by them… and I'm embarrassed by my own lack of courage."

Anna looked over to Grace's side of the bed. Now that her eyes had adjusted to the darkness, she could make out the outline of her. She reached across and touched her cheek. Grace pulled Anna's hand around to her lips and held it there.

CHAPTER THIRTY-SIX

January 2022

Kiruna

Anna woke to an empty cabin. The tight knot in her stomach served as a painful reminder of Rupert's outrage at seeing her and Grace together. *We should have told him sooner. I should have resisted her, insisted that we wait, be patient, and give it time.*

She groaned into the pillow, then dragged herself out of bed and got dressed.

At the lodge, Anna approached the table where they were all seated together. Rupert remained hunched over his cereal bowl as everyone else greeted her.

Grace mouthed, "You okay?"

Anna nodded and tried but failed to summon a smile.

Grace followed her to the breakfast buffet. "He isn't talking to me either," she said, softly resting her hand on Anna's arm.

Anna glanced towards their table. Rupert was staring at them, his lips pursed tight.

"Perhaps we should keep our distance? At least until Rupert has calmed down and we can talk to him," said Anna.

Grace frowned and her hand fell away. "If that's what you want."

Anna sighed. "No, of course, it's not what I want... but I don't want things to be like this either."

* * *

"It's minus twenty-one degrees in Jukkasjärvi, folks, so I hope you're wearing thermals. I've borrowed some extra coats from the lodge if anyone needs another layer," said Roy over the coach microphone.

At the Sami village, they huddled in front of a tipi-like tent, which their rosy-cheeked guide told them was called a Lavvu. Anna hugged her arms around herself. Even with thermals, the bitter cold seeped through. She wished she'd taken Roy up on the extra coat; he'd insisted Edith take one and she looked snug.

Anna glanced across at Grace, who was flanked by Lexi and Toby. *Keeping her distance.* This cold would be more bearable if they were sharing each other's warmth. She closed her eyes to the image of Grace's smooth body and the soft tessellation of their curves when they pressed together. She shook the thought from her head and tried to focus on the Sami guide.

"Today only two percent of Sami work in the reindeer industry, but we continue to keep reindeer..."

After hearing about the lives and culture of Scandinavia's indigenous people, they were invited to feed handfuls of lichen to the reindeer. The guide fielded questions about the traditional herding methods of the Sami people, but again Anna struggled to concentrate. She shuffled from foot to foot; even through her snow boots and thick wool socks, the frozen ground gripped her feet and rendered them painfully numb.

Others in the group were shuffling too. Finally, reading the crowd, their winter-hardy guide ushered them inside the tent where they were greeted by the smoky, rich aroma of lunch being cooked on a roaring fire.

They took seats on hide-covered benches at long tables around the fire. The Sami hosts served them a traditional herder lunch of smoked reindeer meat on warm flatbread.

"Isn't it a bit barbaric that we're eating the flesh of the animals we've literally just been petting?" Lexi curled her lip and poked a fork at the lean brown meat on her plate.

Toby looked at her wide-eyed, before grimacing at his meal.

"Yeah, it is a bit, but if you're hungry enough you'll eat it," Rupert said. He wrapped the flatbread around the meat and took a bite. "Mmm. Delicious."

Toby shrugged and followed suit.

"It actually tastes really good, Lex," Toby said through a full mouth.

"Don't talk with your mouth full, Toby. You don't have to eat it, Lexi. I think they only have two menu options though; take it or leave it," said Grace.

"I think I'll leave it, thanks." Lexi pushed her plate away and poured herself a glass of lingonberry juice from the jug on the table. "You're quiet, Banana, what's up?"

"I'm fine, just defrosting. It was so cold out there," said Anna. *Cold in here too*, she thought looking from Grace to Rupert, who were both staring at their plates.

* * *

After lunch they followed Roy on a short walk from the Sami village to the world-renowned Swedish Ice Hotel: A single-story building made entirely of snow and ice, cemented together by a special mixture of the two called 'snice'. They posed for some group photos before Roy ushered them into the lobby to meet their dedicated tour guide.

The guide escorted them into a vaulted hallway, supported by enormous columns. Huge, intricate ice chandeliers lit their way to double doors fitted with antler handles. The doors opened into a stunningly crafted ceremony room, decorated with ice balloon sculptures of various sizes. They sat on pelt-covered benches and listened to their guide as she explained how this, the world's first and largest ice hotel, is annually recreated.

"It is built using ice harvested from the neighbouring Torne River. Every year artists from around the world are hand-picked and invited to create bespoke hotel suites from the snow and ice. The suites form an art exhibition by day, and by night are rooms for guests to stay in."

When she asked if anyone had any questions, Toby's hand shot up.

"Isn't it freezing sleeping in a room made of ice?"

"That's a very good question." She grinned at Toby, and he blushed.

"The temperature inside the hotel stays at around minus five to minus seven degrees centigrade. So yes, you're right, it is cold. We give the guests special sleeping bags, and they also have access to a heated building in case they get too cold overnight."

"Are the toilets made of ice too? Do people's bums get stuck?" Toby asked and laughter echoed off the icy walls.

"More very good questions. I'm not sure anyone has ever asked me that before." She giggled. "No, the toilets aren't made of ice. They're just normal toilets. So, nobody gets their bum… or anything else stuck." She clapped her hands together. "Okay, if that's all of the questions, then please feel free to explore the exhibition at your leisure and be sure to check out our famous Ice Bar."

"I'm not sure I'd fancy sleeping in an ice room. A bit too cold for me." Edith put her arm around Toby and pretended to shiver. "Shall we take a look at some of these ice sculptures?"

Anna waited in line as the group filed out through the doors; she turned and looked back towards the altar. Rupert still sat on the bench with his gaze fixed ahead. She slowly approached, half expecting him to shout or scowl at her again. When he didn't, she tentatively sat next to him. By the time everyone else had left the room, she'd plucked up the courage to speak.

"Hey. We should talk," she said.

"Yep." He ruffled his fingers through his hair.

"I'm sorry you saw what you saw yesterday. That must have been a shock."

Rupert stared down at his boots and nodded. "Yeah, it was. I spoke to Nicole about it this morning—"

Anna scoffed before she could stop herself. Rupert glared at her; his normally bright blue eyes looked dark and moody. She held up her hands apologetically. He looked back to his boots and continued.

"She said I was unfair to you. She said maybe I didn't understand what was happening and perhaps I'd jumped to the wrong conclusions. Did I jump to the wrong conclusions, Anna? Has something been going on between you and Grace?"

Fuck! Okay… here goes. She drew in a deep breath and exhaled ungainly words that tumbled out and tripped over each other. "Grace and I… there are a lot of feelings between us. It's complicated. It always has been. We didn't mean for this to happen… it just did. I won't say it was a mistake because I honestly don't feel that way about it. But it wasn't planned."

She winced and looked at him. He stared at her through narrowed eyes. She drew in another deep breath. "What Grace and I have right now, it's new. Okay, well not new exactly… we've had feelings for each other for a long time, but the intimacy is new, sort of…" She covered her face with her hands and spoke into her palms. "Oh God, I'm sorry. I'm really messing this up."

"I'm not ready to hear any of this, Anna," he said in a surprisingly calm and even voice. "I can't deal with it right now. There's everything with Gran, and now this. I thought we were close, but we've all been hiding things."

"We hide things because we don't want to hurt each other. I know you understand that. I didn't want you to find out like this."

"It's a lot to get my head around. I need some time."

She nodded. "I know. I get it. The timing is terrible. We need to focus on Gran. We need to help the kids get through you and Grace splitting up. We all need to be there for each other. I promise I won't let anything get in the way of that, Ru." She nudged his elbow with hers.

Unsmiling, he put his arm around her and pulled her to him. The gesture filled her with a warm relief that almost counterbalanced the sickening swirl in her stomach; the feeling that happiness with Grace was about to elude her again.

* * *

Anna and Rupert joined the others in the Ice Bar. Grace looked at Anna and raised her eyebrows. Anna shook her head and mouthed, "Later."

"Where were you guys?" asked Toby. "You missed the sculptures. They were sick. There was this giant lizard and a goat. And like a whole room full of ice chickens!"

"Ice chickens?" Anna laughed.

Edith chuckled. "They really were quite something."

"Here's to Sweden and the ice chickens." Rupert raised his ice flute of Champagne.

Toby giggled and licked the side of his glass.

Lexi scrunched her face up. "What are you doing, Tobes?"

"I wanted to see if my tongue would stick to the glass."

"Can you even call it a glass? Isn't it just an ice? An ice of Champagne." Lexi shrugged and took another sip.

Toby's ice slipped out of his hand and shattered as it hit the floor; the fractured pieces darted away.

As the six of them walked back to their cabins, a luminous green slash appeared across the black velvet fabric of the night sky.

"Look, there." Anna unlinked her arm from Lexi's and pointed at the long thin vertical line.

Gasps of, "wow," and "awesome," chorused from everyone.

The vivid green aurora started to arc, and then another bright green slash ripped into the sky. The two lines twisted and turned together, like a slow-motion ethereal vortex.

Anna tore her eyes away. In the dim light, her gaze met Grace's. More than anything she wished it was just the two of them in this moment. She longed to cup Grace's face in her hands and kiss her like she had that night in Bodø when they'd had their own intimate light show. That had only been one week ago, but it seemed like a lifetime of things had happened in the space between.

Anna glanced at Rupert. His eyes were fixed firmly on the sky and there it was again, that sickening swirl tugging at her core.

CHAPTER THIRTY-SEVEN

September 2009

Sweat dripped down Anna's face and neck. She gritted her teeth against the burning fatigue in her calves and pedalled in time to the remixed bass of the Black Eyed Peas. *Yeah, 'I Gotta Feeling'... that I'm about to pass out.*

"C'mon, ladies. You've got this. One last push. We're almost there," shouted the instructor. Her flawless brown skin glistened in the gym's harsh lighting. She shot Anna a smile and quickly looked away.

Head down and determined, Anna ratcheted up her speed, as if she'd been turbo-charged by the instructor's grin. She ignored the screaming pain in her lungs and pushed through the urge to just flop onto the floor and gulp at the air like a fish flipping out of its bowl.

"...and we're done." The instructor sat up straight, her toned legs still cycling at half speed, making it look easy. "Awesome! Way to go, everyone. Great job today." She raised her hands above her head and clapped. The class took her cue and gave themselves a round of applause.

Anna slumped forward over the handlebars and looked across at Grace, who was mopping sweat from her face with a towel. "What was I thinking, letting you talk me into this? I won't be able to walk for a week."

"Don't be such a pussy. You're worse than Rupert." Grace chuckled. "Come on, surely you've to admit it was worth it for the view?" Green eyes sparkling, she gave Anna a cheeky grin.

Anna groaned. "Yeah, yeah. Alright, it was worth it for the view." A smile crept over her lips and she subtly turned her head to admire the lean and muscular Lycra-clad body of their spin instructor.

It felt weird to be checking out girls with Grace, but weird in a good way. *Perhaps she's finally accepted that I can't live like a nun forever just to spare her feelings?*

"So, you want me to introduce you?" Grace asked, snatching Anna back from her thoughts.

Before Anna could answer, the instructor came bounding over with far more energy than she thought possible after the exercise they'd just done.

"Hey, Grace. Great job today, you absolutely smashed it. You're getting so much fitter. Who's your friend?" she asked, flashing Anna a wide smile.

"Clare, this is my Anna. I mean, this *is* Anna, my sister-in-law. Today was her first spin class, if you hadn't guessed." Grace laughed.

"Sorry, a bit sweaty." Anna wiped her hand on her shorts and shook Clare's proffered hand. "I'd say nice to meet you, but you just nearly killed me, so…"

Clare's laugh was sweet and smooth, like hot caramel. Anna warmed to her instantly and it seemed mutual by the way Clare was smiling at her. Grace cleared her throat, prompting Clare to realise she was still shaking Anna's hand.

"Er, yeah… Anna, you did well, especially at the end there, I saw you digging deep… erm, perhaps I could buy you a coffee to make up for all the mortal peril?" Her confident smile faltered and she rubbed the back of her neck.

"Yeah, sure. That'd be—" Anna stopped and looked to Grace, who was grinning at them.

"Oh, you too, Grace. I probably owe you a coffee as well," said Clare.

"Ah thanks, but I can't today, sorry. I have to pick Lexi up shortly. You two go ahead though." She smiled. "Clare, perhaps you could talk Anna into coming along to the next class? Although I don't think she's going to need too much persuasion." Grace winked at Anna.

"I'll see what I can do. Anna, twenty minutes to get cleaned up and I'll meet you out the front?" Clare bounced on her heels and gave Grace a double thumbs-up. "I will see *you* next week."

Anna and Grace stood side by side, watching as Clare jogged away from them.

"She's such a ride, and that really is one fantastic arse!" Grace tilted her head to get a better angle. "Does my arse look as good as that?"

"Literally no one else's arse looks as good as that. Lycra was invented for that arse."

Grace playfully hit her arm and looked at her. "Come on. The state of you, you'll need all of those twenty minutes to get ready for your coffee date."

Anna laughed and a warm bubble of joy rose in her chest.

* * *

Anna's phone buzzed and jumped its way across the arm of the sofa.

She looked at the screen and smiled.

"Hold on," she answered whilst wrestling with the TV remote to turn down the volume. "Sorry about that. You alright?"

"Yeah, fine thanks," mumbled Grace through a yawn. "What are you up to?"

"Watching crap and eating rubbish." Anna glanced at the almost empty family-sized packet of cheesy nachos perched on her coffee table.

"Ugh, *X Factor*?"

"Yup, nothing else on. How about you?"

"I am home alone, and not embarrassed to say that I just polished off a Chinese banquet all to myself, which I'm washing down with a glass of Pinot Grigio. Rupert's out on Craig's stag do, so he's probably busy stuffing fivers into a stripper's thong, or whatever it is they do."

"I like to think they only do that in the movies." Anna laughed. "Where's Lex?"

"Asleep, at last, although it took what felt like the entire back catalogue of Dr. Seuss before she drifted off. Look at us, rock and roll on a Saturday night. You should've come over; we could've been sad acts together."

"I can barely walk after this morning. I just needed a bubble bath and my PJs."

"So, how did it go?"

"What, the bubble bath?"

Grace tutted. "No, you eejit. Coffee with Clare."

"Oh yeah... good... really good. I like her, she's... nice."

"Nice?" Grace squawked.

"Alright, what do you want me to say? She's really hot and she has a fantastic rack. You already know that because you have eyes."

Grace laughed. "So, do you think you'll see her again?"

"That's the plan… we're going out for dinner next week. That new Brazilian place, I think."

"Now, that's more like it. Who asked who?"

"She asked me."

"Good work, Clare." Grace cheered.

"I hope you're not just pimping me out to get a discount on your spin class?"

"Shit, you've sussed me." Grace's laughter echoed Anna's until the line went quiet.

"You still there?" Anna asked.

"Yeah."

"Thanks for this… I mean, thanks for being like you are about things. It's much better, isn't it?"

"Yeah, yeah it is… I want you to be happy, Anna. I've always wanted that for you, it just took me a while to accept that I didn't have to be at the centre of it." The weight of Grace's words betrayed the lightness of her voice. "I hope I'm making it up to you now."

Anna paused, caught off guard. A friendship with Grace was what she wanted. *Wasn't it?*

Static buzzed on the line, the sound of the space between them. "Love you," she said in almost a whisper.

"Love you too."

CHAPTER THIRTY-EIGHT

January 2022

Luleå

The road to Luleå carved through wide plains of Swedish Lapland; an expanse of white interrupted only by the odd cluster of red wooden houses or spinney of bare trees, huddled together in the Arctic cold.

Anna stretched out, occupying what had become *her* space at the back of the coach. As they neared the end of the journey, the group's collective high was at odds with her mood. She pulled on her headphones against the excited buzz of chatter, opting instead for her playlist as the soundtrack to her thoughts. *What a journey.* She rested her head against the glass.

Frozen landscape blurred by under the pastel-blue sky. *It's true that travel changes you, but this trip has changed everything.* She traced her finger through the patch of condensation, where her breath had fogged the window. Proof that this was all real, it hadn't been a dream, although at times it had felt like it.

Grace shimmied up in the seat next to her. Anna pulled down her headphones.

"Did you win?" asked Grace.

"Huh?"

Grace jutted her chin to the window to where Anna had drawn a hangman.

"Doesn't look like it." Anna wiped the doodle away with her sleeve.

"Ah well, you win some, you lose some... are you okay?"

"I'm ready to go home now. It'll be nice to sleep in the same bed for more than a night or two. I'd say it'll be good to get back to normality, but I'm not sure what that looks like for any of us any more."

"Ha! Tell me about it. I'm looking forward to not living out of a suitcase and not having to wash my knickers in a hotel sink," said Grace.

Anna laughed. Grace grinned and the low sun's warm glow accentuated the gorgeous crinkle of laughter lines around her eyes. Anna felt the urge to kiss her. But she didn't, and her chest hurt with the weight of everything.

"I'm scared," said Grace, in a tiny voice that didn't belong to her. "I don't know who I am without you and Rupert." She rested her head back on the seat and closed her eyes.

Anna had no words. Instead, she took Grace's hand and squeezed. A smile formed on Grace's lips as she squeezed back.

* * *

The orange glow of the setting sun blotted the edges of the horizon as they arrived at their final excursion. A cacophony of howling and barking rang through the air, and the noisemakers jumped around, raring to cut loose on the sledding track.

A burly Swede with a wild grey beard whistled through his fingers to get their attention and instructed them to split into groups of four. The first sled was promised the thrill ride, with the fastest dogs up front and out on their first run of the afternoon. Rupert, Lexi, and Toby jumped in before anyone else had the chance.

"One more person," said the Swede. Edith put her hand up.

"Seriously, Gran?" Anna shook her head.

"One last hoorah." Edith rubbed her hands together and climbed onto the sled, sandwiching herself between Rupert and Lexi. Roy's face looked ashen.

"Hold on tight," instructed their guide. They zipped off through the trees with the dogs in fast pursuit of the snowmobile. Screams and laughter echoed through the woods even when they were long out of sight.

Anna and Grace paired up with Jeff and Stephen. The two chaps sat at the back for ballast, with Grace up front, and Anna behind her. Grace leaned back and Anna wrapped her arms tightly around her waist. Acrid fumes choked the fresh air as the snowmobile fired up and raced off.

"Let's go," the guide hollered and the pack of dogs sped along the well-worn track, effortlessly pulling the sled in their wake. The guide yelled instructions to lean left and right as he steered around tight bends. They caught some air over a bump and Grace screamed when they thumped back down on the hard-packed trail.

"I think a little bit of wee just came out," yelled Grace, her howling laughter audible over the din of the dogs.

"I'm so glad you're sitting in the front," Anna yelled back.

After twenty minutes the dogs pulled to a halt where they'd started the loop.

"That was wild," said Grace, breathless from all the laughing and screaming. Anna took her hand and Grace pulled her to her feet, but she overbalanced and they stumbled backwards, landing in the snowy bank behind them. Grace howled even more than she had on the sled.

"Stop, stop, my stomach hurts." Anna laughed and tears ran down her cheeks.

Bear-like, Jeff towered over them. With outstretched arms, he hoisted them both up at the same time. He looked from Anna to Grace and beamed.

"You know, if I may say so… you two make an adorable couple."

"Oh! We're not… I mean, she's my…" Grace stuttered and colour rose in her cheeks. "She's my—"

"I know, I know." He raised his hands. "Just saying." He gave them a camp wink and looked around grinning at Stephen. "Aren't they cute, Ste?"

"Come on, big mouth. I told you not to say anything." Stephen mouthed, "Sorry," as he looped his arm through Jeff's, and they walked away bickering.

"Well, if anyone knows a good pairing when they see one, it would be those two." Anna laughed. "You didn't have to get so hypertensive about him thinking of us as a couple though."

"I panicked… I'm sorry." Grace bowed her head.

Anna leaned in and kissed her cheek. "Let's go," she said, taking her hand.

They followed the snow-trodden path through a canopy of trees leading to a clearing. In the centre stood a picture-postcard wooden cabin, so perfect it looked edible. Smoke plumed out of the little chimney and festoon lights decorated the eaves and door, inviting them in.

A log fire roared in the centre of the hut, and the groups already back from their sled rides sat at tables around the perimeter. They were served homemade cinnamon buns and wooden mugs of coffee, which had been brewed over the fire.

Their burly, bearded host stood next to the fire and sipped from his mug. "Every day, we Swedes make time for a coffee and cake break… but it's so much more than a sip of coffee and a piece of cake. The tradition of *fika* is a state of mind. It's about making meaningful connections."

"Mmm… I could get right behind *fika*," Edith said through a mouthful of cinnamon bun.

Anna looked over the faces of her family as they laughed and chatted. The firelight danced across their familiar features. All of the rough edges looked smooth in the soft light. Just for that moment, she allowed herself to forget that they were falling apart.

* * *

Anna woke early on the final morning of their trip. She dressed quietly and left Edith undisturbed. In the lobby she paced back and forth until the elevator pinged and the doors slid open, revealing Grace.

"Jesus, Anna. This better be worth it." Grace grinned and pulled on a beanie.

Anna smiled and took her arm. Warm breath misting in the air, they braced themselves against the cold and walked towards the shoreline that could be seen from the hotel. Arriving at a snowy jetty, they walked to the end and Anna tentatively stepped out onto the frozen sea.

"Are you sure this is safe?" Grace pulled her mouth into a grimace.

"They all seem fine." Anna pointed at the people in the distance, walking their dogs, running, and even skating on the frozen water.

"Yeah, but they're… you know…"

"What?"

"Swedish."

Anna laughed. "I don't think that makes a difference." She stamped her foot on the metres of thick ice beneath and Grace covered her eyes with her gloved hands.

"Come on. Trust me." Anna held out a hand and Grace took it.

After a few cautious steps, Grace accepted that the ice was strong enough and, arm in arm, they walked briskly out towards the horizon.

With eyes fixed on the vast frozen expanse ahead, Anna took a deep breath and spoke. "I don't regret a single second of the time we've had together on this trip. It was incredible. I just wish the timing was different and we'd figured things out with Rupert before—"

"Let's not pretend like he's an innocent party in all of this."

"I know, I get that he isn't… but things are messy right now. You've still got to tell the kids. There's so much for you all to work through. You don't need me adding to that confusion. None of you need that."

Grace stopped and turned to look at her. "What are you saying, Anna?"

"I'm just saying that the timing is awful, you've said so yourself. If we hadn't been on this trip, if things hadn't unfolded like they did with Rupert telling me about Nicole, then…"

Grace's face had set into a frown.

Anna faltered and cleared her throat to dislodge the words now sticking there. "Grace… what I'm saying is, we got swept away in the moment, and as wonderful as that was, it's not the right time to start something, is it?"

"So is this you saying that you don't want to be with me?"

"No, that's not what I'm saying at all. Of course I want to be with you, I've never wanted anything more." Anna lifted Grace's hands into her own. "I'm saying that for us to start something right now would be selfish and it would complicate things more than it needs to."

Grace pulled her hands away and covered her face.

"We need to think about Lexi and Toby. We need to think about Gran. It seems as if I'm going to lose her soon enough… I can't bear to lose Rupert as well," said Anna.

Grace dropped her hands from her face, revealing a blank expression. No tears, no words. She drew in a breath and looped her arm through Anna's. They walked back towards the shoreline in silence aside from the rhythmic crunch of their boots on the surface of the deep-frozen sea.

They neared the jetty and Grace stopped. "Things may well be messy right now but there's one thing I'm certain of… I want to be with you, Anna."

Anna gently gripped her shoulders and looked into her face. "I want the same thing… but are you truly ready for that? Have you thought about how complicated it's going to be? People are going to ask questions. People are going to pass judgements, and they'll say all sorts of things about us. Can you deal with that?"

Grace shook her head. "I don't want to think about anyone else, I just want to think about us."

"Yeah, and that'd be fine for a while, but not forever, Grace. I'm not ashamed of who I am or who I love, and I'm not prepared to hide it. I don't want to put extra pressure on you or make you do anything you don't want to, but if we're going to be together, I need it to be real and out in the open."

Anna wrapped her into a hug.

"I love you, Grace Ryan, I always have, I always will. As hard as it's going to be to let you go again, it's the right thing to do. I need to give you some space to work things out so you can be sure of what you want."

Grace's body heaved with a huge sob, and Anna squeezed her tight to bolster her own conviction. *This is for the best… isn't it?*

CHAPTER THIRTY-NINE

July 2010

Anna nestled a bowl of tortilla chips and homemade guacamole on the dining table amongst the many colourful dishes of food that had already been set out. She stood back, took a deep breath, and surveyed the room. What the place lacked in character, they'd made up for in cosiness, with odd pieces of furniture they'd cobbled together, and new things they'd splashed out on, like the plush corner sofa.

She took another deep breath and plumped the cushions. *I actually own a house. Well, half a house... and half a sofa. I'm happy... I couldn't be happier.* She frowned and tried to straighten a framed photo on the wall.

"Everything looks great," said Clare as she entered the room. She flashed Anna a huge grin and wrapped her arms around her. "You're all tense." She moved her strong hands up Anna's back and firmly massaged the muscles around her neck. "Are you nervous?"

"Yeah, a bit. I don't know why," Anna lied and leaned into the shoulder rub.

Without a doubt, the root of Anna's concern was Grace. Despite their blossoming friendship over the last couple of years, Anna could never entirely shake the feeling that it could all derail at any time. Grace seemed to genuinely like Clare, and it was she who'd effectively set them up. Even so, when Anna had shared her latest news, Grace's face registered a flash of something from the past. *Or did I just imagine the flicker of a slow blink? The trace of a faltering smile?* Grace's words had been supportive, but had her voice been higher than usual when she'd said them?

"Oh, that's good. Don't stop," said Anna as Clare moved behind her and kneaded the knots between her shoulder blades.

It had crossed Anna's mind that she was projecting; it was *her* feeling this way and not Grace at all. She could barely even admit it to herself but sometimes she longed for Grace to get possessive over her in the way that she used to. She yearned for the dangerous fever pitch of desire that used to rage between them and sometimes consume her.

"Mmm," Anna groaned.

Clare giggled. "You like that, huh?"

Anna shook her head to clear her thoughts. "Yeah, thanks. Feels better." She turned and kissed Clare's full lips. "I'm fine. Our friends and family are coming over to celebrate our lovely new home with us. Why should I be nervous?" She heard her own laugh, and it sounded shallow and unconvincing.

Clare narrowed her eyes. "Well, how about we pop open one of those bottles of fizz and take the edge off before everyone arrives?" She rubbed Anna's arms and bounced off into the kitchen.

The doorbell chimed. "I'll get it," she called through to Clare. Stopping at her reflection in the hallway mirror, she smoothed her hands over her blonde bob and allowed herself another deep breath before opening the door.

"You're early," she said.

"Makes a bloody change, doesn't it?" Rupert kissed her on the cheek.

"We got this for you, Banana. It's for you and Clare, for your new home." Lexi beamed as she held up a large potted purple orchid to Anna.

"Try not to kill this one." Grace grinned. "I find it fascinating that you can revive animals from the brink of certain death, but you just have to look at a plant and it shrivels up."

Anna laughed. "What can I say? I'm gifted with the fauna, not the flora... but you'll be pleased to hear that Clare has green fingers." Anna wiggled her fingers at Lexi, who giggled. "We already have a very full herb garden taking shape, and she likes to grow her own veg."

Grace smirked. "Do her talents know no bounds?"

"It's like you guys sniffed out the bubbly. Perfect timing," said Clare, open bottle in hand.

"Clare, we got you a flower. I picked it myself!" said Lexi.

"Ah, that's very lovely of you, sweetie. Thank you. Wow, isn't this pretty? Orchids are my favourites." Lexi beamed again and Clare bent down to hug her. "Right, who's for fizz?"

* * *

The small house quickly filled with family and friends, an eclectic mix of vets and personal trainers, plus a couple of their new neighbours. When the sun made an appearance, the party spilled out through the French doors and into the neat little garden. Edith and Marjorie, Clare's larger-than-life mum, seemed to be relishing each other's company. The raucous howl of Marjorie's laugh frequently punched through the air.

"Your gran is an absolute hoot," chuckled Marjorie when Anna came by to top up their glasses.

"Yeah, she is." Anna smiled. "I hope she's not telling too many tall tales about me though." She playfully narrowed her eyes at Edith.

Marjorie sucked air through her teeth. "Oh, I've heard plenty of stories, but for every one she has about you I can match it with two about Clare."

"Ha, do your worst, Mum, I've nothing to hide." Clare approached from behind and rested her warm hands on Anna's hips. "It's this one who's the dark horse, she doesn't tell me anything."

Anna exhaled a laugh and Clare planted a kiss on her cheek.

"Look at her, she's one smitten kitten." Marjorie beamed and held a hand to her chest.

"Ah well, yes. I think it's marvellous when you find *the one*," said Edith with a barely perceptible wink at Anna.

"Amen to that, sister!" Marjorie bellowed and clinked Edith's glass with her own.

Anna's eyes roamed the garden until they landed on Grace, standing alone by the shed. Her auburn hair glowed in the sun as she fidgeted with the empty wine glass in her slender hands.

* * *

"Ah, I'm delighted for you." Grace looked around, "You've yourselves a lovely home here together. It's grand, really grand. And Clare, she's a great girl, she's bang on. I'm pleased you're finally settling yourself down, Anna. You seem so… happy. Really happy. It's grand, sure it is."

"You sound like you're trying to convince me." Anna tucked her hair behind her ear.

"Ha, no, jeez, not at all. I'm happy for you. You've finally found someone who seems right for you. I mean, sure even I'd have bought a house with her if she'd asked me to." Grace grinned. "I'd get to look at that arse every day."

Anna laughed. "Please stop perving over my girlfriend's arse."

An awkward silence fell between them, broken only by voices from the house. Anna looked around and then back to Grace. She shuffled her feet and took a sip of her drink. "I suppose I better go and mingle."

"Wait, just a sec. I, er… I have you a little something. You know, a housewarming present."

"Yeah, the orchid. It's lovely, thank you."

"No, something else. I wasn't sure whether I should give it to you, but I've decided now that I will. I think you'll appreciate it." Grace rummaged in her bag and pulled out a small package which looked like it had been wrapped in a hurry. "It's silly. Just a silly little thing." She shook her head as she handed it to Anna.

"Thanks, should I open it with Clare?"

"No, no. It's for you."

Anna passed her wine glass to Grace, freeing up her hands. Her mouth stretched into a huge grin as she pulled out a packet of yellow washing-up gloves.

"You remember?"

Anna nodded. A bubble rose in her chest and escaped as a laugh.

No one else on the planet would be as delighted to get a pair of washing-up gloves as a present.

"Do you like them?" A smile lit up Grace's face.

"Yeah, I really do, thank you. This means a lot." Anna grinned at the packet in her hands.

"You can, you know, think of me when you…"

"…wash up. Yeah, thanks. I will, I totally will."

Sparks flickered between them like fireflies.

Clare skipped over towards them. "You two look like you're up to mischief, what have I missed?"

"Ah, you know, this and that," said Grace.

Clare looked at Anna, then down at her hands. "Washing-up gloves? We've got a dishwasher."

"Pots and pans," Anna and Grace said in unison before erupting with laughter.

"Ooohkay." Clare smiled and backed away.

CHAPTER FORTY

January 2022

Home

Anna shoved her front door to dislodge the mountain of post that had accumulated behind it. She squeezed through the gap she'd created and shut the door behind her. The cottage was cold and already dark as she'd pulled the curtains closed when she'd left. She set down her backpack in the hallway, scooped up the pile of post and made her way through to the kitchen.

She wasn't much of a tea drinker, but she had to agree with Gran that there was something wonderful about a strong cuppa when you arrived home after a long journey. She dropped the armful of post on the kitchen table, flicked on the kettle, and ducked through the doorway into the snug to light the log burner. The fire took quickly, filling the room with a warm orange glow.

Anna checked her phone whilst she waited for her tea to brew. No notifications. *The others must still be on their way home.* She took her mug of tea through to the snug, tucked herself into the armchair and closed her eyes.

"Good to be home," she said.

Her mind turned to Grace and the last conversation they'd had out on the frozen sea in Luleå. A familiar mix of longing and disquiet churned inside her. She sighed. *Is she thinking about me too?*

A loud pop from the burner startled her. Embers flared from the log being consumed by the fire. She picked up her phone. No notifications. She turned on the TV, flicked through four or five channels, and turned it off again.

She sat up and drained her mug. She took her backpack through to the small utility room off the kitchen. After emptying her dirty laundry onto the floor, she stuffed a load of darks into the machine and set it going. She glanced at the clock on the wall above the sink. *They should all be home by now.* She checked her phone. No notifications, so she called Edith.

"Hey, Gran."

"Hello, darling. Missing me already?"

Anna smiled. Edith's warm voice had a way of settling her. "Of course. Is everything okay at home?"

"I haven't long walked in. Just made a nice cup of tea and put the washing on. How about you?"

"Same." Anna laughed.

"It was a lovely trip but always good to get home, isn't it?"

"Yeah, it's good... er, did Rupert speak to you on the plane? He said he was going to."

"Yes, yes, he did. I'm fully up to speed. I can't say I'm surprised. I'd suspected for a while that there was someone else. He's had a different air about him. Dare I say, I think it's all for the best. Don't you?"

"Er, yeah, I guess... I feel for Grace though."

Edith chuckled.

Anna frowned. "What? Why are you laughing?"

"Oh, I'm not worried about Grace. I think this may have been the kick up the derrière she needed." Edith chuckled again. "Let's be honest, perhaps it's what you both needed? There could be hope for the two of you yet."

"Oh, Gran. I wouldn't be so sure of that. There's so much for them to work through. Divorce is always messy, isn't it? No one is left unscathed. I feel terrible for Lexi and Toby."

"They'll be fine once they get past the shock of it. The main thing is that they still have both their parents alive and well. You and Rupert didn't have that, and if I may say so myself, I think you both turned out okay."

Anna scoffed. "One of us soon to be divorced, and the other *hopelessly* in love with her sister-in-law. Yeah, we're a real poster campaign for the perfect family."

"Still in love then?" Edith asked. Anna could hear the smile in her voice.

"More than ever, I'm afraid." Anna sighed.

"I thought as much." Edith chortled. "So, what's the plan, my darling?"

"There is no plan. She knows how I feel. I'm just giving her some space to figure it all out. She needs time to sort through everything with Rupert and the kids. I don't want us to rush into something until she's ready."

"Well, that's not what I'd call *hopeless*."

"No, I suppose not." Anna smiled.

* * *

Anna slid a frozen lasagne into the oven and set the timer. She hung her clean washing out on the drying rack in the spare room and checked her phone again. One new message; from Tomas, not Grace.

> Hey mate. Welcome home. Can't wait to hear
> all about your holiday. Please don't try
> to come in tomorrow, get some rest while
> you still can, it's been nuts. See you on
> Monday. Mr T x

She replied. The oven timer went off. She let the lasagne cool and ate it in front of the TV. She flicked through the channels until landing on a documentary about penguins, which she was sure she'd seen before. As the flightless birds flapped and waddled across the screen, trying to make their way back to their chicks, she wondered whether Grace and Rupert had told the kids yet. She looked down at her phone. No notifications. Her stomach knotted as she typed out a message.

> Hey. Hope you got home OK, let me know when
> you get a chance. Thinking about you x

Her thumb hovered over the send button. *Should I just wait to hear from her? I'm supposed to be giving her space… but maybe she needs a little moral support.* She pressed send before she could change her mind. She turned her phone face down on the arm of the chair and promised herself she wouldn't look at it for at least an hour.

She loaded her plate and fork into the dishwasher, took her almost empty backpack upstairs and put on her pyjamas and a pair of woolly socks.

Whilst making another cup of tea she reneged on waiting an hour and checked her phone. No notifications. *Why are there no notifications?* Grace had received and read her message.

"Fuck." She screwed up her eyes and kneaded the heel of her hand into her forehead.

She put another log in the burner and dunked a chocolate biscuit in her tea. When her phone pinged, she picked it up so fast she nearly dropped it.

> O.M.F.G Banana!!! I can't believe it. Did you
> know about this? It's totally fucked up!!

Anna's heart lurched. *They've told the kids… shit.* She paced in front of the log burner, biting her thumbnail. Suddenly very hot, she went into the kitchen and opened the back door. A rush of cold, damp night air flooded in. She leaned on the door frame, took a deep breath of the mossy air, and hit the call button. Her anxiety levels increased with each unanswered ring.

She looked at Lexi's message again. Three dots appeared and pulsed underneath before another message pinged through.

> Can't talk. Will call you later, promise x

Nearly two tense hours dragged by before Anna's phone finally rang. The screen illuminated with a photo of Lexi's grinning face. She took a deep breath and answered.

"Hey, Lex."

"Bloody hell, Banana. I can't believe it. They're getting a divorce." Lexi breathed heavily.

"Yeah, I know."

"Why didn't you tell me?"

"It wasn't my place, hon. I'm sorry. Are you okay?"

"Yeah, I guess so. I think it's probably for the best seeing as Dad has another woman. I can't believe he had an affair. What an absolute bast—"

"I know you're angry now, Lexi, but he's still your dad and he loves you so much. These things happen. Relationships are hard. They're messy and complicated. None of it gets any easier as you get older, you'll see."

Lexi puffed out a breath. "I feel really bad for Mum. She seems okay, but she must be hurting."

Anna chewed her lip. "How did Toby take it?"

"He cried a whole lot. He told us he'd got peri-peri sauce in his eye, but he hadn't. He was really upset."

"Oh, bless him."

"He perked right up when Dad said he'd buy him a new computer though. Dad promised to buy me a car too when I pass my test… so that's something."

Anna laughed. "It seems you two are going to do alright out of his guilty conscience."

"Yeah, I suppose. It's just going to be a bit weird. I don't like the idea of us not being a family any more."

"It'll take time but they'll always be your mum and dad. You'll always be family. Perhaps it's better this way? If they don't make each other happy, then they shouldn't stay together. Life is too short."

"Yeah, I guess… but if that's true then—" A symphony of pings chimed in the background. "Oh, shit. Sorry, Banana. I got to take this call. It's Alice. I'll call you tomorrow, yeah?"

"Yeah, of course. Love ya, Lex."

* * *

Anna pulled back the duvet and climbed between her sheets; an incredible feeling after two weeks of sleeping in a different bed most nights. She turned off the bedside lamp and let her head sink into her pillow. Her phone pinged and cast a glow that cut through the darkness, dragging her back from the edge of sleep. She squinted at the screen. *Grace, at last!*

> Hey you. I'd have called but it's late and I
> didn't want to wake you. We told the kids.
> They're OK. Rupert has left. We decided
> it was best just to rip off the plaster.
> Everything feels so weird but I'm OK. We're
> all OK. I miss you. More than anything I wish
> we were together right now. Sweet dreams x

Anna held the phone to her chest and with the image of Grace's face behind her closed eyes, she surrendered to sleep.

CHAPTER FORTY-ONE

February 2011

In the dull dawn light, Anna pulled on yesterday's jeans and a jumper and tiptoed out of the room, avoiding the creaky floorboards in an effort not to wake Clare. She busied herself clearing up from the night before, trying not to clink the bottles and glasses as she collected them from the large wooden table in the centre of the kitchen.

She shrugged on her coat, stepped outside and breathed in the fresh morning air. The brisk, short walk to the nearest boulangerie did wonders to clear her fuzzy head, which was tired and groggy from the boozy late night.

In competent French, Anna ordered an array of pastries and some freshly baked baguettes, which warmed her arms as she carried them back. On her return, the chalet was still as quiet as when she'd left. She got to work in the unfamiliar kitchen, cutting the bread and plating up various cheeses and charcuterie. She piled the pastries into baskets and set them out on the table.

A pyjama-clad Rupert appeared in the doorway, ruffling his fingers through his short blonde hair. "What's all this?" he asked mid-yawn.

"I thought I'd make breakfast before we hit the slopes, soak up some of that booze—"

"Ugh!" He rubbed his eyes with the palms of his hands.

Anna turned back to the counter and started slicing a cantaloupe. "And I do believe it's Grace's birthday today, so I thought it'd be nice to do this for her."

"Oh shit! That's today?"

Knife in hand, Anna spun around and glared at him. "Please tell me you didn't forget, Ru."

Rupert raised his palms. "No, I didn't forget. I just lost track of the days. Easily done when you're on holiday, isn't it? Please don't stab me." He sniggered.

Anna shrugged and resumed her slicing.

"I got her an awesome present. You should've told me you were planning this though… I would've got up with you."

"Oh, this is nothing. We can say we did it together. Here, dry these glasses and put them on the table. I'll get the coffee going."

Rupert caught the tea towel Anna threw at him.

* * *

"Happy birthday, birthday girl." Anna beamed as Grace entered the room.

Grace groaned. "Ugh, don't remind me. It feels like every second of my thirty years is banging through my head right now. How are you two so sprightly? Were we not playing that silly feckin' ibble-dibble game until the early hours?" She took a glass from Rupert and poured herself an orange juice. "Why do I always lose?"

"Because you're a big loser." Rupert laughed and planted a kiss on her cheek. "Happy birthday, old girl."

Grace poked her tongue out at him and took a seat at the table. "Aw, this is very lovely of you both! Mmm… these are my favourites." She picked up an almond croissant from the basket.

"Ready for coffee?" Anna smiled.

"As if you need to ask." Grace closed her eyes and took a big bite out of the pastry. "Mmm… still warm."

The others gradually padded in and joined them around the table. Lexi beamed a gappy grin as she presented Grace with a handmade birthday card.

"Aw thank you, Lex. You've truly captured the essence of me skiing there. And would you look at all of that crazy orange hair spilling out from under the hat." Grace smiled at Lexi's felt-tip drawing and pulled her into a hug.

Grace's youngest sister, Shona, handed Grace a gift-wrapped box. "This is from us lot at home. It was Rupert's idea to get it, so you can blame him if it's wrong."

Grace smiled as she unwrapped the box, revealing a sports action camera. "Ah, this is grand, thanks." She passed it to Rupert, who was craning over her shoulder to get a better look.

"We all clubbed together, it's the latest one out. You can mount it on your ski helmet and get some good films," said Roisin. "If you don't like it, we've the receipt, and you can change it for something else."

"No, really it's grand. Although I imagine it'll be mainly footage of me falling and screaming as I tumble down the mountain on my arse." Grace laughed.

"Ah sure, you can't be worse than me," said Danny. "I can barely stand up yet and to be honest, I'm a danger when I do. I nearly took out the whole ski school yesterday."

"You'll get there with it, mate." Rupert looked up from the helmet installation instructions and smiled. "A few more lessons and he'll be smashing the black runs with us won't he, Lex?"

Lexi gave Danny an enthusiastic thumbs-up.

"Isn't it a bit embarrassing that a seven-year-old girl can ski better than you can, Danny-boy?" Roisin laughed and jabbed him in the ribs.

"Ah c'mon. I'm twenty-six and it's only my first go at it. She's no fear, that one. I've seen her flying down the mountain. I reckon she was born with skis on."

"I can assure you, she was not," Grace said with wide eyes. She grinned at the laughter her comment roused.

"Open my present next, Grace." Rupert passed her a neatly wrapped parcel and watched as she unwrapped it. "I kind of felt disloyal buying it but I thought that's who you'd be rooting for when we go to the game."

"What game?" Grace unfolded an Ireland rugby shirt and held it up.

"That's the next part… open your card now."

Grace peeled open the envelope. "Oh, that's grand. Thanks, Ru. I hope we're sitting with the Irish crowd though." She smiled and pecked him on the cheek.

"Well, what is it then?" Roisin asked through a mouthful of croissant.

"Tickets to the Six Nations. England versus Ireland in Dublin next month." Rupert put his arm around Grace. "We'll go spend a few days with the family whilst we're over there. It's all organised."

Danny and Clare nodded their approval.

"You sure that's not actually a present for you, Rupert?" Roisin rolled her eyes. "For the record, Danny, don't ever go buying me anything to do with rugby or any other sport, for that matter. I would be raging." She jabbed him in the ribs again and he winced.

"I enjoy the rugby, Ros. Sure, not as much as Rupert does, but it'll be fun watching Ireland give England a good hiding." Grace winked at Rupert.

Grace fingered the remaining envelope on the table. She smiled as she pulled out a card with a picture of Boyzone on the front and unfolded the sheet of paper contained within. Anna beamed at Grace's reaction, relishing the glow on her face and the captivating sparkle in her eyes, as they danced over the words.

Grace yelped. "Oh my God, Anna. This is amazing!"

Suddenly aware of everyone else, Anna quickly said "They're from Clare too."

Clare held up her hands. "I can't take any credit; it was all Anna's idea and execution."

Grace squealed. "These include a meet and greet. Anna, this is just…" She turned the card over and examined the photo again. "It's such a shame about poor Stephen. I can't believe he's dead."

Rupert frowned. "Stephen who?"

"Stephen feckin' Gately." Roisin scoffed.

Rupert looked blank.

"You know, Boyzone?" A smirk lifted the corner of Roisin's top lip as she eyed Grace. "I can't believe you're still obsessed with them after all these years, Grace. Stephen was a gay, you know that don't you?"

Clare cleared her throat and Grace shifted in her seat. Danny gently nudged Roisin's arm with his elbow.

She glared at him. "What?"

He jutted his chin towards Anna and Clare. Roisin looked at them and the penny dropped. "Ah, you know what I mean. No offence, ladies."

Clare looked at Anna with raised eyebrows. *Leave it.* Anna subtly shook her head and stole a glance at Grace, who was closely examining the concert tickets.

"Erm, so I get you Six Nations tickets but you're more excited about a boy band that should've been left in the nineties?" Rupert shook his head.

"It's not just any boy band. It's Boyzone!" said Grace. "And with that attitude, I most definitely won't be bringing you as my plus one."

Rupert laughed. "Lucky me."

Grace smiled across the table at Anna. She mouthed 'Thank you,' and blew her a kiss, eliciting a flutter in Anna's chest.

"Right, we better get ourselves dressed and up the hill before it's all hacked," said Rupert. He clapped his hands together and his chair scraped across the floor tiles as he stood up.

"I'm doing a maximum of five runs and then I'm hitting the après bar... which is where you will find me for the rest of the day. It's my birthday... *and I can get pissed if I want to!*" announced Grace.

Danny cheered. "I'm up for that. See you there after ski school."

"Yeah, if you make it out alive." Roisin cackled.

Rupert rinsed the dishes and Anna loaded them into the dishwasher.

"That was a nice present you got," he said.

"Yeah, I saw they were touring and I know she loves—"

"Yeah, exactly... way to trump my gift." He huffed.

"That wasn't... I mean, I didn't intend to do that. She was made up with your gift too."

"Yeah, but yours was better. I saw her face. She lit up." He shrugged. "I should've asked you what to get, you seem to understand her better than I do."

"No, don't be silly. I got lucky. Who knew she'd be so into a boy band from the nineties, hey?" She squeezed his shoulder.

He dried his hands with the tea towel and gave her a flat smile.

"You did good, Ru. She'll have a great time at the rugby. Let's just hope Ireland win."

"They won't." He grinned and left the room.

With his absence she dismissed his jealousy, making way for the image of delight on Grace's face as she'd opened her gift. She loved nothing more than being the reason for Grace smiling like that.

"What are you smirking about?" Clare asked as she slid her arms around Anna's waist.

Anna inhaled. "We're in the mountains, the sun is shining. What is there not to smile about?"

"I don't know, maybe the casual homophobia of a certain person in our group?"

"Hmm, yeah there is that I suppose." Anna chuckled. "It's only Roisin, take no notice. It's her problem, not ours."

CHAPTER FORTY-TWO

March 2022

Anna caught the waiter's eye and ordered another drink. She picked up her phone, sighed and put it face down on the table again. A flutter of nerves rippled through her, like proper first-date nerves. Except this was far from a first date.

The waiter returned with her vodka and coke. The ice clinked against the glass as she stirred it and resisted the urge to gulp it down and order another. She picked up her phone again, this time opening a social media app and scrolling through the feed. She swiped past photos of Shona's new kitten, and Craig's son's fifth birthday party. Her thumb hovered over a photo of the recently married Mel and her wife, enjoying a vineyard tour in the Barossa Valley. *They look so happy. I wish I was in a vineyard... although not with Mel.*

Anna scrolled on and stopped when she reached a post by Lexi, entitled 'Family Trip'. She swiped through the photos. Colourful houses on stilts in Trondheim. Their family photo on Torghatten. Lexi's birthday cake on the train – lit with its eighteen candles. The snowy harbour in Svolvær. Skiing in Narvik. The rainbow clouds near Kiruna. Toby with a reindeer. Toby with an ice chicken. Lastly, the northern lights swirling over Camp Norden. Snapshots of an incredible trip, perfect moments captured forever, which was ironic as nothing would ever be the same again, and things were far from perfect.

Anna clicked the heart symbol and flicked back to the group photo. She pinched her fingers to zoom in on Grace and grinned at the gorgeous face that filled her screen.

"God, sorry I'm so late. I would've messaged you, but…" Grace held her phone up as she approached the table. "Flat battery."

Anna quickly locked her screen and stood to greet her. "It's okay. You're here now."

They embraced, but there was something rigid and awkward about their hug. Anna wanted to kiss her, but instead she sat as Grace removed her coat and scarf.

"It took longer with the lawyers than I thought it would." Grace pointed to Anna's glass. "Do you mind if I have a sip? I'm dying for a drink."

"Yeah of course. Do you want the same?"

Grace nodded. "Damn, that's good," she said as she drained the contents of Anna's glass.

Anna smiled and gestured for two more from the same waiter. "So, did it all go okay?"

"Yeah, as well as it could. It's fairly straightforward seeing as we pretty much agree on what's what… but still, there's this weird tension between us. I guess that's to be expected as we're effectively tearing our lives apart and dividing up the pieces. I think once we're through this bit, we'll be able to move on. We have to, for Lexi and Toby. I don't want this being any worse than it already is for them."

Anna slowly nodded. "It must be tough for you all. Lexi and Toby seem okay though. I saw them at Gran's last weekend."

"I think they know this is all for the best."

The waiter shuffled up to the table and unloaded their drinks from a precariously balanced tray.

"Anyway, enough about all of that. How have you been?" asked Grace.

Anna grinned. "I've missed you. I mean, I've *really* missed you."

Grace smiled and Anna's nerves subsided a little.

"Work has been busy… it's that time of year. But we've just hired two new juniors which will lighten the load. I'll get to spend more time with Gran once they're settled in."

"How is Gran?"

"Oh, you know, taking it all in her stride and still pretending she's fine. I've been taking her to her hospital appointments, so I get to hear the facts and not just Gran's sugar-coated version of events." Anna widened her eyes. "Apart from that, not much else has happened since we got back… oh, I told you that Rupert wanted me to meet Nicole, didn't I? The three of us went out for dinner last week, to that little Italian place Ru likes."

Grace smiled with her lips but not her eyes. "Yeah, how was it? What's she like?"

"It was… weird. It felt really strange being out with them as a couple. She's nice enough but young, I mean, younger than I thought she'd be."

"How young?" Grace raised an eyebrow.

"I don't know… mid-twenties? Same mental age as Rupert." Anna laughed.

"Ugh. Is she disgustingly pretty?"

"Yeah, but in an obvious way… she's not my type."

"Well, that's lucky then." Grace grinned and sipped her drink.

"They seem really happy together," Anna said tentatively.

"I'm pleased he's happy. Genuinely, I am. It's good that he's met someone who makes him feel like that."

Anna traced a finger along the wood grain of the table. "Yeah, it's only fair that he should have that too."

They stared at each other until Grace broke eye contact.

"Did Rupert tell you we've put the house on the market?"

Anna nodded.

"It makes sense. It'll mean we can split things fairly down the middle. It also means that I need to start looking for somewhere to live." Grace took a deep breath. "I've been thinking about going back to Ireland."

"Oh. That's, erm…" Anna's voice drowned in the sudden rush of panic rising inside her.

"Lexi will be off to university in September and starting her own big adventure. So, I thought it might be good timing for me and Toby to have an adventure of our own."

"Yeah. Wow…" Anna attempted a smile but only achieved a grimace.

"Look, I haven't decided anything yet. I'm just thinking through my options. I want to do what's best for Toby. It's a lot of change for him, so we'll see."

"Yeah, sure. Of course. You have to explore your options." Anna forced breaths through her nose until all of her words spilled out at once— "You know you're welcome to stay with me, for as long as you need. Stay forever if you want, I don't mind. My home is yours. I mean that. I know it's not a big place, but we can make it work."

Grace sat forward and leaned across the table. She cupped her hands over Anna's.

"I really do appreciate that, Anna. You were right though, what you said in Luleå about me needing some time and space to figure out what I want."

Unblinking, Anna stared at their hands heaped in a pile on the table. Her fingers were freezing underneath Grace's warm, soft hands and her warm, soft voice was saying words Anna didn't want to hear.

"It was so hard when we first got back from our trip, what with Rupert leaving and not seeing you. But since then, I feel like I've started to get back in touch with myself. I'm learning about who I am, without needing someone else to define me. Does that make sense?"

"Mm-hmm." Anna bit her lip. She tore her gaze away from the pile of hands and looked at Grace. "Actually, no. It doesn't make sense. I don't want you to go to Ireland, Grace. I really don't want that. When I said I wanted you to have space and time… I think what I meant was *divorce Rupert, sort your head out and then be with me.* Maybe I didn't make that clear enough?"

"Honestly, at the time it didn't make sense to me. I felt like you were pushing me away. I was hurting and I was scared, I didn't want you to let me go. I didn't know who I was without you or Rupert."

Anna nodded. She stared at their hands again. At some point, she'd turned hers over. They were palm to palm and she was gripping Grace's warm fingers with her own freezing digits, clinging on like a climber dangling over a cliff.

"I was alone, and I started to ask myself, *who are you, Grace Ryan?* I'd never really had the chance to properly figure it out before life just happened to me. I spent all of those years wanting something I couldn't have. And now I realise, what I want more than anything is the chance to get to know myself."

Why did I ever think it'd be a good idea to give her space? "I'm such an idiot," Anna muttered. "Grace, I want to be with you. I don't care if you never want to tell another soul about us – if that's what's stopping you from being with me. As long as we can be together, that's all I want. I know you want that too… I know you do—"

"Anna, stop… it's not about that, not any more." Grace looked into her eyes. "I know what you want. And it's what I thought I wanted too. But now I have things I need to do, for myself. It's better this way, okay? Trust me."

Anna squeezed her eyes shut to hold back her tears.

CHAPTER FORTY-THREE

November 1967

Edith collected the post from the front doormat and flicked through the small pile on her way to the kitchen. She paused and scrutinised a handwritten envelope, addressed in an unfamiliar scrawl. Her heart lurched as her eyes settled on the North Wales postmark. Instantly, her mind turned to Helene, as it almost always did.

It had been over a year since she'd last seen Helene and she longed to hear from her. Things between them had been so unpleasant at the end that she didn't even have an address for her. She assumed Helene had returned to Wales, for a while at least. She wouldn't stick around anywhere for long. Helene craved adventure and wanted to see the world, which was the main reason things between them had ended the way they had.

Helene couldn't understand why Edith was so reluctant to uproot James and go travelling. Her own voice, edged with bitterness, echoed in her mind with the words that had been the beginning of the end. "Yes, I'm sure it would be wonderful for us… but it's a fantasy. You and me, all of this… normal people don't live this way. James needs stability. He needs normality and above all else, as his mother, it's my job to provide that."

Her hands trembled slightly as she placed the letter on the table.

With a cautious eye on it – just in case it disappeared when she turned her back – she boiled the kettle and methodically made herself a strong cup of tea.

After examining the postmark again – *Definitely a dragon, definitely North Wales* – she sat down, opened the envelope and unfolded the single sheet of paper inside.

> Dear Edith,
>
> I hope this letter finds you well. You don't know me, but I am writing to you with regards to my sister, Helene. I understand from Helene that you are a close friend of hers. I am sorry to have to tell you that she is ill. The doctors have said she doesn't have long left. At best we can hope to have weeks, at worst she only has days. Helene has been asking to see you and your son, in fact she speaks of nothing else when she is able. If you can, and you are willing, I ask that you please come to visit her, I think it would make a dying woman very happy.
>
> Helene is living with my husband and me. We have plenty of room. You, and your son, would be very welcome here. I do hope this letter reaches you in time and I do hope you come.
>
> Yours sincerely,
>
> Carys Jones

With quivering hands, Edith turned the letter over and saw that Carys had written an address on the reverse. She covered her mouth with her hand and drew in a ragged breath through her nose.

* * *

Edith excused herself from work with a phone call about a family emergency. She packed a small suitcase with essentials and waited at the school gates for James. As they made their way to the train station, she told him they were going on an adventure. He bounced around, asking all sorts of questions she didn't have the capacity to answer in any way that would make sense to him.

They boarded the train and took their seats for the long journey ahead. "We have to catch three trains and we won't arrive until tomorrow morning," she told James. *It will be worth it*, she tried to convince herself. As the train trundled along the track, Edith unwrapped a homemade cheese and pickle sandwich and set it out in front of James.

"It's your favourite," she whispered into his ear. She smiled as she watched him eat, his wide eyes fixed on the various shades of green landscape rolling by outside the rain-streaked window.

After a while, the motion of the train rocked Edith to sleep.

She awoke with a jolt as the train pulled into a station.

"James, darling. Time to wake up. Quick, quick." She jumped up and retrieved their suitcase from the overhead luggage rack.

James rubbed his eyes as Edith ushered him down onto the platform. She checked her watch; they'd have to run to make their connection. Edith pulled James along; he was grouchy from being woken so abruptly, and not in the mood for running in the rain.

"Would those feet move a little faster if I told you I had a chocolate bar in my bag?" Edith asked.

James grinned and picked up the pace.

The sour-faced conductor grumbled and shook his head at their tardiness, but he bundled them into the carriage and blew his whistle. Edith puffed a sigh of relief as they took their seats and the train lurched forward. Outside, the grey drizzly daylight faded to dusk, and dusk to darkness, until only the odd station here and there punctuated the inky black night.

James ate the chocolate and he read his schoolbook, tracing his finger along the sentences until his eyes drooped. He leaned against Edith and drifted off. She kissed the top of his head and closed her eyes to the image of Helene, her beautiful smile, the dusting of freckles across her nose, her sing-song accent and funny expressions for ordinary things. She frowned at the thought of the silly argument that had ended it all. *Why had I been so stubborn? Why didn't I run after her and beg her to stay? It was hard enough to lose her once; I can't bear to lose her again.*

She sniffed and wiped away a tear with the back of her hand. *Pull yourself together, Edith. Stay positive. Perhaps Carys was exaggerating or maybe the doctors are wrong? Helene is young and fit… surely, she'll be okay? …I hope I'm not too late.*

The rhythm of the train softly pulsed in her ears – *Helene, Helene, Helene, Helene.*

* * *

"Sorry to disturb you, madam, the train terminates at this station. You'll need to alight here." The conductor gently tapped her shoulder.

Startled, Edith peered around the empty carriage. "Oh goodness. I'm sorry, I must have drifted off."

The conductor gave a hearty chuckle. "You're not the first and you won't be the last. I hope you didn't miss your stop."

"No, this is where we're meant to be." Edith gently shook James, who was slumped against the window.

"Oh right, well, there's not much around here. Are you heading somewhere in particular?"

"We have a connecting train in about five hours' time. I was hoping there might be a waiting room."

"Oh, I see. Well, there is but it's usually locked at this time. We don't get many people passing through here and waiting overnight." He rubbed the bristles on his jowly jaw. "I can unlock it for you and your lad though, and you can make yourselves as comfortable as you can. Those benches are a bit hard, mind. I think there may be a blanket in the station master's office if you'd like me to fetch it for you."

"That's very kind of you." Edith smiled.

Edith held James' hand as they stepped onto the platform. His teeth chattered and she put her arm around his small shoulders as they followed the conductor towards the waiting room. He unlocked the door and flicked the light switch, casting a dingy yellow glow into the room.

"Here you are." He stepped back and gestured for them to enter. "Let me fetch you that blanket."

Edith perched on the wooden bench and set her suitcase down beside it.

James covered his nose. "It smells funny in here." His voice echoed in the sparsely furnished room.

"It's just a bit damp, darling. Better than sleeping outside though, hey?" She pulled him onto her lap and rubbed his back.

The conductor returned with a woollen blanket slung over his arm and a tray loaded with two steaming mugs and a plate of biscuits.

"I hope you like cocoa… and I rustled up a couple of biscuits from the bottom of the tin. They're only digestives, mind. Nothing fancy."

"Thank you so much. You've been too kind," said Edith.

The conductor beamed. "I only wish I could offer you a bed for the night, but I don't think the wife would be happy with me bringing back strays." He chuckled and looked at his watch. "Right then, I best be going. Just leave everything on the bench when you set off tomorrow."

James finished his cocoa. Edith smiled at his sleepy little face and wiped the chocolate from his top lip with her thumb. He nestled his head onto her lap and she tucked the rough blanket around his shoulders.

* * *

At dawn, sunlight sliced through the mist in the valley and illuminated flashes of rugged landscape, as the early morning express charged toward their final destination. A well-rested James bopped around in his seat, pointing out landmarks and asking endless questions. Edith did her best to humour him, smiling and nodding as he chattered away, but tiredness and nerves frayed the edges of her patience. Her eyes settled into a soft focus as she chewed her thumbnail.

As they drew closer to their destination, anxiety twisted in her empty stomach, gnawing away her sense of certainty. *What if she doesn't want to see me? What if we have another argument? What if she's too sick to speak?*

What if I'm too late?

* * *

Edith asked for directions before they left the station and they set off on foot. After an uphill walk, which James complained about the whole way, they arrived outside an imposing stone house. Edith took the letter from her coat pocket and double-checked the address.

"This is it," she said, smiling down at James. She took a deep breath and squeezed his hand. They crunched up the gravel driveway to the front door. Edith tried to steady her shaking hand as she knocked.

The door creaked open, and behind it stood a small but sturdy woman in an apron. One look at her face and a trickle of warm familiarity soothed Edith's nerves; older than Helene, but she had the same kind eyes, and the same dimple in her chin.

"Er, hello. You must be Carys... I'm Edith and this is James."

"Edith! Thank goodness you came." Carys stepped forward and embraced her, taking her a little by surprise. "And young James, hello to you." She ruffled his hair. "Please, come in. You must be exhausted after your trip. Let me fix you some tea. I've just taken some Welsh cakes out of the oven. I bet you've never had a Welsh cake before, have you, James?"

James blushed and shook his head. Carys chuckled and ushered him forward. Edith reached out and grasped her elbow.

"Helene, is she—" Edith whispered.

"Sleeping. She's sleeping, love. Let's get you some tea and then we'll wake her together."

Edith closed her eyes and released the breath she'd been holding since reading the letter.

Carys rubbed her arm. "She is going to be so pleased to see you. Honestly, she hasn't stopped asking for you." Carys grinned as the heat rose in Edith's cheeks.

* * *

With a belly full of Welsh cakes and sugary tea, James settled by the fire with his schoolbook. One of Carys' many cats took up residency on his lap.

"We call that one Mittens," she told him. "Because it looks like she's wearing little white mittens. Although it did get quite confusing when Mittens had kittens."

James giggled and stroked the cat.

Edith followed Carys up the stairs and waited behind her as she softly knocked on a closed door and pushed it open into a clean, bright room. A big brass bed faced a large window, which overlooked a green and rocky hillside shrouded in mist.

"Wakey, wakey, sleepyhead. You have a visitor," said Carys.

Edith stepped out from behind Carys and gasped at the sight of Helene, propped up on several pillows, her bony chest rising and falling with each laboured breath.

Helene rasped and opened her eyes. "Good to see I'm still taking your breath away, Edie," she said with a weak half-smile.

Edith wanted to laugh and cry at the same time. She avoided eye contact with Carys, who was looking at her, smiling expectantly.

Helene strained and held out her arms. "Come here, give me a *cwtch*."

"I shall leave you to it." Carys bowed her head and left the room. The door clicked shut behind her.

Edith leaned over the bed and gently embraced Helene, or at least what little was left of her.

"I came as soon as I heard. You really are sick, aren't you? I'd hoped that Carys was exaggerating." Edith touched her hand to Helene's pale cheek and rested it there.

"It has to be said, I've been better, Edie. I think all of my adventuring has finally caught up with me." Helene smiled up at her. "You look as beautiful as you ever did. Thank you for coming, I'd hoped you would... did you bring my little friend?"

"Yes, James is here as well. I didn't want to overwhelm you, so he's downstairs getting acquainted with the cats."

Helene reached up and held Edith's face in her bony hands. "You're really here."

Edith smiled. "I'm really here."

"Will you lie down with me?" Helene tried to move but her face creased with pain.

"Don't, there's enough room here." Edith lifted the blankets and squeezed into the space next to Helene. Side by side, they stared up at the white ceiling adorned with decorative cornices and an elaborate plaster rose.

Helene eventually broke the silence. "I'm so sorry about what happened between us. I shouldn't have pressured you like I did." She searched under the covers for Edith's hand.

"Don't worry about any of that. We're together now, and that's all that matters. I missed you so much, I don't think a day went by when I didn't think of you." Edith turned onto her side to face Helene and gently leaned in to kiss her. With eyes closed and the softness of Helene's lips on her own, time was erased and she was transported back to the first time they'd kissed.

"I never should have left you, Edie. It's my one regret." Tears welled in Helene's eyes. They looked at each other for a long moment. "Will you stay?"

"Of course. I didn't come all of this way for just one kiss."

"I mean, until the end... I don't know when it will be."

"I'm not going anywhere, I promise." Edith kissed her again.

* * *

The following days passed in a blur. Edith helped Carys around the house and frequently apologised for their imposition. Carys insisted it was a pleasure to have them and it took the pressure off her. Carys' husband, Big Al, was out from dawn until dusk, busy with his sheep. Big Al seemed very taken with his new and eager farmhand, James, who most days returned exhausted and covered in mud, but with a big smile stretching across his little face.

Edith spent most of the time in Helene's room. Carys kept them fed and watered, with frequent trays of her hearty home-cooked goodness. Edith, and sometimes James, read aloud to Helene from the wicker chair in the window, her appetite for adventure sated a little by the stories she chose for them to read: *Gulliver's Travels, Moby Dick,* and of course her favourite, *The Three Musketeers.*

Despite Helene's protests, Edith helped her back and forth to the loo. Helene put up much less protest whenever Edith offered to help her bathe. She reclined in the roll-top tub, smiling at the ceiling as Edith tenderly soaped *every* inch of her. They lay on the bed talking about everything and nothing until all hours. They laughed until their stomachs hurt, and they cried until their tears ran dry. Sometimes they just sat and watched as the daylight changed colour over the hillside, Edith holding Helene whilst she drifted in and out of sleep.

The days rolled into weeks. At the end of the third week, Helene took a turn for the worse. She hardly woke, her breathing became shallow, and her temperature rose. Edith sat by her bedside and mopped her brow with a cold flannel.

Carys called for the doctor. Helene was barely conscious as he examined her. Carys and Edith looked on. With pursed lips, the doctor shook his head and spoke to them in the hallway. They embraced and tried to muffle their sobs when he told them they should prepare for the end.

That night Edith woke with a start to the stirrings of Helene trying to get out of bed and she rushed around to her. "Helene? Darling? Are you okay?"

"Can you help me with something please, Edie?" Helene sounded more coherent and alert than she had been in days.

"Sure, anything you want."

"I want to go outside with you. I need some fresh air."

"I'm not sure we'll make it, my darling. I'm sorry." Edith desperately looked around the room until her eyes fixed on the window. "How about I pull the window open wide and we can sit by it together? Will that do?"

"Yes, good idea."

Edith opened up the sash window as far as it would go and shivered as the cold November air spilt into the room. She took a wool jumper out of the chest of drawers and helped Helene to pull it on, then supported her to stand and walk over to the wicker chair. Edith tugged one of the blankets off the bed and draped it over Helene's tiny shoulders. She knelt in front of her and rested her head on Helene's lap.

"Thank you," said Helene as she stroked Edith's hair. "One more thing though, Edie. There's a wooden box in my top drawer, will you fetch it for me please?"

Edith rummaged in the top drawer of Helene's bedside cabinet and retrieved a small, intricately carved box with a brass clasp. She wrapped a blanket around her own shoulders before returning to her kneeling spot in front of Helene.

"Now this is why I really wanted to go outside. Carys will go berserk if she smells it." Helene laboured a little laugh, which caused her to cough. "She can't kill me when I'm nearly dead already though." She opened the lid and grinned at the contents. She took out a roll-up, placed it between her lips and retrieved a fold of matches from the box.

Edith laughed heartily at this incredible woman, so full of surprises. *So full of life.*

"Here, let me." Edith struck a match and Helene cupped her hands around it to light the joint. Helene took a long draw, inhaling deeply. She held the smoke in her lungs before resting her head back and blowing it out in a long plume. Holding it between her thumb and forefinger, she passed the joint to Edith.

Edith took it gingerly. "I've never tried this before."

"It's nice, it relaxes you. I'd been saving this one for a special occasion… no time like the present."

After a short drag, Edith coughed and spluttered. She waved her hand in front of her face and passed the roll-up back to Helene. They both giggled. Helene stared out of the window at the clear night sky studded with stars. Edith examined her face in the moonlight.

"Are you scared?" she asked.

"Of dying?" Helene took another pull of the joint and exhaled before answering. "No, I'm not scared but that doesn't mean I'm ready to go. I have unfinished business here, you know? But that's different to being scared. I want to stay here with you."

"I want you to stay with me too. *I'm* scared."

"I'll always be with you, you know that. What we have is bigger than life or death. It's bigger than anything our little minds can even think of."

Edith released a sob that shook her body. She turned her face into Helene's lap and wept.

"Shh, Edie. It's okay." Helene stroked her hair. "Look now, I'm just going off on my next big adventure, and one day you'll join me. Not anytime soon though, okay? You have James to take care of."

Edith knelt up between Helene's knees. Helene reached out and wiped away Edith's tears and then kissed her until she was breathless. She drew her in close, wrapping her blanket around the both of them. "I love you," she said.

Edith shut the window and helped Helene back into bed. They were both famished, so Edith fetched some biscuits from the kitchen. They lay in bed making crumbs and giggling about nothing until Helene fell asleep for the last time in Edith's arms.

CHAPTER FORTY-FOUR

April 2022

Anna balanced a tray loaded with Edith's breakfast in her arms as she nudged open the door with her foot. The early morning sun streamed through Edith's bedroom window and danced over her face. Her eyes were closed but a faint smile played on her lips, suggesting that she was awake.

"Morning, Gran."

"Good morning, darling," Edith croaked. "Oh, look at all this. You're spoiling me." She shuffled to sit up.

Anna retrieved her cup of coffee from the tray and eased into the chair beside the bed. "It's a proper spring day out there." She gestured towards the window.

"I can always tell when spring has sprung by the birdsong." Edith smiled as she cracked into the first of the two boiled eggs. "You should be getting back home soon, darling. Things must be busy at work now, surely?"

Anna cupped her hands around her mug and smiled. "Tomas has everything under control. Besides, he'll call me if he needs me… so, you're stuck with me, whether you like it or not, okay?"

Edith bit into a slice of toast and grinned. "It has been lovely spending so much time with you, but I don't want to be a burden."

"Don't be silly, Gran. I'm happy to be here… right, how about I pick up where we left off?" Anna picked up the hefty, leather-bound tome from the bedside table. The well-worn spine cracked when opened at the bookmarked page. Anna cleared her throat and read.

Edith fixed her gaze ahead, listening as she sipped her tea. When she'd finished her breakfast, Anna removed the tray and fluffed the pillows. Edith relaxed back and closed her eyes. Anna continued to read aloud until small snores puffed from Edith's slightly open mouth, then she softly closed the book and tiptoed out of the room.

Anna pulled on Edith's flowery rubber gloves, washed the breakfast dishes, and made herself another cup of coffee. Sitting at the large round oak table, she thought of all the family meals they'd enjoyed in this room; the hundreds of memories that had been made here. In contrast to the spring day outside, heralding new beginnings, a chapter was about to close in their lives; the last doctor's visit had told them as much. The words still echoed in Anna's mind – *I'm afraid she doesn't have long left. It's time to prepare for the end.*

They'd been given the option of moving Edith to a hospice for end-of-life care, but Anna had insisted she would take some leave from work.

"I want Gran to spend her final days comfortable in her own home," she had said. Rupert raised his hands – no quarrel there. Since then, nurses came twice a day and Anna did the rest.

Rupert stayed over on the last two weekends. Between them, they'd managed to get Edith down the stairs and out into the garden for some fresh air. Being outdoors seemed to breathe life back into her, but she tired quickly. It was so hard seeing her like this; her adventurer's spirit was still very much alive, just trapped inside its old, failing vessel.

Anna picked up her phone. Notifications crowded the screen. Messages from Rupert, Grace and Lexi asking how Gran was doing. Anna replied to them all with the same message.

> She's not too bad. Fed and watered, now
> sleeping again. Miss you, love you x.

* * *

Anna hummed along to an old song playing on the radio as she heated a bowl of homemade vegetable soup and sliced a crusty baguette. Startled by a noise, she spun around. The knife in her hand clattered to the floor at the sight of Edith standing in the hallway, her depleted frame swallowed up by her once well-fitted pink dressing gown.

"Jesus, Gran. You should've called out. I would've helped you down the stairs."

Edith chuckled. "No need to fuss. I thought I'd come down for lunch. I feel terrible with you doing all of this running around after me, darling."

Anna took Edith's elbow, steadying her as she shuffled over to her usual seat. Edith winced and leveraged the sturdy table to help lower herself into her chair.

"Do you need some more painkillers?" Anna asked. "The doctor said you can have an extra dose if —"

"No, no. I'm quite alright." She waved away Anna's concern and sniffed the air. "Something smells good. What are we having?"

"Ah, you know nothing I could make would smell this good. This is a Rupert special. He made us up a few meal batches over the weekend."

"Ah. bless him. He's a good boy, isn't he?" Edith grinned.

"Sometimes." Anna smirked.

"How are things with you two now?"

Anna frowned. "In what way?"

"Rupert told me that he found out you and Grace had rekindled something whilst we were on our trip. He said he was a little unfair on you both, and he should have been more understanding. Especially with his own... change of circumstance." Edith raised both eyebrows.

"Oh, right. Okay." Anna chewed her thumbnail. "Well, we're fine. We haven't talked about it since Sweden. Besides, he doesn't have anything to worry about anyway. As I told you, Grace knows how I feel..." Anna sighed and returned to the hob to stir the simmering soup. "It's too late, she wants something else for herself now."

Edith stared out of the window as Anna placed lunch on the table. They ate to the murmur of chatter on a talk radio show.

"Anna, can you remind me, was it Debussy who said that thing? ... you know, about the spaces between the notes in music?" Edith wiped the corners of her mouth with a serviette.

"Erm, I'm not too sure, Gran. I can look it up for you if you want?"

"No, don't worry. I think it was Debussy... but it doesn't matter who said it. The point is, there's no music without silence. Without silence, it'd just be noise."

"Yeah, I guess that makes sense." Anna shrugged.

"Arguably, the most important notes in a song are the ones that aren't even played, those weighty pauses so full of promise. You see, it's the spaces between the notes that make the crescendo what it is." Eyes sparkling, she looked at Anna.

Anna smiled and nodded slowly, although she wasn't sure why Gran was talking about Debussy. *Perhaps it's the morphine.*

"It's not the morphine talking if that's what you're thinking," Edith tutted, and Anna grinned.

"Every day is full of fleeting moments, Anna, but the moments are incomplete without the pauses in between. Do you understand what I'm saying?"

"Sorry, I'm not sure I—"

"You and Grace… you're like the spaces between the notes. You may not have been together all of these years, but don't underestimate the importance of the things you have shared despite that. All of those moments in between." She reached across and rested her hand on Anna's arm. "Just promise me you won't give up on her."

I'm not sure I have a choice, she thought, but as Edith stared into her face, Anna nodded and gently squeezed the frail hand resting on her arm.

* * *

With Anna's help, Edith took the stairs one slow step at a time. Edith strained with the effort of fighting a losing battle. *How cruel that a woman who could once climb mountains without breaking a sweat is reduced to exhaustion after a few stairs.*

"Do you want me to read some more?" Anna asked as Edith settled back into bed.

"No thank you, darling. Will you just sit with me for a while? I'm very tired now. I think I'll sleep soon." Edith grimaced and Anna passed her a glass of water with two tablets. She held out a shaky hand and took them without protest.

"Are you scared, Gran?"

"No, I'm ready, darling. Ready for my next big adventure." She smiled.

"I'm scared of losing you. I don't know what I'll do without..." Anna paused to steady her voice. "I'm not sure I've ever said it, but you've been so much more than a grandmother. You've been a wonderful mum to Rupert and me... I mean, even though we lost Mum and Dad, we... we were so lucky to have..." Her voice broke over words too hard to say.

"I've been the lucky one, darling." Edith smiled across at her. "You two have brought me so much joy. We've had some wonderful adventures, haven't we?" A chuckle rattled in her throat. She closed her eyes and her shallow breath fell into a steady rhythm.

Anna stayed by her bedside, stroking her hand as daylight faded to dusk and the blackbirds sang their evening song. Edith sharply inhaled, drawing Anna's attention back to her face. Perhaps a trick of the low light, but the heavy lines etched into Edith's skin by pain and age seemed lighter. Suddenly, Edith's eyebrows arched over her closed eyes. An upward turn spread from the corners of her lips and her mouth cracked into a smile.

"Hello, you," she said.

Anna sat forward. "Gran? What is it? Who are you talking—"

Edith didn't stir. Her face eased into a wax-like serenity.

"Gran?" Anna reached for her wrist. No pulse. Edith's chest didn't rise.

No breath, no pulse.

"No. Gran. No, no…" she gasped, gulping big breaths as if the wind had been knocked out of her. She collapsed over Edith and sobbed.

* * *

All cried out, and disorientated by the darkness, Anna sat up and rubbed her swollen eyes. Her chest ached, raw and hollow, like the very core of her had been scraped away. She pulled her phone out of her pocket. Squinting against the brightness of the screen, she clicked on her contacts and scrolled to the photo of Rupert, wearing a sombrero and a goofy grin.

"Hey," he answered after two rings.

Anna opened her mouth to speak but her words stumbled over the massive lump in her throat.

"Anna, what's up? Is Gran okay?"

An involuntary sob spilt out of her.

"She's gone, Ru. She's gone."

Silence met her for a long, agonising moment. Then he sniffed.

"I'm on my way."

Anna switched on the bedside lamp. Her tears fell as she stroked Edith's hair and touched her cheek. *Cold. So cold already.* She brought Edith's hand to her lips and kissed it.

"Enjoy your next adventure, Gran."

* * *

News travelled quickly in the small town Edith had called home for over six decades. Friends and neighbours rallied around, helping with the funeral plans, making tea, and filling the fridge with an inordinate amount of lasagne.

In the days that followed Edith's death, Rupert and Anna stayed at the house together, finding comfort in each other's company. With tears and laughter, they flicked through old photo albums and relived childhood adventures. Rupert took notes for the eulogy he would, without question, deliver at Edith's funeral.

One of Edith's friends took Edith's address book and with it the task of informing everyone in it. After a couple of days, flowers, cards, and letters started to arrive at the house.

Anna opened an envelope postmarked North Wales. She unfolded the single page and strained to make out the shaky font looping across the paper.

> To Rupert, Anna, and family
>
> My deepest sympathies on the passing of Edith, I was so sorry to hear. Edith truly was a remarkable woman, and I will be eternally grateful for the joy she brought to my dear sister Helene in her final days. Even after all these years, I sometimes imagine I can still hear their fits of giggles coming from Helene's room. I'm sure they have been reunited now, and they'll be laughing together again.

Losing Helene was, of course, a very sad and difficult time, but despite this, we were able to look back on it fondly as well. It was a pleasure getting to know Edith and James. James was a lovely boy; what happened in Norway was such a tragedy. I stayed in touch with your Gran all these years, and I heard a lot about you. She was very proud of you both.

You had a wonderful grandmother, but I'm sure you don't need me to tell you that.

God bless.

Carys Jones

Anna held the letter to her chest as if hugging its author.

"Oh, Gran. Why didn't you tell me you'd seen Helene again? Why didn't you tell me that she died?"

* * *

After three nights, Lexi and Toby joined Anna and Rupert at the house. With them came more tears, but more laughter too. Their company stirred up Anna's yearning for Grace, and somehow, that made her miss Edith even more. *She's gone, she's gone, she's gone,* she kept reminding herself, although adrift in the fug of her grief, she wasn't clear which of them she was referring to.

The night before the funeral came a knock at the door.

"Get that, will you, Anna?" Rupert called from the kitchen.

Grace stood in the doorway, a bottle of wine in each hand and an overnight bag slung over her shoulder. Anna crumpled to the floor at the unexpected sight of her, overwhelmed by the weight of her emotions.

"Ah come on now, come here." Grace bent and scooped Anna into a hug.

"I thought you weren't… until… tomorrow." Anna sobbed into her shoulder. "I'm sorry, it's a lot and seeing you just…" she sniffled and choked back another sob. "I miss her so much, Grace. I can't believe she's gone."

"I know, I know. It's awful." Grace held onto her and Anna allowed herself to be comforted, surprised by the solace she found in Grace's arms.

"Hey, you made it." Rupert came into the hallway.

Anna extracted herself from Grace's hug and wiped her face with the sleeves of her jumper.

"Yeah, thanks for inviting me. I appreciate that, Ru," said Grace.

"Lex, set another place at the table, will you?" he called through to the dining room, then he put his arm around Anna and squeezed. "Alright. C'mon, frowny face."

* * *

Rupert raised a toast before they ate. "To the indomitable Edith Edwards. Our Gran."

"Our Gran," they chorused.

"She'd love this," said Rupert as he looked over their faces. "You know, having the gang back together." He flashed a smile at Anna and Grace. Lexi and Toby exchanged a look.

"It feels like she's still here," said Lexi.

"Oh, I believe she is," said Grace.

Toby's wide eyes scanned the room. "What, like a ghost?"

Rupert and Lexi laughed out loud.

"No, not a ghost." Grace smiled. "Just her spirit. You know, the essence of Gran. As long as we keep her in our hearts and minds, then she'll always be with us."

Toby looked at Anna, his infallible source of all things rational. She smiled and nodded.

Lexi volunteered herself and Toby to wash up. Toby whined until Lexi promised to let him kick her ass on the PlayStation if he helped her.

Anna, Grace, and Rupert took the remaining wine through to the lounge. Anna lit the log burner and they sat sipping in silence, except for the crackles and pops of the fire taking hold. Anna stared into the flames, chewing her bottom lip as tears brimmed in her eyes.

"Come here, you." Grace held out a blanket-covered arm.

Despite the desperate desire to be comforted, Anna looked over at Rupert. He smiled as if to say, *it's okay*. She shuffled up to Grace and nestled her head on her shoulder. Grace pulled the blanket around her and kissed the top of Anna's head.

"Are you all set for tomorrow, Ru?" Grace asked.

"Yeah, just about. The biggest challenge has been narrowing it all down. There's so much to say about her. Talk about a life well lived."

"Ah, you'll be grand. You'll do her proud."

"I just hope I can keep it together. It's one thing being good at public speaking but another when you've lost your..." He cleared his throat and took a large gulp of wine. He opened his mouth to speak again but hesitated. His eyes flicked between Anna and Grace. "You know, I spoke to Gran... about you two."

"You did?" Grace asked.

He nodded. "She said that I'd been a bit of a prick. I shouldn't have reacted like I did... I don't even know where that anger came from. I was so annoyed that I'd been feeling so bad and yet there you two were—"

"Well, I think we can probably all agree that we've been awful pricks to each other, and settle it there," said Grace.

Rupert fixed his eyes on the glass in his hand and swirled the crimson liquid around. "If I'm honest, I think I always knew that there was this *thing* between you two... like this magic spark. You light each other up, you always have. We never really had that, did we, Grace?"

Grace sipped her wine and shook her head. Anna swallowed and focused on the pattern of the blanket, tracing its lines with her eyes.

"I'm so happy with Nicole, like, so fucking happy. No offence, Grace."

Grace smiled and raised her hand – *no offence taken.*

"I have no right to deny anyone else a shot at happiness. I meant what I said in Narvik... you two are my best friends and I need you both in my life. So, I want you to know that I'm okay with it. More than okay... I think it's great actually." He drained his wine and beamed at them.

Grace inhaled through her nose. In contrast, Anna held her breath, anxious to hear how Grace would respond. A tiny ember of hope ignited, accompanied by the echo of Gran's words – *promise me you won't give up on her.*

"I'm pleased you've reflected on things the way that you have, Ru. Since we got back, I've been doing a fair bit of reflecting myself. I've taken some time off work and I'm going to go back to Ireland for a bit. There's nothing decided, I just want to go and see if I can envisage a life there. A fresh start."

Rupert's eyebrows shot up. "Oh! What about Lexi and Toby?"

"Lexi's off to uni in September, so she'll be grand. I'm going to go to Ireland with Toby in mind. If I think it's right for the both of us, then you and I will work out the finer details. Where he lives, where he holidays and so forth. I want him to have a say in it too." She squeezed Anna under the blanket. "And it's not like I'll be moving to Australia, is it? It's only a short skip over the sea."

"Sure, okay. Wow. Yeah. I'm surprised but yeah… if that's what you want, I'll be supportive." Rupert shrugged and poured more wine into his glass. "And, er, what about Anna?" he asked, as if she wasn't in the room.

Grace scoffed. "When you change your feckin' tune, you sing from a completely different songbook."

"Leave it, Ru." Anna was surprised by the sound of her own voice joining the conversation. "Grace doesn't need that sort of pressure." She buried her face into the blanket to hide her eyes and stamped out the tiny ember that had dared to ignite.

Anna's phone pinged. She pulled it out of her pocket and blinked away tears to focus on the screen.

> Hey. I'm so sorry to hear about your gran. Edith
> was a lovely lady. I liked her a lot. I hope
> you're holding up OK. I'm here if you want to
> chat. Always x

"Wow, was that from Clare? I didn't realise you were still in touch," said Grace.

Anna stuffed the phone back in her pocket. *Shit, she could see my screen.* Heat rose in her cheeks. *Seriously, why am I blushing?*

"We're not really *in touch*. She just messaged about Gran. I suppose someone must have called Clare's mum. I'm pretty sure Gran stayed in contact with Marjorie, although I'm not sure Marjorie ever forgave me."

"Joyce literally called everyone in Gran's phonebook. We've been getting messages from all sorts of randoms I'd never even heard of." Rupert shrugged.

"Ah, that was nice of Clare to message you," said Grace. "Especially after everything—"

"You know, I never really understood what happened with you two. You seemed so settled with her. It was weird how it just ended. One day, just…" Rupert wiped his hands together, "…so long, Sporty Spice."

"Don't, Ru." Anna shot him a look. "Clare was decent, she was good for me. Too good. I was the one who cocked it all up. *One big cock up* should be my relationship status. I'll add it to my Tinder profile."

Rupert laughed out loud.

Grace shifted her weight and Anna lifted her head to look up at her.

"Stay there. I'm just moving my leg… it's gone a bit dead." Her arm tightened around Anna's shoulder and she kissed the top of her head again. "I didn't know that you're on Tinder," she muttered.

CHAPTER FORTY-FIVE

July 2012

Anna examined her reflection in the bathroom mirror. She could've sworn she saw a grey hair in her left eyebrow the other day, but she couldn't find it now. She smiled to check for crow's feet and frowned when some faint lines appeared around her eyes. *It's like the last few years crept up and then just pounced overnight. How is it possible that I'm thirty today? I still feel twenty-one.* She held her forefingers to her temples and pulled the skin tight. *There, that's better.*

"The taxi will be here in five," Clare shouted from downstairs.

"Shit," Anna muttered. She rummaged for her eyeliner in their shared make-up bag.

This whole thing had been Rupert's idea, not hers. She'd have rather they had a nice meal and be able to hear the conversation. But no, Rupert wanted to have a night out or as he put it, "celebrate the death of our twenties by getting shit-faced and dancing like no one's watching."

"Except *everyone* will be watching because we'll be in a crowded club, and by midnight you'll be puking in a pint glass and I'll be holding your hair back," she'd said.

"It's my birthday too, Anna." He sulked until she gave in.

"Oh come on, it'll be fun!" Clare had tried to reassure her. Anna hadn't been reassured.

Anxiety twisted her gut at the thought of Clare. Usually, life with Clare was uncomplicated but things had been a bit off lately. Clare seemed distant – working longer hours and taking on more clients. She'd been acting secretive and shifty with her phone, never leaving the room without it and flicking the screen away from Anna's view. *Maybe she's seeing someone else?*

Anna tried to shrug off her concerns as insecurity spurred by her approaching milestone birthday. She also wondered whether her unease was a projection of her own conscience. Being honest with herself, she spent far more time thinking about Grace than she did about Clare.

"Anna, are you nearly ready?" Impatience edged Clare's voice.

"Yep, just a sec," Anna called through the door as she blotted her lips on a tissue.

At the start of the year, Rupert had secured a promotion, and ever since, he'd become consumed by work. Grace had turned to Anna for company. They'd been hanging out, a lot. Sometimes with Clare, but more often it was just her, Grace, and Lexi. *How I like it best,* she thought, and her stomach churned.

Last week, after a lovely day trip to the beach, they were saying their goodbyes on the doorstep. Anna kissed Grace's cheek and lingered longer than she should have, inhaling the sweet scent of her. Grace turned her face and their lips were millimetres apart. The air fizzed in that effervescent way it only ever did with Grace, and as always, the edges faded out.

A passing dog barked, Anna stepped back and they laughed. In the warm, stuffy evening air Grace had shivered and rubbed tell-tale goosebumps from her bare arms. *Does she feel it too?*

With Rupert's absence and Clare being so aloof, Anna could almost justify her feelings. *Almost.* Being really honest with herself, a tiny bit of her hoped Clare *was* cheating – it would partly alleviate her own guilt. But the rest of her was livid at the thought of Clare's infidelity. *We've built a fucking life together, how could she? I bet it's a bendy younger woman, who has no trouble at all with her downward dog.*

"Anna. Come. On. The taxi's here," shouted Clare.

"Sorry, sorry. I'm coming." Anna smoothed her hands over her hair and pouted her lips. She rarely wore lipstick but tonight she'd gone with red. After a final check in the mirror, she skipped out of the bathroom and down the stairs.

Clare stepped back and looked her up and down. "Wow. You look, just... wow!"

Anna swallowed to suppress an acidic twinge of guilt about her recent line of thought. She kissed Clare on the cheek, leaving behind a red lipstick mark.

Clare grinned and stared at her with hungry eyes.

Anna squirmed. "Stop it, you're being weird! Come on, let's go."

* * *

"Skywalker!" Rupert bellowed from across the room and threw his arms up. Anna and Clare made their way over to the cordoned section, reserved for 'Ru & Anna's Big Birthday Bash'. Balloons and banners announced their thirtieth birthday to the world.

Rupert scooped her into a bear hug. "Many happy returns of the day, old girl."

"Likewise, old boy." She laughed and looked up into his smiling face. *Lucky bastard, he hasn't aged at all. He looks knackered, but no older than he did ten years ago.*

"Let's get this party started," he shouted over the music.

"If we have to," she said.

He hollered in the direction of Joe and Craig, who were ordering drinks at their private section of the bar. "Boys, you know what makes me happy?"

"Tequila!" they both yelled back.

This is going to be messy. "I don't know how you guys can still drink that after uni." Anna grimaced, already dreading the hangover.

Clare smiled and squeezed her hand. "This isn't so bad, is it? I'll go get us some drinks; you want the usual?"

Anna's eyes followed Clare's athletic body as she made her way to the bar. Clare stopped to greet some of their friends and she leaned in to whisper something to one of them. They both looked around at Anna and grinned. She waved but they turned back to each other… *more whispering.*

The heavy bass of the music pounded in her chest as Anna scanned the room, searching for Grace. They locked eyes. Anna smiled and mouthed, "Hi."

Grace abruptly ended her conversation and walked towards her. Eyes locked. *Mutual permission to stare.* They embraced and Grace said something Anna didn't catch.

"Sorry, what?"

Grace leaned in again, her breath hot on Anna's ear. "I said, you look incredible."

"Oh." Anna grinned as a bubble of happiness burst in her chest. "You don't look so bad yourself." Heat rose up her neck and into her cheeks.

Two vodka and cokes and at least three tequila slammers later, Anna's feet forgot she couldn't dance. *Last Nite* by The Strokes pounded out of the speakers and magnetised her towards the dance floor.

"Tune!" she yelled as she pulled Grace, Rupert, and Clare along with her. Tune after tune – The Kooks, The Arctic Monkeys, The Fratellis. More tequila – Kings of Leon and Queens of the Stone Age. In a kaleidoscope of light, Rupert threw elaborate shapes and Clare matched them with her own. Amidst the frenzy of limbs and laughter, Anna's eyes kept dancing their way back to Grace, mesmerised by her silk chiffon top. It shimmered like liquid gold around her torso, as she swayed her hips.

"This DJ is a fucking god!" Anna screamed as the intro riff of *Mr. Brightside* blasted out. Arms flailing in abandon, like an inflatable tube man, Anna gave it her all and reduced herself to a hot, sweaty mess by the end of the track.

"I need the loo." Anna caught her breath as she joined the line outside the women's toilets. She leaned against the wall and smiled to herself, for once enjoying the warm tingle of alcohol coursing through her bloodstream. A hand brushed her arm and she didn't need to turn around to know whose it was. Women muttered and tutted as Grace cut into the queue. Anna leaned back into her and they laced their fingers together. Her heart raced at Grace's hot breath on her neck.

"Do you know how much I want you right now?" Grace whispered into her ear.

Fuck. Anna closed her eyes and squeezed Grace's fingers in her own. They reached the front of the queue and giggled as they shuffled into the first available cubicle together, ignoring more tuts and murmurs of disapproval.

There were a million other places she'd have preferred to be with Grace, but they were here, and the moment was now. The air not only fizzed, it pulsed.

With the flimsy cubicle door locked behind them, they entangled in a frantic embrace. Grace's hands in her hair, on the back of her neck, feeling their way over her breasts and between her legs, groping at the seam of her jeans. Grace hitched up her skirt and firmly pushed Anna's hand into her lacy pants. Anna's fingers dived into her wetness. Grace moaned out loud and Anna covered her mouth with her free hand. Grace tugged at the button of Anna's jeans until it released, and then she worked her fingers inside the denim, inside her pants, inside of her and right to the core of her aching, desperate need.

"Oh fuck… yes… fuck." Anna gasped staccato words in between staccato breaths.

"Fuck, you're so fucking hot." Grace panted into her ear and bit the top of it.

They breathed heavily in between manic kisses as they brought each other to the edge. Sparks fizzed behind Anna's eyelids as she came, the waves of her orgasm flowing with her final thrusts into Grace, who threw her head back and gave a guttural groan.

Breathless and panting, they stared at each other.

"I can't believe we just did that," Anna whispered.

"Me neither, but you've no idea how long I've wanted to." Grace grinned, her mouth smeared with what was left of Anna's red lipstick.

"I think I have a fair idea." Anna laughed and let her eyes drink in the stunning, dishevelled woman in front of her.

Grace smoothed down her skirt and adjusted her top. She held her palm to Anna's cheek. "They'll be wondering where we've got to."

"I just need a minute. I did actually come in here to pee. Maybe you should go on ahead of me?"

Grace laughed. "Oh yeah, sorry not sorry I gate-crashed your loo break. See you back out there then."

"Wait," said Anna as Grace moved to unlock the door. "We need to fix this. You look like the Joker." She rubbed her thumb across Grace's lips in an effort to remove the lipstick smudged over them.

They stared into each other's eyes. *Fizz, fade,* they kissed again, *electric.*

* * *

Anna returned to Rupert filling a tray full of Champagne flutes. "What's all this?" she asked and tried to swallow the guilt rising in her at the sight of him. Suddenly she felt very sober and a little bit sick.

Rupert smiled and gestured to the half-dozen bottles of Moët sitting in an ice bucket.

"I know you got a promotion and everything but you're being a bit flashy aren't you, Ru?"

"It wasn't Rupert, it was me." Clare appeared and beamed at her. She looked over to the DJ booth and signalled something with a raised hand. The music screeched to a stop and groans of protest emanated from the dance floor. In a complete change of tempo, Adele started singing out the words to a song Clare had once proclaimed as 'theirs'.

Conscious of everyone staring at them, Anna fixed her wide eyes on Clare. "What's going on?"

Clare smiled and took Anna's hands. "I don't mean to steal your thunder on your big birthday. I checked with Rupert, and he said it was alright with him."

Anna looked from Clare to Rupert. He was all drunken smiles and thumbs-up.

"Anna, I love you. I want to spend the rest of my life trying to make you as happy as you make me." Clare exhaled a shaky breath, got down on one knee and brandished a small, black, velvet box containing a sparkly ring. "Will you marry me?"

Fuck was the only word in Anna's mind, and it took all her effort not to let it come out of her mouth. Her heartbeat drummed in her ears as Adele tried to make them feel her love. *I should've never left the toilet cubicle. Grace and I... we could've been happy there.*

Clare looked up at her with her big, beautiful smile. Her brown eyes brimmed with love and hope for their future together. *How am I supposed to say no?*

"Yes," she said in a tiny voice and she forced a smile. A look of relief washed over Clare and she jumped up and threw her arms around her.

Everyone cheered and clapped, even more so when the DJ changed the track.

Rupert thrust a glass of Champagne into Anna's hand, Clare clinked it with her own, and she kissed her. Anna let *her fiancée* kiss the lips that had just been extremely unfaithful. *So why does it feel like it's Grace I'm being unfaithful to?*

A blur of people congratulated and hugged them. Trance-like, Anna accepted the well-wishes, but a rush of panic filled her chest, overtaking the flood of guilt that had surged before it. For the first time since she'd said 'yes', she dared to look around for Grace.

Anna's eyes flicked from face to face, until there she was, across the room. Jaw clenched; hard stare fixed on Anna. Grace's green eyes raged, wild like an angry ocean.

Anna wanted to run to her, hold her, kiss and taste her again. But her arm was tethered to Clare's, her feet rooted to the spot. "Sorry," she mouthed.

Unblinking, Grace downed the glass of Champagne in her hand. She tore away her dagger-like stare and whispered something into Rupert's ear. And without a backward glance, she left.

Rupert followed her, passing through a gauntlet of back-slaps and taunts from his rugby mates.

"Someone's on a promise!" one of them jeered, to a sickening chorus of laughter.

Anna's heart sank.

CHAPTER FORTY-SIX

May 2022

With a heavy heart, Anna stood by the barrier separating those who were leaving from those being left behind. Grace turned and waved before disappearing through the entrance to Departures. *Why does it feel like this is the end?*

Anna smothered a sob with her sleeve and there she met with the lingering scent of Grace's sweet, musky perfume from when they'd hugged their goodbyes. *If you love someone, set them free,* she reminded herself. But what she really wanted to do was tie Grace to a chair until she saw sense. Until Grace was ready to love her in the way she wanted to be loved. *But if you have to lock someone up until they love you, then it's probably you who should be locked up.*

"Cheer up, Banana. She's only going to Ireland for a few weeks. You'll see her again soon enough." Lexi's voice jolted Anna back to awareness. *Shit.* She'd come to support Lexi, not the other way around. She sniffed and stretched her lips into a weak smile.

"I know. I'm sorry, Lex. I'm going to miss her, she's been my rock since Gran—" Tears prickled in her eyes and she blinked hard to fight them back.

"I'll miss her too, but I think she needs to make this trip… *to find herself,* or whatever." Lexi grinned and rolled her eyes. "Anyway…

I'm absolutely starving. Can we go home and order that pizza you promised me?"

"Come on, let's get back to the car before I have to re-mortgage my house to pay for parking." Anna looped her arm through Lexi's and they weaved their way through the terminal. "We're not getting pineapple all over the pizza though, I mean it."

"We'll have to get two then. I need the pineapple."

"You're an animal. Like your father."

Lexi giggled and Anna smiled, grateful not to be going home alone. As much as she wanted to curl up and cry, she'd have to keep her shit together for Lexi.

* * *

As stuffed as the crust she'd ordered, after half a large pizza and two glasses of wine, Anna relaxed back into her armchair.

Lexi lounged on a large cushion on the floor and scrolled through movie titles on the screen. "Any preferences?"

"Watch whatever you want… maybe something light and funny," said Anna. "Just not a rom-com." *Watching other people's happy endings will likely send me over the edge right now.* She brought her sleeve to her nose and inhaled Grace's scent again. "Have you heard from Toby today?"

"Yeah, I messaged him earlier. Dad and Nicole took him to the cinema. He seems happy staying with them. I think he really likes Nicole, probably because she lets him play his stupid video games as much as he wants. Dad wants him to like her, so Tobes is getting away with murder."

"What do you think of Nicole?" Anna topped up her glass and added a splash more wine to Lexi's too. She still found it strange to be drinking with her niece, the little girl she'd watched grow up.

"I didn't want to like her but she's actually pretty cool. It was so weird seeing her and Dad together at first though. Like, I literally wanted to puke watching them all loved up. The way they look at each other... it's... ick." Lexi shook her head as if trying to expel the repulsive thought.

Anna grinned. "It's because they're in loooooooooove."

"It's just weird for me. I mean, I never saw Mum and Dad like that together. They were always kind of cold and, more often than not, bitching at each other. I just figured that's how married couples were." Lexi shrugged. "Ooh, what about this one? I really rate her. She was brilliant in that one with the guy who could time travel. It was really funny."

"Is it a rom-com? Are there any romantic sub-plots? Will there be a happy ending?"

"Er, dunno... maybe... oh here, it says 'scenes of an explicit sexual nature'."

"Then nope. Keep scrolling."

Lexi spun around on the cushion. "Anna, can I ask you something?" *Uh-oh! She never calls me Anna.* "Sure, anything."

Lexi's eyebrows pinched together. "Do you love my mum?"

Anna chuckled. "Yeah, of course. Why are you asking me that?"

"No, I mean... do you *love* her?"

Heat rose in Anna's cheeks as Lexi's eyes bore into her. *Ah fuck it,*

I'm not going to lie. "It's complicated, Lex… But you're an adult now—" She swallowed a large gulp of wine. "Yes, I do *love* her. Very much so."

A disarming look of delight dawned on Lexi's face. "I knew it."

Anna snorted her wine.

"I totally knew it." Lexi bounced on the cushion as words excitedly spewed out of her. "I told Alice and Switch that there was something between you two. They said I was just trying to be cool… you know, having a queer mum as well as a gay aunt, but I said 'having LGBTQQIA people in your family doesn't make you cool by default, *being an ally* is what makes you cool'. That shut Alice right up, but Switch carried on being a douchebag… although I suppose they are non-binary so they can have the final say."

Mouth open and eyes wide, Anna stared at her.

Lexi smiled, reached across and put her hand on Anna's knee. "Really, Banana, I always thought something was going on with you and Mum."

"I can't believe… what the… really?"

"Honestly, ever since I was little, maybe about eight years old, I used to think that Mum had accidentally married the wrong twin. It's not that I don't love Dad. I mean Toby and I literally wouldn't be here if it wasn't for him…" She raised her eyebrows. "But there's just a vibe with you and Mum… you're always happiest when you're around each other."

"Wow." Anna puffed her lips and slowly exhaled. "That's incredibly mature of you, Lexi."

"Woke, I believe is the term, Banana. I'm woke."

Anna smiled and shook her head. "If you've wondered about it all this time, why did you keep it to yourself?"

"I've wanted to ask you about it so many times. I wanted to ask Mum too, but it felt kind of strange… y'know… because of Dad. I didn't keep it to myself though, I plucked up the courage to ask Gran about it once."

"Huh! And what did Gran say?"

"Gran said that love is a complicated thing, but everything will be alright in the end. And if it's not alright, then it's not the end… so, er I guess she didn't tell me anything." Lexi shrugged.

"No, she just quoted John Lennon at you. Good old Gran." Anna smiled. Somehow, through Lexi, Gran had managed to tell her exactly what she needed to hear, at exactly the right moment.

Lexi raised her hands. "Well then…?"

"Well then, what?"

"What are you going to do about it? Mum isn't with Dad now. You're both young… *ish*, free and single. In fact, you've been a desperate singleton for as long as I can remember."

"Oi!" Anna threw a cushion at her. "Single, yes. Desperate… not so much."

Lexi laughed. "Seriously though, what have you got to lose?"

"Isn't it weird?" Anna grimaced. "People will think it's weird. Your mum and your aunt hooking up."

"Who cares what people think? I don't."

"Your mum cares. I'm not sure she'll ever be able to get over that. And it's not just about us, is it? What about Toby?"

"He's nine and he's more woke than me."

Anna chuckled. "Yeah. Okay, well she's gone to Ireland to *find herself,* so what do you suggest?"

"She'll be back, and she'll have realised that she's lost without you." Lexi grinned and turned back to the screen. "Right, we're watching this one. No arguments." She pressed play on a cheesy old rom-com they'd both seen at least a hundred times.

Anna groaned but offered no further protest. A tiny ember glowed in the darkness that earlier threatened to engulf her. A smile crept over her lips. She covered it with the sleeve of her jumper and breathed *her* in.

CHAPTER FORTY-SEVEN

October 2012

Anna poured milk from a small stainless-steel jug into a ludicrously large mug of coffee. The teaspoon obnoxiously clinked as she stirred, the loudest sound in the near-empty coffee shop. She glanced across the table at Grace; arms folded and jaw clenched. *Hostile.*

Anna directed her gaze out of the window. Afternoon traffic queued along the high street and red taillights refracted in the droplets on the rain-spattered glass.

They hadn't seen each other or even spoken since *that* night, over three months ago, one or the other making excuses to absent themselves from family engagements. Avoidance seemed to be their mutual, unspoken strategy. Not a second had passed when she hadn't thought about Grace; from the highs of erotic flashbacks of their reckless encounter to the lows of being racked with guilt and feeling really fucking angry that Grace had been so fucking angry with her.

But she was here to make things right. She rolled her shoulders to relieve some of the tension she was holding there. "Thanks for coming, I wasn't sure you would."

"Hmm." Grace fixed her with a penetrating stare, before turning her attention outside again.

"Look, Grace, I wanted to see you… I mean, I've been thinking a lot… thinking about us, and what happened and—"

"How's the engagement going?" Grace asked flatly.

"Didn't Rupert tell you?"

Grace looked at her with a blank expression.

"I called it off. Clare and I, we split up. I moved back in with Gran. My commute is a bit shit but it's fine for now. It was the right thing to do." She shook her head. "I can't believe he didn't tell you."

Grace uncrossed her arms and shifted in her seat. "I hardly see him. He's always at work."

Tension spiked the air between them and silence descended again. Anna tried to sip her coffee but it was too hot, so she put the mug down. She clasped and unclasped her hands.

"I think you've made a mistake. You should marry her. I don't know why you've ended it." Grace's voice had softened, as had her stare.

Anna narrowed her eyes. "What? Why would you say that?"

Grace pursed her lips, withholding a response.

Anna scoffed. "You clearly weren't happy about it. The way you walked off like that, you didn't even give me a chance to speak to you. Seriously, what the fuck was I supposed to do, Grace?"

Grace's shrug irked Anna even more.

"You know what I've been wondering…" Anna's voice shook with anger. "Did you know before we fucked that she was going to propose to me? Is that why you came and found me?"

"What? No! Of course I didn't know. Jesus, you must take me for one cold-hearted bitch if you think that of me." Grace's shoulders drooped and her features softened; the angry mask slipped, revealing the hurt underneath.

Anna sighed and slumped back into the faux leather tub chair. "I don't want to fight with you, Grace. That's not why I asked you to meet me… it wouldn't have been right of me to marry Clare when I'm in love with you. I can't get past it. I want *you*. I love *you*."

Grace's eyes flicked down to the table. "I feel the same, I do but—"

"But nothing." Anna reached across and took her hands. "I've given this a lot of thought. I know there'll be consequences, but let's stop wasting time… we love each other. What we have when we're together, it's like nothing else. You and Rupert don't make each other happy, so leave him."

Grace squeezed her eyes shut and hung her head.

"Grace, listen to me. We'll work it out. Lexi will be fine. Ru will be okay. We'll make him understand. I think he knows deep down anyway. And your family, maybe one day they'll accept it, who knows? But this is about us. It's right for us, you know it is."

"No, Anna. I can't…" Grace's voice cracked and her tears splashed onto the table.

"Yes, you can," Anna said firmly and squeezed Grace's hands. "You were prepared to do it before, when I came back from Australia. It was you who suggested it. You were going to leave Rupert, but I was with Mel and it—"

"I'm pregnant."

"What?"

"You heard me."

Anna flopped back in her chair again and put her hands on her head.

"Rupert doesn't know yet. No one does. I'm only three months gone."

"Three months? Oh God, please tell me it wasn't *that* night?"

"No. But close enough. Rupert and I, we hadn't, you know... for a long while. But after what happened with us. I felt terrible, and I was angry at you, and frustrated because our lives are such a feckin' mess and, fuck, it just happened—"

"Yeah, I get it." Anna held her hands up. She sat forward and rested her forehead on the table, breathing deep breaths through her nose to quell the bilious churn in her stomach. She squeezed her eyes shut in the hope that when she opened them again she'd no longer be on this nightmarish merry-go-round that was her life with Grace.

"Do you think you'll be able to sort things out with Clare?" Grace asked softly.

Anna sat up. "No, I can't do that. I've hurt her enough. She's a good person, she doesn't deserve that. She deserves someone who can love her properly."

"So do you. But I can't—"

"I know."

"I'm sorry for everything. This isn't what I wanted either, but it's happened, and I have to make the best of it. You won't leave again, will you? I know it's selfish of me to ask that of you, but I can't do this without you." Grace teared up again.

"Don't get upset." Anna reached across and took her hands. "I'm not going anywhere. I promised you that before, remember?" She held eye contact with Grace and mustered a smile. "We can't keep doing this to each other though, it's torture."

Grace nodded.

"I will always love you, Grace, but we need to bury this." Anna traced an invisible line between them, back and forth with her finger. "We need to forget we were ever lovers. Forget that we were ever anything more than friends." Anna's voice frayed and she cleared her throat. "We need to get over it once and for all. It has to be our promise to each other. We have to hold one another to it. No matter how hard it gets, we can't talk about our feelings because look where it always ends up."

Grace nodded. "Okay, yes, it'll be like a pact. I promise to be good." She held up her three middle fingers, "Brownie's honour, I will never, ever again seduce you in the ladies' lavatories."

Anna smiled weakly. "Nor anywhere else?"

"Nor anywhere else."

CHAPTER FORTY-EIGHT

June 2022

With eyes fixed on the sliding doors, Anna chewed her bottom lip and waited. Nerves tightened the knot in her stomach as people started to trickle through the gateway of International Arrivals.

Aside from the odd text message, they hadn't spoken the entire month Grace had been away. Anna restrained her thumb on the many occasions it hovered over the call button, out of respect for the time and space Grace had requested.

Now her mind raced through all of the possibilities, coloured with either hope or despair. She'd recovered from heartache with Grace before; she could do it again, but bolstered by the chat with Lexi, Anna clutched at the hem of her promise to Gran.

Promise me you won't give up on her.

Around her, people smiled and hugged as they reunited with their loved ones. Anna scanned the steady flow of faces filing through the doors. Then through a sea of people, there she was. Grace's green eyes swam through the crowd until they found Anna's and her face radiated a smile that set Anna's insides alight.

Fizz, fade… *for fuck's sake. Stop it.* Anna mentally pumped the brakes. *Don't get ahead of yourself.*

Her heart pounded as she folded Grace in her arms and melted into the embrace. *How will I ever be able to let you go again?* Anna gripped her more tightly yet and squeezed her eyes against the sudden urge to cry. She turned her face into Grace's hair and breathed in her sweet, musky scent.

As if Anna's thoughts spilt into Grace's words, she whispered into her ear, "You smell so good."

Anna grinned and reluctantly extracted herself from the hug. "Shall we?" She took one of Grace's bags and they walked towards the car park. Lots of smiles and shy stolen glances, but no words. Anna bit her lips together to dam the flood of questions she was bursting to ask. *Too soon. Give her time. Don't be needy*, like everything balanced on a tightrope of good timing.

✳ ✳ ✳

Buckled up and behind the wheel, Anna reversed out of her spot and fumbled for her ticket to exit the multi-storey. Grace flicked on the radio and Jo Whiley's *Shiny Happy Playlist* filled the spaces between their stilted small talk. *How was your trip? How's your family? How's Lexi getting on at yours? I hope she hasn't been too much trouble. Have you heard much from Toby? It seems like he's getting on grand with Nicole. Is Rupert still smitten? Has work been okay?* Their back-and-forth edged around the elephant in the car.

"Thanks again for picking me up, I could've caught the train."

"No, it was my pleasure." Anna smiled and tapped her thumbs on the steering wheel in time to the *You & Me Song*. She checked the mirrors and indicated to leave the motorway. "You know what, let's go the back way. It doesn't take much longer and it's a nicer drive."

"Now, are you sure you don't mind me staying at yours? I don't want to put you out."

Anna tutted. "Hardly. Although you might be putting Lexi out a bit. She's well and truly settled into the spare room. You'll either have to share with her and all her crap, which is somehow everywhere… or we can flip a coin for who gets the sofa."

"Or I've a better idea… how about we both stay in your room?"

Anna's eyes flicked from the road to Grace, who was grinning. "Okay, yeah… that's fine too. I don't mind… if you're okay with that."

"Why wouldn't I be?"

"I, er… well, I wasn't sure, with you wanting space… if you still needed space. I guess we'll be sharing a tent at Glastonbury, so I suppose it's the same thing. We're both adults. I won't jump you in the night." Anna cringed and wished she'd opted for a breezy, 'Yeah, no worries', instead of all the stupid shit that had just tumbled out of her mouth.

Grace laughed. "That's a shame."

"Er, which bit?"

"That you won't be jumping me in the night. I kind of hoped you would."

Anna glanced across at Grace, who had turned her attention out of the passenger side window. *Now, the time is now.* She accelerated towards a lay-by and pulled over, switched off the engine and unclipped her seatbelt. Avoiding Grace's stare, Anna tunnelled her vision out of the windscreen and fixed her eyes on a gnarly oak tree. Golden light filtered through its leaves and dappled the bonnet of her old Defender.

"Grace, I don't want to pressure you, but I need to know. Either we're together or we're not. I can't deal with the head-fuck of not knowing which it is." Anna rested her hands on the steering wheel and her head on her hands. She closed her eyes and braced herself.

Grace placed a hand on Anna's shoulder and spoke softly. "I kind of thought it was obvious with that hug at the airport. I'd have never let you go if you hadn't let go first. We'd still be standing there, hugging like two big feckin' eejits."

Anna's breath quickened but she remained frozen in position; head glued to her hands, hands glued to the wheel.

"If you'll still have me, Anna, I'm yours. I always have been, like that was ever going to change. I was hoping we could chat this through over a Chinese and a bottle of wine but here we are. I'm back. I'm here to stay for good. Forever. With you. You and me. Anna and Grace. Grace and Anna. Let's finally feckin' do this."

Anna lifted her head and tears streamed down her face as she twisted towards Grace.

Grace cupped Anna's cheeks in her hands. "Are you going to kiss me or not?"

Anna's smile erupted and she leaned in. Their lips met in a long, happy, wet, and tender kiss. Of all the reunions they'd had over the years, this was by far the sweetest. *Mutual permission to love.*

When they broke away from their embrace, Anna's flood of questions burst the dam. "What about the kids? What about Ireland?"

Grace made wide eyes. "I do believe Lexi has given us both a good talking-to. The kids will be fine."

Anna smiled and nodded.

"As for Ireland… it will always be part of who I am but I realised I outgrew it a long time ago. It wouldn't be starting a new life moving back there, I'd be putting on an old coat that no longer fits… besides, I don't want a new life. I want this life, with you."

Anna exhaled a shaky breath. "What about your family?"

"Now there's a story. I fetched myself a stiff drink, sat them all down and I told them what I should've told them a long time ago." Grace grinned.

Anna raised her eyebrows, willing her on.

"I told them I've met someone, and I've fallen in love. Ma was all like, 'Ah now that's lovely, especially after Rupert has gone and divorced you.'" Grace stared at her intently and a cute grin curled up the corners of her lips. "…And then I told them it's you."

"Oh fuck!"

Grace laughed. "Yeah, exactly. You literally could've heard a pin drop. Nothing but silence until Shona piped up. God love her, she got up, came over, wrapped her arms around me and said, 'Love is love, if she makes you happy then I'm happy for you.'"

"Oh, Shona. Love her." Anna smiled.

"But Roisin sat there with a face on her like a smacked arse. After Shona said her piece, Ros huffed. I asked if she had something to say and you know what the stupid cow said?"

"I dread to think."

Grace affected a shrill voice and parodied her own accent. "'I think it's disgusting and it's not fair on the kids, especially Toby, he'll grow up thinking he has two mams and not knowing where he came from.'"

Anna scoffed a laugh. "Is she for real?"

"I told her that although Toby's only a child, unlike her he's not as thick as shite so I'm pretty sure he'll figure it out. But then, out of nowhere, Shona piped up again. She never stands up to Ros, but she just came out with it like—" Grace smirked and shook her head.

"What? What did she say?"

"She said, 'What I think is *disgusting*, Roisin, is how you've been carrying on with at least two of Danny's mates behind his back.'"

"No." Anna gasped. "Is that true?"

"It sure is. I was back long enough to get all the gossip. It's a small town. The dirty, judgemental little tart, sitting up there on her high horse but not realising her knickers were on show for the world to see." Grace chuckled. "Anyway, it took the attention off me. Roisin started bawling and ran out the room. Mammy ran screaming after her."

"Blimey!"

"Yep, talk about throwing stones in glass houses."

"Your ma and da, are they okay now about what you told them?"

"They'll need some time. I think Ma has only just got over you coming out to them at Roisin's wedding… and when was that, like 2008? So maybe we'll give them a few years."

"And how do *you* feel?"

The warm golden glow of the fading day outlined Grace's face as her eyes met Anna's. Her lips quirked into a smile and she slowly nodded as she took Anna's hand.

"Free… I feel free."

CHAPTER FORTY-NINE

April 2013

Anna stroked Grace's hair back from her drenched forehead and held her hand as Grace squeezed, panted, and pushed. "I'm so sorry I haven't been able to get hold of him."

"It's okay. I don't care. You're here." Grace looked up and smiled until her face screwed up with another contraction.

"Yeah, but it should be Rupert's hand you're breaking, not mine. It wasn't me who got you into this state."

"I wish it had been," said Grace.

The young nurse raised her eyebrows and shot a look at Anna.

Anna shrugged and muttered, "It's the drugs talking."

Grace panted. "It's not... the feckin'... drugs."

"Okay, another big push for me, Grace," said the nurse. "We're almost there. I can see the crown."

"It's wearing a crown? Is that why it feckin' hurts so much?"

Anna laughed louder than she should have.

Grace screamed, panted, pushed, and in a rush of amniotic fluid, it was over. The baby wailed and Grace collapsed into Anna's arms, crying, sweaty, and exhausted.

Anna clutched Grace's head to her chest and kissed the top of it. "Shh, it's okay. I'm here."

* * *

"Pick up, pick up, pick up," Anna muttered as she paced up and down the strip-lit corridor with her phone pressed to her ear.

"Hey, what's up?"

"Fuck, Rupert. I've been trying to get you all afternoon."

"I've been in a workshop and the reception is a bit shit here. You okay?"

"Grace has given birth to a boy."

"What?"

"It's a boy. You have a son, Ru. He's perfect."

"Oh fuck. He's early. Grace isn't due for another week yet. I was supposed to be there. Fuck. Is he okay? Is Grace okay?"

"Yeah, they're good." Anna smiled into the phone. "Grace is exhausted and emotional, but she's fine. They're both fine."

"Oh wow… I have a son. Tell them I'll get back as soon as I can. I'll be on the first flight home, okay?"

"Don't worry. I'll look after them until you get here."

"I know you will…" his voice choked. "Anna?"

"Yeah?"

"Thanks for being there."

"Always," she said.

CHAPTER FIFTY

June 2022

The low sun cast a majestic, early evening light over the euphoric crowd gathered in front of the iconic Pyramid stage. Deep within the throng of sweaty, singing people, Anna stood with her arms around Grace, who leaned back into her as they swayed together.

After a few songs, Noel conceded to please the crowd and the High Flying Birds gave over to an Oasis set. The sound swelled with at least a hundred thousand voices chorusing the lyrics to *Wonderwall*. With her hot body pressed against Grace, Anna closed her eyes and summoned that sticky night, twenty years ago, when they met. When fizz, fade... *fuck*, she'd fallen so hard for the first time, but not the last. As if compelled by the same thought, Grace turned around and looked at her with those ocean eyes and a disarming smile that Anna couldn't resist.

Wonderwall reached its final refrain and Anna captured Grace's lips with her own. She kissed her like she wished she had on that first night. She kissed her for all the years they'd wasted; for all of the winding roads and blinding lights, and the heart-wrenching times they'd hungered and pined for what they couldn't have. But most of all, she kissed her because now they were here, together.

Grace broke away, still breathless from *that* kiss, "I was going to ask

315

you if you wanted another drink…"

"Oh," Anna laughed.

"…But perhaps we should go and, er… check on the tent instead?"

Anna answered with a grin.

They laced their fingers together and wove their way out of the crowd.

THE GREAT ARCTIC
ADVENTURES TOUR

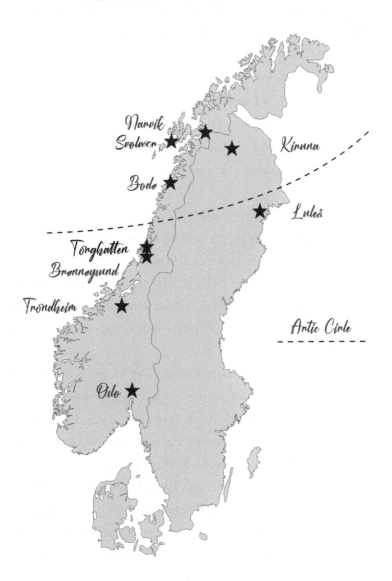

ACKNOWLEDGEMENTS

Firstly, bottomless thanks to my wonderful wife, Shannon. You've been there through everything. And more importantly, you're still there. If it wasn't for our amazing adventures, I never would've been inspired to write this story. Thank you for loving Anna and Grace (almost) as much as I do. And for loving me, in the way that you do.

To my amazing mum, Glenda – thanks for always being my loudest cheerleader. And for your unwavering belief in my ability to do absolutely anything – although I think that might be part of my problem!?

To Roberta, the best mother-in-law a girl could ask for – I appreciate your hearty support and encouragement. And to the rest of the Aussie contingent, you're my family.

To my besties, Si and Nina, Carrie and Nina – thank you for indulging me and making me feel like anything is possible. Without you guys, life would be less. (Si, I hope you've finally read it... c'mon, only thirty-eight chapters to go).

To my early-draft readers, Marie, JoJo, Cait, Victorian-Simon, Lisa, Steve, and Jas – your encouragement and support were absolutely crucial for me in those early stages. And a special mention to Matt – If it wasn't for you holding me to account, I probably wouldn't have started, let alone finished this book. Thank you for being annoyingly curious and enthusiastic. And, yes, "It's an actual fucking book!"

Thank you to my 'critters' on Critique Circle for helping me to take the whole thing apart and put it back together again (and for making me see that needed to happen). I learned so much from the 'friends' I found on CC – with special mentions to Jenny and Janie.

An extra big thank you to Sophia Blackwell for the incredible editing efforts. I'm so pleased I got to work with you. Your corrections and suggestions have helped me to make this book (even) better. I'm hugely grateful for your input.

Thank you to Kevin at Bookcoversonline for the truly awesome design work, typesetting, and for your patience whilst I tried to figure out what the hell I'm doing.

To Shelley and Lars at www.lifejourney4two.com – your awesome account of hiking Torghatten mountain was invaluable to me when writing about it.

Thanks to the lovely group of travellers we met on the Great Rail Journeys Arctic Explorer Tour in January 2022 – it truly was the trip of a lifetime (because of you) and I hope this fictionalised version of our trip brings back some fond memories.

Thank you to you... Yes you, reading this right now. If I know you then I've probably nagged you into buying this... but kudos to you, you're actually reading it (this bit at least). If I don't know you, then thank you for taking a chance on an indie author – I'm so grateful that you did and I hope you are too. It would be fan-feckin'-tastic if you could take the time to drop a review (Amazon, Goodreads, social media... wherever), and let me ...but more importantly, the rest of the world know what you think.

Lastly, thank you to everyone who has supported, advised, encouraged and been there on this new and exciting journey with me. If it wasn't for you, and everyone mentioned above then there wouldn't even be a book.

ABOUT THE AUTHOR

Pip Landers-Letts lives a full and happy life in the UK with her wife, Shannon and their two young 'kids', Mouse (the cat) and Roux (the dog). When she's not hanging out with her imaginary friends, she loves travelling, being in the mountains, making delicious food – and eating it, pouring good wine – and drinking it. This is her debut novel, but if you like it she'll write more.

You can find Pip online, so do reach out and say 'Hi', she'd love that.

www.pipwritesfiction.com

Instagram: @pipwritesfiction

Made in the USA
Las Vegas, NV
21 August 2024

94128104R00181